VALLEY OF THE RAYS

AJ BAILEY ADVENTURE SERIES - BOOK 7

NICHOLAS HARVEY

HarveyBooks LLC

Printed in the United States of America

First Printing, 2020

ISBN-13: 979-8690969776 (Amazon only)
ISBN-13: 978-1-959627-07-4 (IngramSparks)

Pier photograph by Drew McArthur

Cover design by Wicked Good Book Covers

Mermaid illustration by Tracie Cotta

Author photograph by Lift Your Eyes Photography

This is a work of fiction. Names, characters, businesses, places, events and incidents are either the products of the author's imagination or used in a fictitious manner unless noted otherwise. Any resemblance to actual persons, living or dead, or actual events is purely coincidental.

Keith & Casey Keller, and Tony Land, kindly provided their permission for their names to be used in a fictitious manner in the story.

DEDICATION

For Cheryl, my mermaid.
Nothing else matters.

1

OXFORD, ENGLAND – SATURDAY

At fifty-five years old, Simon Lever had been a good-looking man, with a healthy physique and a full head of slightly greying brown hair. At fifty-six, he lay weathered, tired, and barely conscious in a John Radcliffe Hospital bed. The cancer, and equally so the treatments, had left him beaten and defeated as his last days ticked away in a haze of pain-medicated delirium. He fought desperately to stay awake and aware when his family were in the room, but his windows of lucidity were quickly diminishing. His son, Martin, was thirteen. Old enough to understand the situation, yet too young to comprehend why his father, who had always been the pillar of strength, confidence and guidance in his life, could not fix this problem. The boy vacillated between tears, cheery denial, and escaping into the latest game on his mobile phone.

Simon grew up playing video games, through the evolution from Pong to the latest high definition, data-intensive, Internet-linked grandiose productions. He loved connecting with his son through entertainment and technology. He had made his fortune via computer technology and built his current corporation, Graph-icWell, a provider of stock photography, video and music, to be a leader in its field. With his son's keenness in computers and programming, he felt sure Martin would take over the business after he finished his schooling. He was now painfully aware that would be a day he himself would not witness. As the cancer had steadily drawn the life from Simon, he had carefully organised and arranged as many details as possible at GraphicWell, to ensure the company bridged the time from his departure to the day his son would assume the helm. He had a strong, technically innovative managerial group in place, but he knew he had been the captain of the ship, and much had fallen upon him to lead and direct the firm in the ever-changing world of technology. His two best friends and former partners in his first firm, Russell and Paul, who had joined him soon after he had formed the company, would be there every step of the way.

His wife, Tamsin, had worked alongside him for eighteen years. She had been hired as his personal assistant while he was in the throes of divorcing his first wife, and they had quickly moved from professional to intimate. He had never resolved in his mind whether subconsciously he had been desperate for another relationship after his first wife's infidelity, or if Tamsin was indeed the soulmate he felt she was. After nearly sixteen years of marriage, a wonderful son, and a life he could not imagine without the two of them, it wasn't important anymore. They now faced a life without him, and it centred his concerns around the challenges that lay ahead for them. Tamsin had come back to GraphicWell after Martin was born, and while she had never quite understood the computer science, she had displayed an impressive acuity for the business side. She would now take the reins, as she had progressively done during his decline in health, and he prayed she could maintain the critical balance between the creative geniuses, with their scattered brilliance, and the market foresight needed to keep the company headed towards a successful future.

Simon stirred as he heard his wife's voice in the room.

"Sorry, my love. There was a line in the coffee shop and then the phone started ringing. How are you doing?" she said in her firm voice with a hint of an upper-class English accent.

He forced his eyes open and did his best to smile. "I'm fine. Maybe we can knock off early today and slip in a game of tennis at the club?" he quietly chortled. His infectious laugh, that could brighten a room and turn any meeting around, lost to the disease that ravaged his body.

Tamsin rolled her eyes and smiled, her long auburn hair glistening in the stark lighting of the hospital room. My goodness, she's beautiful, Simon thought, as his thirty-nine-year-old wife put her warm hand on his, carefully avoiding the drip line and heart-rate lead.

"Then we'll clean up, grab a bite at La Cucina, before you take me dancing."

He groaned. "We must invite Nico and Michael along if we're going dancing. I'll succumb to my mandatory one dance, then those two can whirl you around the floor, and I'll watch you, loving every second."

"I'll never understand why you dislike dancing so much, you're a wonderful dancer," she said, sipping her coffee.

"All men hate to dance. We dance to get the girl. Once we have the girl, we see no need to dance anymore," he croaked.

She shook her head. "Not all men. Nico and Michael love to dance." She quickly held up a finger and frowned at her husband. "Don't you dare say it."

Simon chuckled, which led into a wheezing cough, and she squeezed his hand. She gave him the time to settle down and even out his breathing.

"I'll bring Martin back with me this afternoon," she said, "Hopefully his match goes well this morning."

Simon nodded. "You should have gone with him. I hate the idea neither of us are there."

"He'll have plenty of football matches…" she said before trailing off, and it was his turn to squeeze her hand. They had never realised how difficult it was to have conversations that avoided any reference to the future. Until the last few months. Their world had taken a significant shift at 10:15am on September 2nd. That was the day they sat before the doctor, the cancer specialist, the best chance they could find, and heard the word 'terminal'. When they had received the prognosis after Simon's cancer had first been discovered, the message had been grim. Statistics of survival rates were daunting, but survivors there were, and Simon Lever was no ordinary man. He had been the smartest boy in his classes, the captain of the school's football team, had exemplary grades in university and was the brains behind two start-up companies, the first of which he and his partners sold for millions before GraphicWell. Simon Lever was well above average at everything. If there was a way to survive this latest challenge, he would find a solution. There had always been hope. Until September 2nd. The unfathomable had become a reality. 'Quality of life' had replaced 'alternative treatment' in the discussions. Once hope was removed, Simon felt like the passenger in a car plunging off a cliff in slow motion. The outcome was inevitable and guaranteed, and the devastating cruelty of knowing the timing of his own death squeezed the life from his soul. Time with Tamsin and Martin was the only thing that kept him fighting, as a clock ticked loudly in the background.

"Text me his result, you know he'll forget," he said, changing the subject. "At least it's a nice day for once." He added, looking over at the blue sky beyond the window of his private room.

Tamsin glanced over her shoulder at the sunshine seeping past the partially opened blinds. "He won't forget," she said.

Simon knew his wife would text their son and remind him, and he smiled as his eyelids grew heavy again.

2

GRAND CAYMAN – SATURDAY

The rigid inflatable boat, or RIB for short, bobbed on the gentle swells, tethered to a mooring ball outside Grand Cayman's North Sound. AJ Bailey sipped from a canteen of water and grinned at the man sitting across the boat from her. Jackson Floyd was tall and lean, with long dark hair tied back in a ponytail and a neatly trimmed beard adorning his handsome face.

"What?" he asked, squinting against the bright Caribbean sun.

"Huh?" she replied.

"You're grinning like you know something no one else knows," he said in his soft, Californian accent. "How about you share?"

AJ's un-English tanned face blushed. "I'm just happy," she replied, beaming. "Is it okay if I'm happy?"

He laughed. "It's not just okay, it's preferable. I'm glad you're happy."

"I can't believe you're finally here, that's all. It seemed like it would never happen and now it has and I'm happy," she said and fidgeted awkwardly, her purple-streaked, shoulder-length blonde hair sprinkling sea water across the side of the boat.

"It did feel like the world was conspiring against us for a while," he admitted. "The quarantine here felt like forever.

Knowing I was on the island and you were just a few miles away was tough. Longest two weeks of my life."

AJ couldn't stop smiling. She felt like an idiot sitting there with a permanent grin, but the glow that emanated from inside wouldn't allow the muscles in her face to relax. The long-distance relationship they had begun well over a year before had meant sporadic time together. Jackson worked aboard Sea Sentry's marine conservation ship, which passed through the Cayman Islands on its way south and returning home to the US, allowing them a few days together each time. He had planned to move to the island earlier in the year, at the end of his tour, but the COVID-19 virus turned everybody's world upside down. He volunteered for another tour with Sea Sentry rather than sit at home in San Francisco, until eventually the Cayman Islands began cautiously opening its borders. The small, self-governed, British overseas territory had eradicated the virus from its three islands over the summer months, and committed to keeping it that way. They both agreed fourteen more days was well worth the wait.

AJ stood and took off the long-sleeved sun shirt she had worn to protect the full-sleeve tattoos down both her arms from the hot UV rays. She pulled her wetsuit up from around her waist and nodded at Jackson.

"Come on then, we've been up for forty-five minutes, the fishies are waiting for us."

He stood and steadied himself as the 30-foot RIB rocked with their movement on the gentle swell of the north side. It was a beautiful day with a few wispy clouds scattered across the bright blue skies. They had arrived early, and their first dive had been off the steep drop-off that surrounded Grand Cayman. For their second dive they would stay shallower and cruise the top of the wall and the reefs below the boat.

Jackson pulled his wetsuit up and reached for the string on the rear zipper. "Better be some sharks this dive. You promised me sharks if we got out here early enough."

AJ donned her buoyancy control device, or BCD, the vest with the dive tank strapped to it containing an air bladder that helped the diver maintain stability as the surrounding water pressure increased with depth.

"I have my dive knife so if we don't see any I'll give you a little slice and I'm sure they'll show up," she joked.

"Great plan, thanks." He grinned as he too geared up.

They sat on opposite sides of the boat and with a quick nod they simultaneously back rolled into the clear, warm water. They met under the boat and from 60 feet above the sea floor they could easily see the beautiful reef below through the gin-clear water. They dropped down and finned towards the drop-off where the wall plummeted away to over 1,000 feet before incrementally stepping down to over 6,000 feet less than a mile farther offshore. The sea fans barely swayed, with the subtle surface swells the only movement of the water. Flashes of blues, greens and yellows darted about the coral heads as myriads of fish went about their daily search for food and shelter from the predators. A large grouper hung still, with his jaw wide open allowing tiny blennies and shrimp to clean his mouth and gills; a free meal and an assurance the big fish wouldn't close his mouth and snack on the cleaners.

AJ tapped a stainless-steel carabiner against her dive tank to get Jackson's attention and pointed down beyond the wall to deeper water. Two eagle rays majestically fluttered their wings as they rose from the depths to hunt along the edge of the North Wall. The two divers hung motionless while the broad rays cruised past them and glided away to the west. AJ could see, Jackson, behind his regulator, had a big smile on his face. She led them farther along the top of the wall and hoped a shark or two would turn up; she loved to see that smile. This was uncharted waters for AJ. She had never felt this way about someone before. A late bloomer from tomboy to pretty teenager, she had always been cautious and selective with whom she shared her time, and her bed, with. But, at thirty-years-old – nearing thirty-one – she had sampled enough relationships that were good, but not all she had hoped for, to know Jackson was something different. Their time together had been short bursts of intense days while he was on the island, followed by months of longing and weekly Internet calls. She knew their time apart fuelled the intensity of their four or five days together, but she had a calmness about their relationship she had never known before. For a while, she had allowed her self-doubt to bore holes in her belief that he was committed, but he had constantly reassured her, and slowly her doubt ebbed away. Patience is considered an emotion, as well as a skill. AJ liked to think she had developed her skill in the emotion no one had ever accused her of possessing, but she knew it was Jackson's easy-going, relaxing nature. He had helped her feel confident in what they had, and willing to wait whatever time it took for them to be together. Now they were, and she wondered if this was the happiest she had ever felt.

AJ noticed Jackson had paused and was hanging upside down, peering under a small coral head. She finned back and he signalled for her to take a look. She came in close but couldn't see anything extraordinary. The usual damsels flitted about and she spotted a Christmas tree worm still spreading its two feathered crowns despite the movement close by. Jackson pointed under the coral head and AJ eased closer and looked carefully. A tiny object, no bigger than the fingernail on her little finger and resembling a dice, bobbed and skittered about. It was a juvenile smooth trunkfish. Rare to see because of their size and keenness to remain hidden from predators, the little black fish with yellowy white spots would one day grow into a clothes iron-shaped adult. AJ wiggled in excitement and smiled so wide she made her mask leak. Okay, she thought, maybe now I'm the happiest I've ever felt.

They pulled back from the coral head to leave the trunkfish in peace, and AJ looked at Jackson, tapping her dive computer watch. He checked his own computer and signalled back with one finger, then seven fingers, indicating he had 1700psi of pressure remaining in his air tank. They had been down over twenty minutes, so AJ whirled a finger in the water, telling him they should turn back towards the boat. He was still over half the 3,000psi they had both started with, so they could take their time and still return under the boat with a safe reserve. They moved a little farther away from the drop-off, swimming over the reef that gently sloped towards the North Sound several hundred yards south, where the coral reached up just below the surface, dividing the open ocean from the sound. They paused several more times to observe and marvel over fish they rarely saw, and for a flounder changing colours as it camouflaged itself against the reef. After another fifteen minutes, AJ looked ahead and could see the mooring line stretching from the stainless-steel eyelet in the sea floor, up to the surface where her RIB lazily swayed. She heard the deep drone of a boat engine at the same time she noticed something large moving towards them. She nudged Jackson to get his attention, but he was already watching the shadows at the edge of their visibility. AJ was filled with awe, and relief, as the reef shark made its way towards them with barely a movement from its tail. Mildly curious, the shark circled them, hoping they had speared a lionfish it could steal for an easy meal. Its seven senses, two more than humans have, quickly determined the divers had nothing to offer, and it continued its hunt along the coral wall.

Jackson held up an okay sign with his hand, and AJ was overjoyed to see the big smile was back on his face. As they both watched the shark disappear, AJ realised the engine drone was now close by, and growing louder. Sound carries farther through water than air, but distinguishing direction becomes much harder. The human ear is tuned to detect the slight difference in timing that sound reaches each ear, but that timing changes underwater and confuses the auditory perception. To the divers, it sounded like the boat was approaching from every direction. A hull appeared, approaching from deeper water, and AJ wondered why anyone would choose to pass by so close to a moored boat displaying a diver flag. The engine note changed, and the boat slowed as it coasted towards the mooring buoy that Arthur's Odyssey, AJ's RIB, was moored to. Jackson looked over at her and held up his hands questioningly. AJ shrugged her shoulders and stared at the hull, trying to recognise the boat from below. It was almost twice the length of her RIB, a single screw, and the bottom needed a good cleaning and some fresh paint. Beyond that, she had no idea what, or who, was paying them a visit.

They ascended to 15 feet where they would hang for three minutes on their safety stop, allowing excess nitrogen that had accumulated in their systems to dissipate before surfacing. While AJ impatiently watched the seconds tick away, she racked her brain trying to think who she knew with a boat like the one now sharing the buoy above them. Her friend, fellow dive boat operator and mentor, Reg Moore, had three boats, but they were all 36-foot Newton dive specials, the same as her other boat, and what bobbed above her was not a Newton. The only dive operation with a bigger boat was the live-aboard charter that took divers to all three islands in the archipelago, comprising Grand Cayman, Cayman Brac, and Little Cayman. Their boat was much bigger still, and would never double tie to one of the standard mooring buoys placed by Cayman's Department of Environment specifically for the dive boats. She was stumped. Whatever it was had a deep draft and the people aboard must not know double tying to the buoy was illegal, not to mention annoying and poor boating etiquette. Finally, their three minutes were up, and she led Jackson to the steps hanging between the twin outboards of her RIB. AJ clambered aboard and looked over at the strange vessel as she dropped her gear to the deck. It looked like a fishing boat, with a long, open rear deck, an enclosed wheelhouse with a covered area extending behind it, and a pale, slightly overweight man wearing a gaudy blue seersucker shirt adorned with marlins, waving to her.

3

GRAND CAYMAN – SATURDAY

The middle-aged man slipped the hat from his head to reveal his receding hairline, waved it in the air and called over in an American accent. He shouted as though he was communicating between two mountain peaks.

"Hi there! How was your dive?"

AJ looked at Jackson, who had followed her onto the boat and now dropped his gear next to hers. He looked as dumbstruck as she felt.

"Can I ask you why you've tied your boat to the mooring we were already on? Are you in some kind of trouble?" AJ called over the 10 feet between the sterns of the two boats.

The man put the hat back on his head and looked around a moment, appearing to gather his thoughts. "Well yes, and no," he replied with an awkward smile. "I do need to get to the island, so I was wondering if you two might be heading that way anytime soon?"

"Do you have a mechanical problem with your boat, sir?" Jackson asked.

The man looked back and forth between the two divers, his

brow furrowed. "No, boat's fine. I just need a ride over to the island if you'd be so kind."

"Are you from Grand Cayman, sir? You know the borders are closed, right?" AJ said, slipping her wetsuit down around her waist and grabbing a towel.

The man fidgeted on his feet and looked down at the deck, nodding his head. "Yup, I am aware. But if I could just get a ride over to the island, I can handle all the official paperwork."

AJ thought for a moment. Something struck her as very odd about the whole situation, but the man appeared almost bumbling in his manner, uncomfortable and out of place somehow. He certainly didn't look at home on a fishing boat, despite his attire.

"I'm sorry, sir, but you'll need to go around the island to the George Town harbour and radio in to the port authority. They'll be able to direct you from there and can point you to a visitor's mooring," AJ said firmly. "I can call them up on the VHF if you like?"

The man looked up, no longer smiling. He shook his head, looked towards the wheelhouse and beckoned someone to join him. A dark-skinned man with dreadlocks, scruffy tan shorts and a stained, white tank top, stepped from the door and walked over. AJ and Jackson both watched, still confused by the situation and unsure how they should be reacting. The loud shirt man nodded and his friend reached to the back of his shorts. His hand returned holding a gun.

"Mother..." Jackson said and stepped in front of AJ. "What the hell do you want?"

The man shook his head again, his smile returning. "I want what I politely asked for," he replied, holding both hands up, "I'd simply like a ride over to your lovely island." His hands dropped to his sides. "But now we're gonna play it my way as you two decided to make it difficult."

A third man came out of the wheelhouse and walked over. He too was dark-skinned and dressed in tattered shorts and a loose-fitting tank top. AJ couldn't believe they were being held up at a dive mooring on the North Wall. She hated guns, and it seemed like she'd had encounters with more than a few over the past couple of years. She stepped from behind Jackson, although she was flattered his first reaction was her protection.

"Put the gun away, sir, there's no need for that. We'll take you where you want to go. Believe me, you don't want to get caught in the Cayman Islands with an illegal firearm, they take it seriously here."

"That's more the spirit," the man said. "Throw a rope over so we can pull the boats together and tie them to those things we have on the side."

"Cleats," AJ said, trying not to laugh despite the gravity of the situation. "We can throw a line over and you can tie off to the cleats."

The man nodded and seemed unfazed as the two men she assumed were Jamaicans, did their best to hide their smiles. Jackson threw a line across and one of the crew pulled the sterns of the boats together and tied the line to a cleat on their gunwale. The second kept the gun pointed across at the RIB.

"Okay, so here's what we'll do. You," the man in the marlin shirt said, pointing at Jackson, "you'll come over here and stay aboard with these two. I'll join the young lady over on your boat and she'll be my taxi. Once I've concluded my business on the island, we'll come back and everyone can go our separate ways."

Jackson didn't move. "How about I stay here and we'll both take you ashore."

The man laughed. "See this guy next to me with the gun in his hand?" he waited for Jackson to nod. "Well, the gun says you'll do what I say, and what I say is, you come over here. I'd like you to do that now, please."

Jackson looked at AJ. She smiled as best she could. "Don't worry, it'll be fine, I'll run him back and forth and this will be over."

Jackson nodded and her heart skipped as she saw the concern, fear, anger and love all from one glance into his eyes. He nimbly jumped from the rubber side of the RIB up to the gunwale of the fishing boat, then stepped down to the deck.

"Thank you," the man said and looked at how he might manoeuvre himself from one boat to the other, clearly nimbleness not being in his repertoire of skills. He sat on the gunwale and swung his legs over to dangle them over the side with the RIB still several feet below him. He then appeared to realise, somehow, he had to get from there across the inflatable side of the RIB. He shakily lowered himself from the gunwale and attempted to stand on the side of the RIB while the other four all watched in a mixture of amusement and disbelief. Neither of the Jamaicans made any effort to help the man as he reached with his foot for the rubber side and the boats both rocked in the soft swells. Just when AJ was convinced the man was going to fall, he lurched towards the RIB, stepping on the rubber gunwale, and half bounced, half fell into Arthur's Odyssey. Miraculously, he landed on his feet, which, by the look on his face, surprised him as much as the onlookers.

"Okay," he said, quickly regaining his composure. "I am armed with a cellphone." He reached into his shorts pocket and retrieved a mobile. "Every hour, on the hour, I call these guys on the phone. If I don't call... Is he your husband?" he asked, pointing again at Jackson.

"Boyfriend," AJ replied, before she could decide if that was the strategically correct answer.

"Right, well if they don't get my call on the hour every hour we're gone, you get to find a new boyfriend."

The Jamaican with the gun pointed it at Jackson's head for emphasis.

"Okay, we get the point," AJ snapped. "Throw off the line, so we can get going." She barked in the second Jamaican man's direction while she strode to the bow and released the RIB from the mooring buoy. Marlin shirt man teetered and wobbled about, finally hanging on to the t-top frame over the console. AJ started the twin outboards.

"Cellphones," the man said, holding out a hand.

"We're out on the water, we didn't bring them," AJ answered, feeling pleased she thought of the retort so quickly.

The man tilted his head to one side and looked at her with a bored expression. "Really? Please, just give me the phones."

She realised it was a weak play. Reaching under the console, she retrieved both their mobile phones and handed them to the man.

He clumsily powered them down, with an arm looped around the frame to steady himself, then slipped them in his khaki cargo shorts pocket. She was surprised and relieved he hadn't tossed them overboard.

"Your boat's staying here? On this buoy?" she asked.

"Yes. Why?" the man queried.

AJ shrugged her shoulders. "It's a dive mooring, bit strange an offshore fishing boat being moored to it. But, whatever. Your call," she said and went to put the RIB in gear.

"Wait," the man said firmly, and looked around the seas. "Where would a fishing boat moor up around here?"

AJ looked over her shoulder and tried to keep an even expression despite her surprise the man had taken the bait.

"Inside the cut would make more sense. Besides, it's flat calm in there. It would be more comfortable while they wait."

"Where's the cut? What do you mean? Over there?" he pointed across the shallow reef to the North Sound.

"Yup. There's a mooring just inside the cut in that calmer water. People aren't using it at the moment," AJ explained in a half truth.

The man looked back at the fishing boat, which they had drifted away from. The two Jamaicans were watching unenthusiastically with Jackson standing beside them.

"Follow us," the man shouted. "You'll wait inside the gap over there."

"Cut," AJ corrected, as she put the RIB in gear and idled around to face Stingray Deep Channel through the reef.

She motored slowly until the fishing boat was free from the mooring, then eased the throttles forward and took a wide arc, lining up straight through the cut. She wished there was an option where the shallower draft of the RIB could clear, but the fishing boat would not. If she could catch them out, Jackson might be able to swim for it in the chaos, but the reef was clearly shallow everywhere but the three cuts, and she guessed the two men aboard were no dummies. Once into the North Sound AJ turned right and ran parallel with the outer reef for a few hundred yards. The water glistened a bright yellowy green from the sandy bottom of the sound, only twelve or fifteen feet below. She backed the throttles down and coasted towards a buoy ahead. Looking back, she saw the fishing boat chugging along in her wake and she pointed to the white buoy, now off her starboard side.

The man looked over the side through the calm, clear water. "What the hell are they?" he exclaimed.

AJ looked over the side at the large, grey disks with long tails, skimming around the sand by the boat.

"Stingrays," she replied flatly.

"Stingrays?" the man said, still sounding alarmed. "Like the things that killed that Australian guy? You know, the animal man."

"Yup," she said. "Steve Irwin."

The man stared at her. "What the hell are you doing bringing us to a death pool of stingrays?" he clung to the t-top frame. "They'll shoot your boy over there if you so much as try to push me in."

AJ laughed. "Irwin's accident was a freak deal. The stingrays are harmless, we feed them by hand and hold them in our arms. Worst thing you'll get from a stingray here is a love bite."

"A what?" he asked, still clutching the aluminium frame.

"A love bite," she repeated. "Hickey I think you call it in America. They feed by sucking shellfish from the sand and crevices on the reef. Sometimes they'll give you a little kiss if you have some squid juice on you. Give you a big old love bite."

The Jamaicans tied the fishing boat to the mooring buoy and looked over the side at the stingrays in mild curiosity.

"What is this place? Why are they all here?" the man asked, still wary.

"Valley of the Rays," AJ replied. "Farther over there on the sandbar is Stingray City. That's where they bring the tourists to splash about in waist-deep water. Here is the original spot where they first dived with all the stingrays in the early 80s. The fishermen would come through the cut and clean their daily catch, here in the calmer water. Pretty soon the stingrays figured out they could grab an easy meal, and they'd meet the boats every day. Now the tour boats feed them so they keep coming."

"People pay to get in the water with a creature called a stingray?" he said, emphasising the sting part of the word and shaking his head. "Unbelievable."

AJ didn't care whether the man believed any of it. The important part was she had persuaded them to move inside the sound where they were more likely to be spotted and on a mooring that was currently off-limits during the pandemic restrictions. Now, she could only hope a Marine Police Unit patrol boat, or someone from the Department of Environment, would happen by.

She looked over at Jackson standing on the deck of the fishing boat. The Jamaicans hadn't tied him or restrained him in any way, until now at least. If there was an opportunity to slip away, she was confident he would take it.

"I'll be back as soon as I can," she shouted over to him.

He smiled, and she eased the throttles forward, turning the RIB south-west across the North Sound.

4

OXFORD, ENGLAND – SATURDAY

Tamsin sat next to the hospital bed and stared at her dying husband. Simon had been asleep when she had returned. Martin had retreated to the chair by the window where he was playing a game on his mobile, with earbuds shutting out the confusing world around him. A magazine lay across her lap from which she had idly read a few articles with little interest. One of the many tragedies for old and sick people in their final time was their cruel lack of energy. At a time when every hour could be counted in fathomable fractions of their remaining existence, their loved ones were forced to watch it ebb away in meaningless sleep. Would it be easier to endure if the man she loved had been swiftly taken? Tamsin pondered the point daily, and still had no discernible answer. The sudden wrenching of a healthy person from the world held the bitter theft of future times, yet saved the agony of watching the one they love slowly decay into an undignified end. Her own father had been taken when she had been a teenager. A car crash. But the pain was not comparable. Her father had been a cold, distanced man who divorced her mother when Tamsin was a toddler. She had spent little time with him for most of his remaining life, and when he deemed her worthy of his presence, she had always felt like an intrusion and an inconvenience. She glanced over at Martin, engrossed in his game. When her relationship had developed with Simon, one attraction had steered her into loving the man more than any other: he was the inverse of her own father. He wanted a child as much as she did, and she was confident he would be a devoted parent. She hadn't been wrong. Their son was the priority in their lives, and despite their hectic corporate distractions, they had made sure at least one of them attended every event in the boy's life. One more change, she thought with a sigh, when 'parents' become the singular 'parent'.

Tamsin's mobile vibrated in her lap, and she studied the text message. It was their company solicitor asking if she had time for a call. She looked at Simon, who appeared to be in a deep sleep, and then turned to check on Martin. He was still a million miles away, his face buried in his mobile with his fingers frantically working the screen. She stood, picked up her Louis Vuitton handbag and walked to the door, looking back at her son, intending to signal her intention of being gone a short time. He was oblivious to her movement, so she left the room and walked down the hall to the nearest lift.

Outside the hospital the afternoon sun felt warm on her face, offsetting the slight chill from the autumn breeze. Tamsin took a cigarette from the pack in her bag, lit the Benson & Hedges Gold and slid the pack and lighter back into the bottom of her bag. She took a long, easy draw that filled her lungs with smoke, and her conscience with guilt. When she began working at GraphicWell she had been a social smoker in the evenings and didn't smoke during the day. When she and Simon began seeing each other, she quickly learnt he had never smoked and couldn't abide the habit. She had sneaked a puff or two every now and again since, when out with girlfriends, but had hidden it entirely from her husband and for all intents and purposes quit entirely, until the last few months.

There were other things she had kept from her husband, but he had been happy to leave the past in the past, so she had gladly complied. Her mother had remarried, and chosen poorly for a second time. Her stepfather was involved with dubious characters – if she put it kindly – an outright crook if she was honest. He treated her and her mother well, but their home was a constant meeting place for his 'business associates'. Tamsin's first job after university was helping her stepfather coordinate and manage the various comings and goings of his associates, and the large sums of cash that changed hands. But that was a life she had left behind; as much as you could ever put those events and people in your past.

An occasional cigarette calmed her nerves, and the few minutes' break helped her refocus and make it through the day. At least that's what she told herself. As she stood outside the hospital, with too many doubts weighing on her mind, she would take any calming she could get before speaking with their solicitor. Again.

"Hi, Andy," she said when the man answered, before taking another drag from her cigarette.

"Hello Tamsin, I apologise for the need to disturb you," he greeted her politely.

"That's okay. Simon is sleeping right now, so I was able to slip out for a few minutes," she said, and noted how tired her own voice sounded.

"I have a couple of points we need to go over if possible, but I believe I have workable solutions for you on both," Andy offered. "The first is regarding the apartment in Spain. I've been in touch with our office in Madrid and they are going to add you to the corporate owner-ship of the Spanish holding company Simon purchased the apartment under. It will require his signature on some paperwork, I'm afraid, but they assure me they will have that paperwork to me by midweek. To set up a power of attorney for the Spanish would be troublesome, espe-cially as it couldn't be you, being an interested party. You're on all the personal accounts there, as you know, which makes things easier."

Tamsin exhaled a stream of smoke, "Okay, that's how we must do it then. He should be home next week, we're planning to move him Monday. Have the papers delivered to the house and I'll courier them straight back."

There was a slight pause. "Does that mean he'll be under hospice care at that point?"

"Yes. Yes, he will," she replied quietly.

"I'm very sorry, Tamsin," Andy said carefully. "I can't imagine how difficult this must all be for you and your family."

"Thank you, Andy," she said, stubbing the cigarette out with her shoe and regaining strength in her voice. "What else do we need to cover? I should be getting back upstairs."

"Right, of course. Well, the other matter is in regard to the will itself. I had one of my associates go over it one last time, and he raised a valid point about the wording regarding your son."

"Martin? What do you mean?" she quickly questioned.

"Well, as you know, this will was written some time ago, so I imagine Simon left it open in the event you two had more children. The will doesn't specify Martin, it uses the broader term of children, which is standard language, but it can simplify matters if it specifically named Martin," Andy explained.

Tamsin frowned and thought a moment. "I don't really see what difference it makes, Andy? We only have one child, so surely there's no issue whether it says child, children or Martin? You know how important it is to Simon..." She checked herself for a moment. "To us both, that Martin is the priority. Simon has set everything up with him in mind."

"I do understand that, which is the only reason I'm mentioning the point. But, you're right, ultimately it shouldn't matter," Andy confirmed. "But the probate court may require a due diligence on unnamed claimants to the will, and having Martin specified can make things simpler. The onus is on the executor of the will to identify all beneficiaries, and they'll be more comfortable making a cursory search if Martin is named."

"Simpler how? If they're going to do a due diligence search anyway, what's the difference?" Tamsin turned and walked towards the door to the hospital. "I assure you, there won't be an issue. I really should be getting back inside, Andy."

"Of course," Andy replied, sounding harried. "I'm so sorry to bother you Tamsin. Please give my best to Simon."

Tamsin hesitated at the door and considered berating the man for trumping up ways to log more billable hours, but she held herself back. Andy had been nothing but supportive and diligent, and Simon trusted him implicitly. He was doing the job he had been charged to do, and it was her nervous feeling and frustration causing the problem.

She took a deep breath. "Thank you, Andy. Look, unless you feel it's vital to change that language, I'd really prefer Simon didn't have to re-sign that complete document again. It's not the signing that's the strain, he just can't help worrying about these things when they're put in front of him."

"I understand, Tamsin, it would just be an amendment page, but I don't think this is vital. It may cause a few weeks of delay, but in the big scheme of things that's not a problem," Andy said, sounding relieved. "It's far more important to keep Simon's stress to a minimum. You all have enough to contend with."

They said their goodbyes and Tamsin walked back inside, pressed the button, and waited on the lift. If she was going to succeed in running GraphicWell for the next ten years, she would have to do better than getting worked up like that, she told herself. Simon had shown her by example how to balance their life between the company and their family time. She just had to put her feet into the prints he had left behind. Great in theory, she thought, words are cheap, but she had to make it happen. Take a breath, she reminded herself, even when the answer or reaction appeared easy, take a breath and turn the problem around in your mind before responding. Simon was so good at doing that. She was aware no one ever knows what another human being is thinking. They surmise based on their actions and history, but somehow, Simon could put himself in other people's shoes and understand their perspective more clearly than anyone she had ever met. Things that would madden her, Simon could logically explain by observing through a different lens she hadn't considered. Tamsin knew she would never be great at that, but with patience, and the knowledge that it needed work, she was determined to improve. Keeping her quick temper in check would be crucial, but she was filled with a deep-seated, single-minded determination to make it all work. Her father may not have seen her potential, but Simon had, and she reminded herself every day of the faith he was placing in her.

"I didn't see you leave," Martin said, pulling the earbuds from his ears as Tamsin entered the room.

She smiled. "You were intensely waging battle with your game, so I didn't want to interrupt. Has he woken up?"

Martin shook his head.

Tamsin looked at her watch. "Well, I shouldn't have any more work calls today," she said, sitting in her chair by the bed. She waved to her son. "Come over, we'll stay until he wakes up. We can spend a little time with him, then we'll head home and get you ready for your friend's party."

Martin came over to the other chair by the bed and sat down heavily, idly spinning his mobile around in his hands.

"I know it's hard, Martin, but Daddy is tired. He'd love nothing more than to be chatting with us whenever we're here," Tamsin said softly.

"I know," Martin replied.

"He always tells me to wake him when we're here," she whispered, more to herself than her son, "but I don't have the heart to disturb him while he's managing to rest. So much of the time he only naps and keeps waking up."

She almost said "with the pain", but stopped herself.

"I'd rather be here, even if he is asleep," Martin said, and Tamsin couldn't reply. She held her breath and forced her eyes to stay open, two tricks she had learnt to keep the tears from coming. She reached over and stroked her son's curly brown hair. Most of the time he pulled away when she did that, but this time he didn't.

"When is Dad coming home?"

5

GRAND CAYMAN – SATURDAY

As the RIB skimmed across the smooth waters of the North Sound the man looked down at the sign on the side of the console, then back at AJ. "You're Mermaid Divers, I presume?"

AJ nodded without looking his way.

"What's your name?" he asked.

"AJ," she replied curtly, although she wondered if she should engage the man in conversation. She had no idea what he was up to on the island, but it was obviously illicit, and now she was enabling him. She needed to think clearly and try to learn more about him. She was hardly a fighter, but he seemed the furthest thing from a threatening man that she could imagine, and she was starting to consider how to take him out, and still get Jackson safely back. If she was going to make a move, it needed to be right after his hourly call so she had the most amount of time to rally help and get back out to the fishing boat. Which wouldn't necessarily be where she had just left it.

What would Reg do, she thought, if he was in my shoes and it was Pearl who was being held? Reg Moore wasn't just her mentor and close friend, he was also a father figure on the island with her own parents being so far away in England. Her family had met Reg when they tried scuba diving for the first time while on holiday in Grand Cayman, 16 years before. They had all stayed in touch and it was Reg who had guided AJ through the process of becoming a scuba instructor, landing her first job in Florida, and then coming to Cayman and working for Pearl Divers, Reg's growing business. Reg and her father had conspired to help her launch her own dive operation and the former British navy man and his wife, Pearl, were family as far as AJ was concerned. At 65, Reg was still a broad-shouldered bear of a man, so the answer to her question was simple; once out of sight of the fishing boat, Reg would have grabbed this bloke by the throat and forced him to release Pearl. For the 5 foot 4 inch tall AJ, at half the weight of Reg, that wasn't quite so easy.

"AJ? Like the two letters, A and J?" he asked.

"Just like," she replied.

"What does A and J stand for?" he queried further.

She sighed. It felt creepy giving this man any personal information about herself. She had also realised neither he nor his men had taken any precaution in hiding their faces. According to the movies, that meant they either didn't care about being identified, or intended to wrap things up so the witnesses would never tell.

"Annabelle Jayne," she answered, "but everyone calls me AJ."

She noticed the man looking her over and suddenly felt incredibly vulnerable. She still had her wetsuit pulled down to her waist and a bikini top on. She felt his eyes studying the purple streaks in her blonde hair then moving down to the full-sleeve tattoos on both arms, pausing at her chest on the way.

"You look more AJ than Annabelle Jayne," he said, and a chill ran through her.

She reached under the console and retrieved her long-sleeved sun shirt. The shirt felt like a layer of armour being slipped over her, as she removed her naked flesh from his view.

"What do I call you?" she asked, as she stepped out of her wetsuit.

He smiled, seemingly happy she had decided to converse. "Call me Pascal."

"Pascal?" she said, unable to hide her surprise. "I didn't peg you as being French."

"I'm not," he replied, looking slightly uncertain.

"Oh. Pascal like the unit of pressure?" she asked, thinking maybe she was misunderstanding him.

"No. Well, yes. Same guy. But I'm more on the side of the mechanical calculator. You know, problem solver," he said with a tone of pride.

AJ looked at him as they skipped across the calm water of the sound towards Governors Creek and the Yacht Club marina. "I don't really get it," she said carefully, not wanting to annoy the man.

"Pascal, he invented the first mechanical calculator you see… and the unit of pressure, of course." He looked at her as he hung to the frame as though his own life depended on it.

"Okay," she replied, still confused.

Pascal shook his head. "It's what I do, you see, I'm a problem solver. I solve problems for people. Problems they can't figure out on their own."

"Oh, I see. A play on words. Or a play on themes I suppose," AJ said, nodding. "Although, to be honest, so far you've only caused me problems, so the analogy doesn't really work from my perspective."

He laughed. "True, but you're not paying me."

"If I paid you, could we go back out and get Jackson and forget about this whole thing?" she asked, knowing the answer.

"You can't afford my price, I'm afraid. We'll get this all done as quickly as possible and then it'll be like it never happened," he replied.

"It's a bit confusing," she said, "your codename thingy."

He frowned. "How so?"

"Well, don't more people know about the unit of pressure, rather than the calculator part? I didn't know he invented a mechanical calculator."

"Not any old mechanical calculator. The first mechanical calculator," Pascal corrected.

"Okay, first. But even so, I'm afraid I didn't know that. Bit obscure, don't you think?" she said carefully, unable to stop herself.

"Yes, well, perhaps you skipped that day in school," he replied, and looked away.

AJ decided she wasn't very good at this banter business, and focused on aiming Arthur's Odyssey at the canal leading to Governors Creek.

After several minutes she eased the throttles back so the RIB came off plane and settled into the water as they entered the canal. The man had been studying his mobile and AJ caught a glimpse of the screen when he looked up as they slowed. He was in the map program with their position on the island a red dot moving in real time with them.

"Where are we going?" she asked.

"You have a vehicle at your dock?" he countered, looking a little green.

She wondered how he knew she had a dock over this side of the island but quickly realised if he had searched Mermaid Divers in the map function it would have shown him both her West Bay and Governors Creek locations.

"Sure. I have my van."

"Okay, go to your dock and we'll take your van," he said, now typing on his mobile phone.

"Looking down is the worst thing to do," she said.

"Huh?" he replied, pausing whatever he was doing on the mobile.

"Looking down," she repeated. "It'll make you feel seasick. You don't look so good."

He shook his head. "I'm not really a boat guy. I prefer dry land."

She looked at him with a hint of disdain, which she tried her best to hide. "No shit."

He frowned back at her with a look more akin to hurt than anger, and she felt a pang of guilt.

"Look at the horizon," she said, wondering why on earth she should possibly feel bad about insulting a kidnapper. "Sometimes the gentle waters can mess you up as bad as the rough."

He nodded and glanced over at the expensive waterfront homes on their right.

"How did you handle the open ocean?" she asked, thinking about the fishing boat and how it had to have come from another island somewhere. That would mean at least 200 miles across the sea.

"Dramamine," he replied. "And I need to get some more while we're here."

"Where is it you need to get to, anyway?" she asked. "It's a small island, I can probably tell you how to get there."

He laughed, and replied without looking at her. "You're going to take me wherever I need to go."

AJ looked ahead at Governors Creek, opening up before them. Creek was a misleading name for the large lagoon, separated from the North Sound by a rim of mangroves and lined with expensive homes and boat docks. She turned north towards the Yacht Club marina where she kept the RIB for much of the year. It was strange to think of help being a few feet away, yet she was incapable of reaching them. People were going about their day completely unaware that Jackson was being held hostage at gunpoint, and a man armed with nothing more than a mobile phone and a threat rendered her powerless. AJ was confident she could save herself at any chosen moment, but Pascal's hold on Jackson was an effective deterrent. She had also noticed his mobile was password locked, not by fingerprint, and he was careful to shield the screen when he used the code. All she could do was continue playing along and hope an opportunity presented itself.

"So, we're going to drive around the island I've lived on for over ten years, and you, who's clearly never been here before, are going to tell me turn right, turn left, stop here?" she asked, pushing for more information.

He let out a long sigh and looked at her. "Are you going to be a pain in my ass?"

"No," she replied, holding up a hand. "I'm trying to make it easier on both of us. If you just told me, 'take me to Bodden Town', I could drive you to Bodden Town and you wouldn't have to fuss around with directions you'll probably get wrong. You should know, Google maps for Grand Cayman aren't entirely accurate."

He let out another accentuated, dramatic sigh. "Alright, alright. I have an address on Melmac Avenue in George Town. Do you know where that is?"

She nodded. "What's there?"

He groaned. "You said it would be easier if I told you where we were going. How is asking a hundred more questions easier for me? Do you know where Melmac is or not?"

"Calm down, don't get your knickers in a knot," she replied. "Melmac is between Walkers and South Church Street, but all that's there are a few homes. That's why I asked."

"45 Melmac, it's a house I'm looking for," he said. "How far is it from your dock?"

"There's no traffic with the borders closed, so fifteen minutes I'd guess. It's the other side of downtown George Town. But nothing's very far away on an island that's only 22 miles long," she said politely, trying to keep him talking as she rounded the corner of the marina.

"Good, maybe we'll get lucky and wrap this up quickly," he mumbled.

"That's it? You just need to see someone at this house?" she asked, knowing she was risking angering the man. "You couldn't call them, or send an email?"

AJ cut left into the channel between two jetties and noticed the docks were pretty much deserted. Whoever was going out had already left, and it was early for the dive boats to return. Few were going out as their only customers were still locals and most people were being careful with their spending.

"Because I don't know if the person I need to contact is still there," he shared absentmindedly, surveying the marina as they idled along. "If they are, this will be quick; if they're not, it may take more time and some searching."

AJ put the motors in reverse to bring the RIB to a stop, then skilfully backed the boat into its spot. "Who is it? Maybe I know them. Like I said, this isn't a big island, there's a chance I know them or at least recognise the family name. Couple of calls and I bet I can track down whoever it is." She offered as she cut the motors.

"No calls, no other people involved," he said firmly, "You'll drive me to Melmac and we'll go from there. Maybe stop at a drugstore on the way."

"Pharmacy," she corrected. "They say pharmacy here. I've always wondered why they call them drugstores in America. Sounds like a dodgy place where some bloke in a hoodie and jeans hanging off his arse offers you weed and ecstasy."

She hopped from the boat to the jetty, which appeared to startle Pascal.

"Hey," he shouted, "what are you doing?"

She looked back at him. "Tying the boat up," she replied calmly. "They tend not to stay put if you don't."

He looked around, seeming to realise he had made more noise than he intended. "Yeah, of course. Go ahead. And I'm guessing the term drug didn't have the same connotation it does today, when they named the stores."

AJ tied the stern line to a cleat on the dock and looked back at the strange man in her boat. "Are you staying there or coming with me to Melmac street?"

Pascal squinted up at her and then at the jetty, seemingly determining his best method of exiting the boat. She guessed from his prior performance, stepping on the soft gunwale over to the dock was not appealing to him.

"You, and your boat, are a pain in the ass," he mumbled under his breath.

6

GRAND CAYMAN – SATURDAY

AJ had hoped to see someone she knew at the marina, thinking somehow she might covertly alert them to her crisis. On the other hand, she had no idea how to do that, and was more likely to raise suspicion in Pascal without drumming up any help. Either way, it didn't matter. The jetties were deserted, and they left in her van without incident. She exited Yacht Drive and turned left at the roundabout onto Esterly Tibbetts Highway, the bypass that ran through what was now known as Seven Mile Corridor, according to the estate agents. Grand Cayman was an odd-shaped island, the shallow North Sound taking a scallop from the land mass, leaving a narrow strip of land about a mile wide between the west side of the sound and the famed Seven Mile Beach. She was now heading south down that narrow strip towards George Town, the capital of the Cayman Islands. They drove in silence for several minutes until Pascal finally spoke.

"It's really flat," he said, looking out the passenger side window.

"You mean the island?" AJ asked, unsure.

"Yeah. There're no hills anywhere," Pascal replied. "Even from the water I couldn't see any hills or higher ground."

AJ negotiated the next of what seemed to be an endless series of roundabouts, her fifteen-passenger van lumbering its way around the curves.

"I think officially the highest point on the island is just shy of 60 feet above sea level. That's over on the north side, inland from the coastline a bit."

She pointed to her left over the mangroves lining the highway. "But that peak you see over there is unofficially the highest point. That's called Mount Trashmore. It's the rubbish dump."

The very top of the pile of refuse could just be seen above the brush as they approached, and a small plume of smoke rose into the air before being swept away by the stiff breeze.

"It catches fire a lot," she added.

Ahead, they neared a busier and larger roundabout with signs to the airport to the left and George Town to the right.

"You said there's a pharmacy around here somewhere?" Pascal asked.

AJ thought for a moment. "Actually, there's one just off Smith Road near the hospital. We're going that way anyway if you want to stop."

Pascal nodded. "Okay, stop there," he replied, looking around at the businesses and offices lining the highway on the outskirts of town.

AJ continued over a traffic light and yet another roundabout until the airport could be seen on their left beyond a cricket field. At the next light she turned right onto Smith Road, where larger office buildings and a few retail stores occupied both sides of the road. She wondered how this would work. Was he planning on going in and leaving her in the van, or would they both enter the store? She couldn't imagine he would leave her alone outside. But if he did, what could she do in the few minutes he was in the shop? If she drove off, Jackson was a phone call away from a bullet. She may well be able to raise the alarm and perhaps capture Pascal, but that wouldn't make Jackson any less dead. They went through a tiny roundabout, nothing more than a painted circle on the tarmac, where Smith Road became Walkers, with the hospital on their left. She continued to run scenarios through her mind. After 150 yards, she slowed and turned right on Leafy Lane, then quickly left into the car park before a building signed 'Valu-Med Pharmacy'. AJ parked the van and left the engine idling, looking over at Pascal.

"There you go," she said.

"They speak English here, right?" he asked, staring at the storefront.

"Yup. The locals have quite an island accent, but they usually soften it for foreigners to understand."

Pascal looked over at AJ. "You're going in," he said, to her surprise. "Do you have money on you?"

Taken aback, she fumbled around and realised her wallet was in her rucksack, still on the RIB. She reached over to the glove box, and Pascal flinched.

"Don't worry, I'm just getting some cash. I keep emergency petrol money in here," she said, digging around and coming up with a Caymanian twenty-dollar bill. "You want Dramamine, right?"

Pascal relaxed. "Yes, get as much as that'll buy you."

AJ nodded, and opened the driver's door.

"Hey," Pascal said firmly, and she looked back at him. "You're thinking about how you might call for help, or contact someone while you're in there." He glanced at his watch, and continued, "In about 10 minutes from now, my men either get a phone call from me with the appropriate code, or they take your hip-looking boyfriend out on deck and blow his brains out. There is nothing you can set in motion that will save him in those ten minutes. If capturing me is worth more to you than his life, go ahead, make a move. If not, I suggest you buy Dramamine as quickly as possible and come back to this van."

AJ tried to speak, but her mouth was dry, and the words wouldn't come. It seemed Pascal had read her mind. She could easily fall foul of underestimating her captor, and this was a good reminder that this was unlikely to be the man's first venture into the world of kidnapping. She nodded and left the van with her legs shaking, closing the door behind her. Her limbs felt like stiff, leaden appendages that required concentration to move in the direction of the doorway. A wave of nausea swept through her and she jumped out of the way, awkwardly startled, as a lady exited through the automatic sliding doors. Come on, she thought, get it together. She knew there was still a window of opportunity present, but she needed to think clearly and act swiftly. Inside the store, she scanned the signs at the end of the aisles and headed down the one marked 'allergy and cold medicine'. She frantically hunted for sea-sickness pills, unsure if she was in the right aisle or not. She spotted a lady stocking shelves one row over and called to her over the merchandise rack.

"Excuse me, I'm looking for Dramamine, where would I find it?"

The dark-skinned, middle-aged Caymanian lady looked up and smiled. "End of the aisle you're on, miss, just down there," she said in her musical island accent, pointing to the end nearest the pharmacy counter in the back.

"Thank you," AJ replied, and hurried down the aisle.

The selection was annoyingly broad with versions marked original, chewable, kids, or non-drowsy, and all available in different-sized packaging. Below were generic and alternate brands. She scanned the prices on the generic, original formula packets, deciding she'd prefer her kidnapper drowsy. She chose the greatest number of pills twenty dollars would buy and rushed back to the front of the store to the checkout counter. No one was there. AJ looked around and spotted the lady who had helped her, slowly making her way over, hobbling along on what appeared to be sore knees.

"Coming right over," the lady said softly. "These pins ain't what they used to be."

AJ smiled and tried her best not to look impatient. "That's fine, I appreciate the help."

The lady made her way behind the counter and took the glasses hanging from a string around her neck and slipped them over her ears. She looked at the register and pecked in a login code with one finger, before turning to AJ.

"Right then. Find everything you needed, young lady?" she enquired.

AJ slid the packet across the counter. "Yes, thanks to you I did. Just the Dramamine today."

The lady took the packet and ran it across the scanner built into the counter, where it didn't beep. She peered at the packet over her glasses, turned it over, and slid it over the scanner again. It beeped and she smiled in satisfaction, or relief, AJ couldn't tell. AJ held out the twenty-dollar bill.

"That's seventeen dollars and ninety-nine cents CI," the lady said and took the banknote, "out of twenty."

She poked at some inputs on the touchscreen, and the register sprung open. She retrieved a couple of one-dollar bills and scraped a penny from the register, before closing the drawer and handing the change to AJ.

"Here you go dear, two dollars and a penny change."

AJ took the money while the lady reached below the counter for a bag.

"I don't need a bag, thank you," she said politely. "But I was wondering if I might ask a strange favour?"

Two minutes later, AJ hurried out of the sliding doors and walked across the car park to the van. She was pleased to see Pascal still sitting in the passenger seat, where he appeared to have stayed. She opened the driver's door and stepped up into the seat, handing the packet of Dramamine to the man, and closing the door.

"Look at me," he demanded sternly.

She turned and faced him.

"Did you make a phone call while you were inside?" he asked calmly, studying her face with his oddly bulging eyes.

She breathed gently and took a moment to reply. "You told me not to. I'm not an idiot."

He kept looking at her, searching for any signs of deceit,

without saying another word. She maintained his stare until he finally looked away.

"Okay, let's go," he ordered.

AJ put the van in reverse and carefully backed out of the parking spot. She had always been a terrible liar, but she had recalled a scene from a movie where someone had explained their trick for lying effectively. They thought of something distracting, like doing math problems, or counting the freckles on the face of the person they were lying to. Anything to make the lie a secondary thought. She had chosen to name the countries across Europe, starting with England, and heading south. She had distracted herself so well, she had almost missed answering his question, but maybe, she thought, maybe it actually worked.

She turned right on the narrow Leafy Lane, then right again on Walkers, and followed it around the curve to head south-west for less than half a mile. Melmac was a minor road on the right that headed towards the ocean on the south side of George Town, and she turned in cautiously, looking for house numbers. Two hundred yards up the lane on the right-hand side was a neatly kept bungalow with the number 45 on the gate leading to the front door.

"Keep going," Pascal said, and AJ cruised slowly by the home, both of them staring at the well-groomed front garden.

Melmac was a short street. AJ soon arrived at the junction onto South Church, with the Caribbean Sea beyond the homes and condos in front of them. Pascal looked around them.

"Turn around and go back up the street," he said, gesticulating back the way they had come. "I want you to park one house away from 45."

AJ nodded and backed into the short driveway of the house on the corner, before slowly rolling back down Melmac. He pointed to a spot by some large shrubs on the right side of the street, and she pulled over and parked.

"Can you park like this here?" he asked.

"Yeah, you can park facing either direction on a street here, same as England," she replied, truthfully.

Pascal sat back in his seat and looked over at the little bungalow.

"What now?" AJ asked, leaving the engine running for the moment.

"Now? Now we wait," he replied quietly.

AJ hit the buttons on the door panel to put the windows down.

"What are you doing?" Pascal quickly barked.

"I'm putting the windows down so I can switch off the engine," she replied, continuing to hold the buttons.

"It's hotter than hell and half of Georgia out there, why on earth would you turn off the air-conditioning?" he retorted.

"Because I don't want to pump emissions into the air unnecessarily," she said, and shut the ignition off.

Pascal shook his head as a bead of sweat already dribbled down his tall forehead from below his hat.

"Emissions my ass, fire this thing back up and give me some AC, damn it."

AJ considered telling him no, but she figured it would prolong a battle she would ultimately lose, and reluctantly started the van and put the windows back up. They sat in silence for a few minutes until Pascal took his mobile, hid the screen from AJ as he entered his code and dialled a number.

After a brief pause, he spoke into the phone. "It's Pascal. Everything is good. 56." He then hung up.

AJ committed the words and numbers to memory by repeating them over and over in her head. Somewhere once she had heard that the brain needed to hear something seven times for it to stay lodged in the grey matter. She had no idea if that was true, but she repeated it nine times to be sure. It was 11am. Five plus six was eleven. Could it be that simple, she wondered? She did not understand how it would help her to know the code, as surely it needed to be spoken by Pascal, or someone doing an accurate impression of the American man who held her hostage. That certainly wasn't her.

7

OXFORD, ENGLAND – SATURDAY

Simon heard voices in his room, slowly becoming recognisable as he emerged from his hazy sleep. He lay still and listened to his wife and son, enjoying the sound of his family without the further awkwardness of being involved in their already awkward conversation.

"The earliest they could set everything up at the house is on Monday, so we can't move him until then," he heard Tamsin whisper.

There was a pause before Martin spoke. "I just don't see how the doctors can still try things, you know, test or whatever, if he's not in the hospital."

His wife's voice was patient, sympathetic, but firm. "Darling, we've covered this. I know it's hard to accept, but they've done all of that. All we can do now is keep him as comfortable as possible, and spend as much time as we can with him."

Simon wanted to open his eyes and take over the conversation. Do what he had always been so good at – talking to people. He would discuss, persuade, and motivate until all parties aligned and headed down the same path. A cohesive unit, organised and enthusiastic to forge ahead with a plan. But he held back. His eyes stayed closed, and he lay still despite the discomfort he felt in his body, and his soul. Tamsin would handle these situations alone, and he dreaded to think of the difficult times that lay ahead for her, and for Martin. He knew she needed to pave her own path through this unchartered territory, and he should allow her the freedom to handle it in her own way. While he was the captain of his corporate ship, he was not a micro-manager. With every problem he solved, he relied on his business analogies to shape his personal decisions, and his personal ethics to guide the boundaries of his company. He had always pictured his companies as a foot-ball pitch. He marked the lines around the field; he set up the goal-posts and explained the rules, clearly and precisely. His role was to build the environment and set forth the objectives, then sit back and let the people do what they did best. He could never under-stand the idea of hiring intelligent, creative people, and then restricting their play with overbearing rules and mandates. Everyone needed to make a bad shot now and again – it was part of the learning process. If play ran outside the sidelines, he would be there to nudge them back onto the pitch, keep play within the broad guidelines he had set, and aimed at the goal. His wife possessed an inner strength that he admired, respected and had stood toe to toe with on more than a few occasions. He had faith she would rise to this challenge both with their son, and with GraphicWell.

"It feels like we're giving up," Martin mumbled.

Simon heard his wife take a deep breath and once again he fought the urge to intervene. "I know it feels that way, darling, but you've seen all the prodding, poking and testing they've tried over the last few months. He doesn't have the strength for any more, and they've exhausted everything they could try. It's time Daddy comes home. Home to us. We have to make the absolute best of these days ahead. This is a precious and important time, Martin. In years to come, when we look back, we'll want to feel like we squeezed everything we could from these moments. Leave nothing unsaid to your dad, let him know how you feel about him, okay?

Of course it's important for him to hear, but it's crucial for our own peace of mind for the rest of our days."

Silence fell about the room, and Simon choked back the tears. He realised there was no way to love this woman any more than he did at that very moment. He opened his eyes and soaked up the image of her beautiful smile, lighting up as she saw him wake.

"There he is. Hope you got some rest, my love," she said warmly.

Martin sat forward in his chair beside the hospital bed. "Hey Dad," he said, and Simon noticed the boy's eyes were moist.

"Hey champ. Nice win this morning," Simon said in a crackly voice and Tamsin reached for the glass of water next to the bed.

Simon sipped through the straw, his head tilted to the side, making it easier to swallow while he was lying down.

"I don't think I played very well, but I did make the pass for our winning goal," Martin explained. "Coach kept telling me to push forward more, but they had a demon centre forward and I was the only one that could keep up with him. That's how they scored the first goal. We were all pushing forward, then we lost the ball, and he was gone."

Simon smiled as Tamsin put the glass of water down. He glanced up at her. "You should have woken me when you got here."

Tamsin shook her head. "You needed the rest. We weren't sitting here long." Which was a white lie, and they both knew it.

Simon turned back to his son. He loved hearing Martin enthuse over his football. He preferred to watch him play, but short of video highlights from a parent's mobile phone, he would never see his son on the pitch again. Martin didn't have the skills that Simon had possessed as a youth, but the boy was a student of the game, and he was the fastest kid on the team. He might be the fastest kid in the local league, Simon pondered proudly. Martin had chosen football and Simon was glad he had never pushed him into the game, or pressured him to perform. When Martin had asked for help or coaching, he had provided it. Beyond that, he had left him to pursue the sport at his own pace and interest.

"How's that put you in points?" Simon asked.

"We're second, but it's early. We've only played five games. Once we're ten into the season, we'll have a better idea of who's our biggest competition," Martin said, stopping abruptly on the last part and looking down at the linoleum floor.

There was that ugly reference to the future again. The elephant in the room can be uncomfortable. The entire herd made it hard to breathe.

"One game at a time, right?" Simon quickly continued. "What have you two got planned for the rest of the weekend?"

"Well, we were going to spend the afternoon with you," Tamsin picked up in a cheery tone, "then Martin has a birthday party he's been invited to this evening." She looked at her son with a wry smile.

"I thought parties still weren't an option with the restrictions?" Simon queried.

Tamsin winked at her husband. "You tell him, Martin."

Their son shifted uncomfortably in his chair and shrugged his shoulders. "It's no big deal. It's a distanced party where we'll all be seated away from each other but in a big circle. They have games set up, and the food is individual takeaway from a restaurant. It's safe and everything."

"There's only eight kids too, so I think it's nice Martin was picked to go," Tamsin added, and Simon noticed she still looked like she was dying to say more.

"Whose birthday is it?" Simon asked and got an eyebrow raise from his wife.

"Just a girl in my class," Martin blurted, and blushed.

Simon turned to Tamsin. "Honey, would you see if the shop downstairs has one of those fruity yogurt things in the tube you've been bringing me? I think I might be able to eat one this evening."

Tamsin reached over and squeezed his hand. "It might take me a few minutes, there's normally a queue at this time of day. I need to check my voicemail too, so I'll do that while I'm downstairs."

"No problem," he replied, smiling back at her as she stood and walked to the door.

Simon waited until she had turned the corner before talking. "Move into your mum's chair here," he said, pointing to the vacant seat closer to him. "Now, whose party is this?"

Martin sat and shook his head, looking anywhere but at his father. "Just a girl in my class, it's really no big deal. I'll be super careful, I promise."

Simon laughed, as best he could without coughing again. "Son, I have no doubt you'll be safe and I'm sure your mum has made sure the party is well organised and safe. What I want to know about is this young lady that's requested your presence."

Martin blushed again and grinned uncomfortably. "Come on, Dad, it's just a school thing. A chance to see some kids from class while we're studying from home."

"Son, do your old man a favour and humour him. I'm gonna miss out on some stuff down the road here, so let me in on this one while I can enjoy it," he said with amusement.

"Jeez." Martin wriggled. "I don't like talking about this stuff, Dad."

"Hey kiddo, the first thing to figure out is that it's normal to think about the girls, and all the guys are thinking about them too." He checked himself for a moment. "Well, most of the guys anyway. There's some that'll lean another direction, and that's okay too. But, what I'm trying to say, son, is you'll be treated however you act about this."

Martin looked up at his father. "How do you mean?"

"If you act awkward around the girls, or about the girls, that's how the girls, and your friends, will treat you. If you're confident and treat it as if it's normal and no big deal, which is how it should be, you'll find everyone is more likely to handle it the same way. I mean, they'll give you a hard time at first, the other blokes I mean, but that's jealousy. Believe me, son, being confident and relaxed about talking to the girls will set you apart and you'll find girls will want to talk to you."

"But, Dad, I don't know what to say to them, I've tried to talk and I kind of seize up."

"The first thing to remember, is my number one rule," Simon said, looking at his boy.

"Tell the truth," Martin replied promptly. "I know, Dad."

"Good, but don't forget that, okay? There'll be times when it's hard to do, or tempting to say what a good-looking young lady wants to hear," Simon continued, making sure his point was clear. "But a little fib needs a bigger lie to support it and then there's no turning back. If you don't have the truth, you have nothing, son."

"Okay, Dad, I promise I will," Martin replied impatiently, wanting to get to the helpful part.

Simon chuckled. "Alright, talking to girls. It takes some practice, son, but the key is to have a bit of a plan. Think about it this way. What would you like to be asked about if they came up to you?"

Martin shrugged his shoulders, but he was no longer blushing. "I don't know. Football, I guess."

"Exactly, and what's football to you?"

"It's what I like to do, I suppose."

"Bingo. Now think about what they like to do, and ask them about that," Simon explained, revelling in this moment of intimacy with his son. Shortly, Martin would be alone in the world to figure out these things and all his father could hope for was to share a brief insight that may help him along the way. Of course, his wife was stunningly beautiful and would be the CEO of a successful corporation, so he had no doubt another man would fill his shoes in time to come. It was a painful thought, despite his desire for Tamsin to be happy. He tried to push it from his mind.

"I don't know what they do. Text each other every five minutes. Go shopping. They talk about clothes and music all the time," Martin replied, thoughtfully.

"What about sports? Who is this girl anyway, whose party is it?" Simon pressed, now his son was opening up.

"It's Alison, I don't think you've met her. She joined our school at the end of last year. Her parents moved here from down south somewhere," Martin said. "She plays tennis."

"There you go, you have two great subjects already. Find out where she moved from, and ask her about that. There's plenty of conversation there, right? Her old school, the town, does she miss her friends? See, loads to talk about." Simon felt a weariness descending upon him again, and a frustration grew at the same time. These were the moments he was to be robbed of and he felt teased by this disease, by this fate. He was allowed a fleeting glance into the world he would not be a part of.

"Tennis, you said," he continued, grimly hanging on before his mind slipped away. "Plenty to chat about there."

Martin looked at his dad with his brow furrowed, and Simon squinted, forcing his eyes to stay focused.

"Dad, she's, umm," the boy struggled. "Well, I think Mum's okay but Dad, you should know too, her dad is a black man," he finally managed to say.

Simon smiled. "I hope you don't think that would bother me, Martin," he said weakly.

"No, I didn't think it would, Dad, but I guess I didn't know for sure."

Simon felt himself slipping and fight as he may to stay with his son in this beautiful moment, the cancer and the medication conspired to steal away what might have been. He would move heaven and earth for his son. In his mind, there was nothing he wouldn't do to protect his boy and secure his future. But what he couldn't do was stay with him in that moment.

"I knew a wonderful black girl, many years ago..." he mumbled, before finally succumbing to restless sleep.

8

GRAND CAYMAN – SATURDAY

Under the shelter of the extended roof off the back of the wheelhouse, the two Jamaicans had set up some crates as a table and two chairs on the deck. One of them disappeared into the cabin below for a few minutes and returned with a scruffy-looking case that he placed on the makeshift table.

"D'ya play the game, mon?" he asked in his thick Jamaican accent as he opened the case to reveal a well-used backgammon board.

Jackson had noticed the two men conversed with each other in patois, the native Jamaican tongue, but used English to address him.

He shrugged his shoulders. "Sure, I know how to play. It's been a while though."

He had never been held hostage before, but if he had been asked how such a scenario played out just an hour before, this was not the answer he would have come up with. The men had not restrained him; they had given him a bottle of water and the gun was tucked sloppily in the back of the one man's shorts. They seemed completely relaxed and not in the least worried about Jackson attempting to escape.

"Thas good enough, brudder, is like ridin' dah bike, mon," the unarmed man said, and pointed at the crate across from him. Jackson sat down and the man began arranging the pieces to their starting positions on the board. Jackson leaned in and helped.

"What should I call you guys?" Jackson asked, glancing from the seated man to the other, who leant against the wheelhouse.

The man standing laughed, revealing a mouthful of misshapen white teeth. "Call me Boss-Man if ya like, mon, seeing as I'd the one wit dah gun."

His partner laughed too, and leaned back on his crate. "Me is Ganjaman, an' everybody call him Fatty."

Jackson looked at Fatty. Neither of the two men had any fat on their bodies, they were both wiry framed and lean. Fatty grinned back at him.

"Not all o' me's fatty ya see," he said, and they both burst out laughing again.

Jackson smiled and took a sip of water, giving them a minute to settle down. "How do you know the other man? The guy that left with my girlfriend? He doesn't really seem like someone you two would hang out with."

Ganjaman shook his head. "Dat fool? It just be a job. We don't know 'im no more than know you." He looked over at Jackson. "Now, put your money on dah table."

Jackson held up both hands. "I don't have any money, we were just diving. I don't take a wallet underwater with me."

Ganjaman swung around and looked at where the RIB had been alongside the fishing boat. "Bet dere's some cash on dah boat doh. Shit, shoulda had a look see 'fore dey took off," he said.

"Wallet's in the centre console," Jackson explained. "Your buddy's probably gone through it by now."

"No matter," Ganjaman said with a wave of his hand. "You can owe me what I win from yer now." Then he laughed. "Gonna take all ya got when dah boat back anyhows."

He looked up at Fatty. "Let's burn one real quick now, 'fore we show dis white boy how to play dis game."

Fatty looked at the cabin door nervously. "Don't be foolin' about, he smell it an all."

Ganjaman screwed up his face. "Nonsense, brudda, we go to dah back der, and everyting be all right."

He got up and walked towards the stern, digging in his shorts pocket. Fatty started after him and Ganjaman stopped and turned around.

"You gotsta watch 'im now. I'll trade wit yer when I burn dah half," he said indignantly.

"He ain't going nowhere," Fatty replied, without pausing. "He smart he know it don't matter weddah he standin' or floatin'." He shoved his sidekick towards the stern. "Anyways, yer not leave me none last time, your half ain't da same as half to nobody else. More like dah mostly all, what I been seein'."

Ganjaman pulled a joint and a lighter from his pocket and paused before he lit it. "Not my fault yer half dah top half. I gotta burn tru yours to get to mine."

Fatty snatched the joint and lighter away, lighting it up and taking a long draw.

Ganjaman looked back at Jackson, still seated on the crate. "You hear that now, mon? Your girl ain't knowing either way. She just hadda think you still here."

Fatty handed the joint to his friend as he released a plume of thick, pungent smoke. "It ain't no ting to me either way."

Jackson caught the cold stare from the man and guessed he was telling the truth; these two didn't care whether he lived or died. They both turned to face the water with their backs to him, and traded the joint back and forth, laughing and chatting. Jackson sat and watched, wondering if there was anything he could do to get away. But they were moored in crystal-clear water, miles from land, without another boat within 1,000 yards. They could take their time untying from the buoy and motor after him before he could swim away. He would be a sitting duck.

Jackson never heard the wheelhouse door, or any steps on the deck. The first he knew was a voice booming from just behind him as he watched the two Jamaicans getting high.

"You two!"

Jackson started, and swung around to see a tall, muscular man with a shaved head staring across the deck. He was neatly dressed in a pale blue linen shirt and beige slacks that fitted his athletic form like a magazine model. Ganjaman quickly threw the remainder of the joint away and they both loped back across the deck. They weren't laughing anymore.

"Stay here and watch him," the man growled in an accent Jackson couldn't place. "We're not paying you to get stoned."

He had a dark unshaved shadow across the lower portion of his face, and a swarthy complexion that suggested southern or eastern Mediterranean. He finally looked at Jackson with dark, penetrating eyes, before turning and going back into the wheelhouse and down the steps into the cabins below.

The two Jamaicans mumbled and complained in patois, but returned to their spots.

"Don't be mattering no how, plenty to go round when dis over wit," Ganjaman said, waving a hand at Jackson. "Go, man, roll to see who start."

Jackson tossed one of the dice across the crate next to the board and rolled a six.

"Shit," Ganjaman said in a long drawn-out groan. "Dis boy luckier dan you," he said, glancing up at Fatty before he rolled a three.

"Maybe it's you no good at der game, ever think about dat?" Fatty ribbed him.

Ganjaman waved him off with a bony, long-fingered hand and looked at Jackson. "Not dat I care, but what they call you?"

"Jackson," he replied and rolled a double four to start, much to Ganjaman's chagrin and a cascade of what he could only assume were curse words in the man's native tongue.

Jackson moved his two pieces eight spots while Ganjaman made a theatrical show of shaking the dice in his hand, before rolling a two and a four across the wooden crate.

"Who's the scary dude?" Jackson asked, as Ganjaman moved one of his pieces to a safe point. "He your boss or is he with the other guy?"

"You ask too much," Fatty barked. "Ain't your worry who's who. If you lucky, you live out dah day, and we be gone."

Jackson picked up the dice and rolled again, this time using a two and a five to move one piece into his home section of the board.

"He is a scary mudda doe, dat be dah trut." Ganjaman said quietly. "Nuttin' dat man don't see. We just hired by dem two for da job. Be glad get dah cash and see dah back of dem both."

"Tru dat." Fatty nodded. "Man gimme dah creeps. Like he a cat or some ting, never hear him move, and den he right der, mon."

"He just stays down in the cabins?" Jackson asked casually, hoping the two would keep talking.

"Damn glad he do," Ganjaman said and rolled the dice.

The third man on the boat had changed everything for Jackson. The two Jamaicans were undoubtedly street hustlers and petty thugs, but they were sloppy and careless. He wouldn't be surprised if they started drinking or smoking again as the day wore on, and he had been sure he would get a chance to grab the gun from Fatty. If he timed it right, after the man who had taken AJ called, as he had done at the top of the hour, he would have almost sixty minutes to raise the alarm and for the police to find AJ on the island. But now he had the man who resembled a mixed martial arts fighter to contend with. A guy that scared the hell out of the two men who were happy to kidnap, and at least threaten to murder, was probably someone he should be worried about too. Even if he got the gun and controlled the deck and the Jamaicans, there was no telling what MMA guy would counter with. Jackson felt sure Fatty's gun wasn't the only one on the fishing boat.

"Your go, mon, quit your day dreamin'," Ganjaman urged, and Jackson gathered up the dice.

He rolled a double three and moved his pieces, taking out a stranded checker of Ganjaman's in the process.

"Shoot dis mudda now, Fatty," Ganjaman shouted, and jumped up from his crate. "Why we grab dah luckiest white boy on dah planet?"

Jackson froze for a second, wondering what the man was about to do, but Ganjaman burst out laughing.

"Guess if he'd dah luckiest, he not be here on our boat wit dah gun up his arse."

"Ain't he lucky. It you dat unlucky," Fatty said, laughing himself. "It you been holdin' me back all dees years. I be rid o' you no good, boat anchor, unlucky, sorry excuse for dah black man, den maybe I bin king o' Kingston by now."

Ganjaman threw his arms up and roared with laughter. "Me bin holdin' you back, you sayin'? You be fish food floatin' in dah harbour it not for me."

"Tru dat," Fatty replied, still in fits of laughter. "Aside from dat, I be better off."

"Aside from dat, nuttin'," Ganjaman retorted, sitting back down. "Dead be dead anytime o' day, hah there, lucky white boy Jackson?"

"Tru dat," Jackson said, and the two Jamaicans roared with laughter one more time.

9

GRAND CAYMAN – SATURDAY

Ten minutes felt like a fortnight to AJ. Sitting, staring at the bungalow while time crawled by, took her further away from the top of the hour and ate into the margin of time she would have to bring in help. Lunging across the front of the van seemed like a clumsy and ineffective way of neutralising Pascal. He may not be physically intimidating, but he still outweighed her by a lot, she guessed, looking over at his pudgy frame. She needed a weapon of some sort. She made a mental note to place a billy club or a tyre iron in the driver's side door pocket, just in case she was abducted in her own van by a strange American man in the future. She thought about what she could do if she had a club of some sort. Was she willing to swing it and hit the guy in the head? It was one thing defending yourself while being attacked; from past experience she knew survival instinct took over and she would fight like a cornered alley cat, but she wasn't sure she could initiate such an act of violence. Smashing another human's skull while there seemed hope for a less vicious solution made her feel ill, and she doubted she could use a weapon if she had it.

"Why are we just sitting here?" she asked. "If you need to meet whoever lives there, why don't you knock on the door. Or can't you call them? This doesn't seem very efficient."

Pascal kept staring out the windscreen. "I don't know if the person I need to meet with lives there," he said.

"Even more reason to go ask, surely?" AJ persisted. "What do you need this person for, anyway?"

Pascal sighed, and turned towards her. "Does the concept of sitting still and being quiet mean anything to you? You have no idea of the situation. So just do as I say, and you can go back to your boyfriend, and your scuba diving, and your sweaty little island life before the day's out. Okay?"

AJ stared back blankly. "You're right, I don't know the situation, which is why I'm asking. I'm sure I can help if you're searching for someone, and that would speed up this entire process of getting you on your way, and me back to my life. I'm sure you have some grandiose plan, but to be honest, it seems rather poorly organised from my seat."

Pascal's shoulders slumped, and he shook his head. "Are you always this difficult?"

"I'm not difficult," she replied indignantly, "I'm offering help and solutions."

"You're a pain in the goddamn ass, that's what you are," he groaned, turning back to the bungalow.

"Are you planning on kidnapping whoever it is you're looking for?" she persisted, undaunted by his prickliness.

"No," he replied curtly.

They both sat up straight and fell quiet as the front door to the bungalow opened and an older white lady stepped outside. She wore a broad sun hat and carried a small plastic bucket along with a foam pad in her hands. She nudged the door closed behind her and looked around her front garden. Choosing a spot to start, she slowly walked over and placed the pad on the ground and the bucket alongside. She carefully dropped to her knees on the pad and began plucking weeds from around her plants in the flower bed.

"Okay, you like talking so much, here's your chance," Pascal said.

"What?" she said, wondering what he could possibly have her do now.

"You're going to walk over there and ask that lady how long she's lived there, and what happened to the previous owner. Get an address if you can," Pascal explained as though he were asking her to grab a bottle of milk for him, at the market.

AJ presumed Pascal had needed her for the ride to the island, and kept her around so she wouldn't report him, and then for the ride back to his boat. But now it was becoming apparent he didn't want to be seen and was using her so he didn't have to be. The wispy hairs on the back of her neck stood up and tickled at the realisation he was fine being seen by her and Jackson, yet no one else.

"If you know who the previous owner was then why don't you tell me? She's much more likely to be helpful if I ask if she knows what happened to Betty, or whatever their name is," AJ reasoned.

He turned and leaned over, waggling a finger at her. "Listen. Enough of this bullshit. Get out of this van, walk over and ask that woman about the previous owners. Get names, get an address, get anything you can, then come back here and tell me exactly what that old lady says. I'll be watching every move you make, every mannerism, and I read lips pretty well too. If I sense any funny business I'm making the call, you hear me?"

AJ nodded. She had found the edge she could push Pascal to and needed to be careful. Of course, once he made that call his mission was over, she had no incentive to comply, and he would be on the run. She let that thought swirl around her mind for a moment as she stepped out of the van. Testing him further would be playing Russian roulette with Jackson's life, but she couldn't let the fear paralyse her to the point of inaction.

She walked across the road and paused at the gate to number 45 Melmac.

"Excuse me, madam, I was wondering if you could help me?" she called out in a pleasant tone.

The lady looked up from her gardening and squinted at AJ as the bright, late morning sun hit her face. "Oh, hello," she said and struggled up from her knees to walk over. "What can I help you with?" she asked in an upper-class English accent.

AJ forced a smile. "I was actually trying to track down the previous owners of this house. You wouldn't happen to know where they moved to, would you?"

The lady looked thoughtful. "Gosh. Haven't thought about the Thompsons in years. We've lived here since 2003. Well, I say we. It was we when we moved here, just me now," she said with the pain in her voice of a widow missing a part of her life that left her incomplete.

"I'm very sorry," AJ said softly, feeling guilty for stirring up the poor woman's loss.

"That's okay," she said, and smiled. "The Thompsons you're looking for? Let me think." The lady wiped beads of sweat from her forehead, then rested her hands on her hips. "They moved to the north side, if I remember correctly. Had some family over there, I recall. I think they lived here while their children went through school, but once the youngest married, they sold up and moved."

"You wouldn't happen to remember where exactly, by any chance? Do you have an address for them? Perhaps in the sales paperwork," AJ asked.

"Oh my, that paperwork is probably long gone," the lady said, her brow furrowed. "Hurricane Ivan hit a year after we moved in and flooded every home all around here. As you can see, we're a bungalow, so we were knee deep in sea water. We lost all kinds of paperwork, photo albums, you name it. Mind you, I don't know that we ever knew their new address, I'm not even sure they'd bought another home by the time we closed the purchase of this place. I'm sorry."

"That's okay, like you say, it was a while back," AJ replied.

"Their children are probably still in town here, maybe they can help," the lady added.

"How many children did they have?" AJ asked. "They would all be married adults by now, surely."

"Three I think, but we only met the youngest. She was getting married right around the time we bought the house. Only reason I remember, was one time when we came over to see the house, she was trying on her wedding dress. Lovely dress it was too. Shaw, I think. She married a chap named Shaw."

AJ thought for a moment. She needed to go back to Pascal with something more than 'north side somewhere', or this ordeal would keep dragging on. She couldn't figure out what he could possibly want with a seemingly normal older couple on the island, but he said he didn't plan to kidnap them. Of course, as he was already a kidnapper, the idea he was lying was hardly a stretch. Still, she needed something more. The sooner they could track down these people and return to the RIB, the better chance she had of getting Jackson back.

"Do you recall the Thompsons' names? Maybe I can find them through some other records," AJ asked.

The lady paused and looked at AJ with a hint of suspicion. "Why is it you're trying to find the Thompsons? I don't think you said."

"No, I didn't, I'm sorry," AJ answered, buying time while she scrambled to think. "They have some money coming to them from their mortgage payoff on this place. It wasn't discovered until now, they just did an audit. I do freelance work like this sometimes, finding people and whatnot. Usually they owe money, but this one's fun as they're actually getting some money back. Their first names are on the paperwork I'm sure, I just can't remember them."

AJ was surprised the lady appeared appeased by her hastily invented story, and she felt guilty again for telling a lovely older lady a lie. She resolved to come back when this was all over and apologise. Assuming she survived whatever this was.

"Hope they pay them the interest on 17 years. I guarantee the mortgage company would add it all up with late fees thrown in if it was the other way round," the lady said, shaking her head.

"Damon was the father, I remember that. Wife's name began with an 'A' I think, but it's escaping me, I'm afraid. Andrea? No, that wasn't it, Aldrea, no that's not even a name," she mumbled. "Of course, these days people call their children any odd thing. Apparently good old normal names don't work anymore. Poor kids spend their lives explaining how to pronounce the pile of letters their silly parents thought would make a good name."

"That's funny," AJ chuckled. "Unique isn't always better."

"Exactly," the lady agreed, firmly. "Alice! That was the wife's name, Alice. See, it's all in there," she said, tapping the side of her hat. "Just have to shake it around a bit sometimes to get the right stuff to fall in to place."

AJ hoped she would have the opportunity to revisit this delightful lady. She guessed a chat over tea would be quite entertaining. She extended her hand. "Thank you so much for your help. My name is AJ by the way. Spelt 'A' and 'J'."

The lady shook her hand with a smile. "You're welcome, nice chatting with you. I'm Kate, spelt the only way I've ever seen it."

AJ walked back across the road and glanced up at the van. She could see Pascal watching her with his mobile in his hand. She got back in the driver's seat and shivered at the cold inside the vehicle. She reached over and turned the air conditioning fan down from overdrive to one. Pascal stared at her.

"Thompsons are the family that used to live there. Sold to this lady, and her now-deceased husband, back in 2003. They moved to the north side of the island, but she doesn't know the address. Their first names are Damon and Alice," AJ told him and realised how thin the information sounded.

"That's it? She bought a house from them but doesn't have a forwarding address for their mail or anything?" Pascal asked impatiently, his thumb hovering over the screen of his mobile.

"Wouldn't matter anyway," AJ quickly retorted. "Cayman doesn't have home delivery of mail, everyone has a PO box."

"How far away is the north side of the island?" he asked.

AJ shrugged her shoulders. "It's only about 10 miles for a bird, but there's only one road that cuts across the middle of the island to the north without going all the way around the East End. It's probably twice that to Old Man's Bay, then whichever way along the north coast you want to go from there. Lot' of locals live over there, but they're scattered all along the coast."

Pascal stared at her, his jaw twitching and his large, bug-like eyes unblinking. She noticed a vein beginning to bulge in his forehead and worried he was about to explode.

"None of that is useful," he seethed.

"I'm sorry, but that's all she knew," AJ replied quietly. She didn't want to rile him any more than he was already, but she felt frustrated the man had shown up, threatened their lives, and was clearly unprepared. "Couldn't you have done a bit more research before you showed up here?"

He took a long inhalation that seemed to suck all the freezing cold air from the van. "Of course we did research," he growled, "but there's not much of public record on this damn island, and your government offices don't have phone numbers. You have to go by the freaking office in person. And guess what? We're in the middle of a worldwide pandemic, so they don't want you going by the office."

"We're over the pandemic," AJ mumbled.

"What?" Pascal huffed.

"The Cayman Islands have been free of cases for months, that's why there's border restrictions still in place. Until the rest of the world gets their shit together, we can't risk bringing the virus back onto the island. Haven't you noticed no one has to wear masks or social distance here?" she said, glaring at the man.

"Don't look at me like that, I don't have the damn virus," he retorted.

She scoffed, and they fell silent except for the fan blowing cold air through the vents and the idling engine.

"How about the phone book?" she said.

"What?" he said, looking at her perplexed. "You have a phone book?"

"Of course," she replied.

"And people still have their phone numbers in it?" he said, still sounding amazed.

"Yeah. I mean, it's mainly the older locals that are in it, especially those without Internet, but you're looking for some older locals, right?" she explained, hoping this might calm him down.

"Where do we find a phone book?" he asked, his tone softening.

She shrugged her shoulders. "Any house or business has one."

"Okay then," he said, "get me a phone book."

10

GRAND CAYMAN – JUNE 1997

Simon stepped from the door of the plane, to be greeted by heat and humidity that hit him like he had opened an oven door. By the time he descended the steps and began walking across the concrete towards the small terminal building, his jeans were clinging to his legs and sweat beaded on his forehead. He hadn't been on a holiday, not a proper holiday at least, since he was a teenager when his parents took a summer trip every year. At 33, it had been a long time coming. He could feel his pale English flesh cowering beneath his short-sleeved button-down shirt and the exposed skin of his arms and face glowing. The only relief was a stiff breeze that swept across the airport, swaying the palms lining the pathway in front of the terminal where a three-piece island band greeted the travellers.

"Brilliant!" his friend Russell enthused, walking behind him, "bloody brilliant."

"Bloody hot," the third member of their group of computer programming bachelors, Paul, said, less enthusiastically.

Simon grinned. They had all been working ridiculous hours for as long as he could remember, but finally the project was complete, the cheque was in the bank, and they were taking the week away they had promised themselves for over three years.

They entered the terminal below a sign welcoming them to Grand Cayman. Inside, a rush of air-conditioned chill met them as they followed the small hanging signs directing them to the choice of two immigration counters for non-residents.

"Blimey, it's better in here," Paul mumbled. "I might have to find indoor entertainment, it has to be fifty degrees outside."

"No bloody way, mate," Russell replied loudly, slapping Paul on the shoulder. "Wait till we get to the beach. Get a daiquiri in your hand with a pretty little umbrella stuffed through a slice of pineapple, sit back in one of them fancy beach chairs, and watch the ladies, barely wearing bikinis, parade themselves around before our eyes."

In front of them, two overly tanned ladies in their fifties, dripping in gold jewellery and designer island wear draped around their paunchy figures, turned and one of them winked at Russell.

"Ladies," he said, and winked back, nudging Paul, who blushed with embarrassment.

The two women stepped up to the immigration counter.

"See! Even you might get lucky, Paul," Russell added, not as quietly as he thought he was being.

Simon couldn't stop smiling. He figured all he had to do was watch his two friends all week and he would have the best entertainment he could possibly imagine. Eleven hours of flying in first class from Heathrow had seen Russell get fairly sauced on free drinks, fall asleep and snore for five hours, then wake up sober and get sauced again. Paul had been engrossed in his Nintendo Game Boy for most of the flight. They made up an odd threesome, but having worked together since their early twenties, meeting at a software company after university, and going on to start their own firm, they had a solid friendship that accepted and embraced their quirky personalities.

They stared at the immigration stamp in their otherwise empty passport pages as they walked to the next area where the baggage carousel entered through rubber flaps and made a serpentine loop before exiting. Bags were starting to come through and the two tanned ladies each dragged a pair of huge suitcases from the belt. Russell gallantly assisted and hauled the behemoths aboard a couple of luggage carts.

"Isn't that yours, Russell?" Simon called, as a tattered old duffel bag rolled past.

Russell tore himself away from the ladies, who appeared in a hurry once their bags had been retrieved, heading for the spa most likely. Simon spotted his suitcase, and they waited a few minutes until Paul's two matching bright yellow hard cases wound their way towards them.

"Bloody hell, Paul," Russell said, shaking his head, "you could spot those from a satellite."

Paul struggled to drag the first case from the belt, bumping into other travellers as he chased the conveyor along. Simon pulled his second case from the belt to save it doing an extra lap.

"What on earth do you have in these things?" he asked as he struggled to lift the case onto a cart.

Paul manhandled the other bag onto the cart and panted for breath. "I may have over-packed a little, but I like to be prepared."

"Seriously, what do you have in there?" Russell asked, slinging his duffel over his shoulder as the three headed towards the customs desk, Simon pulling his suitcase on wheels and Paul pushing the over-weighted cart.

"I wasn't sure if it would be cold at night, so I packed warm clothes, and then something to wear to dinner each evening. Some shorts and tee-shirts for the beach. A towel, of course."

"A bloody towel? You packed a towel?" Russell said, laughing loudly. "We're staying at this plush gaff on a Caribbean island and you didn't think they might at least have towels?"

Paul frowned. "I don't like hotel towels."

"You brought flannel pyjamas too, didn't you?" Russell teased. "Come on, admit it, you have flannel bloody pyjamas in there, don't you?"

Paul blushed a little. "Just two pairs…"

He couldn't finish his reasoning as Russell's laughter drowned him out. Simon couldn't help chuckling along with him, and the customs official looked at them with amused patience.

"Anything to declare gentlemen?" he asked politely in a rhythmic island accent.

"Yup," Russell said, with a serious expression. "I'd like to declare my friend here is smuggling two pairs of flannel pyjamas into your beautiful, and extremely hot island. I recommend you send him home with a note, and tell him not to return until he removes his head from his rectum."

The official looked from Russell to Paul, who was muttering a mixture of excuses and insults to Russell.

"You gentlemen enjoy your stay. Welcome to the Cayman Islands."

Much to Paul's relief, the shuttle to their hotel was waiting for them outside at the kerb. Much to Simon's relief, the tanned ladies were not staying at their hotel. He wasn't sure he could handle Russell launching himself at them again. He was pretty sure the Oxford Street shoppers were in search of bronze-muscled, exotic tennis coaches, not pasty English computer boffins. The shuttle driver gave the three a stream of local information as he left the airport, headed across the northern side of George Town and turned right on West Bay Road behind Seven Mile Beach. Their heads were on swivels as the local man pointed out his favourite restaurants, bars and shops, where they should use his name for extra special service. Simon held back a laugh. He was sure the service was the same, but the driver was bound to get a kickback, and he admired the man's entrepreneurial eagerness.

After five minutes' driving, with glimpses of the bright blue ocean between buildings on their left, the driver pulled into the car park for the Westin Casuarina. The hotel was a five-storey sprawling building along the waterfront that had just opened two years prior, according to their driver, who wrapped up his speech at the lobby doors and sprung from the van. He had no sooner unloaded their bags when a porter whisked them away on a cart and beckoned them to follow along. Simon tipped the driver and thanked him before following Russell, who was once again explaining to Paul how much female flesh would be on display by the swimming pool.

"Simon Lever," he told the polite lady at the front desk who had greeted him with a broad smile and a welcome.

"I see you have three adjoining rooms, Mr. Lever, would you like to leave them all in your name, or add your friends to the rooms?" she said in perfect English with a hint of an accent he couldn't place.

He looked at her name tag, which read Anita, Austria. He pulled his corporate credit card from his wallet and tapped it on the desk, thoughtfully. Pausing, he glanced over at Russell who was strutting around the lobby, commentating on everything that caught his eye, which was mainly members of the fairer sex. Simon turned back to Anita.

"Let's have the chaps give you their own credit cards. I think using this might be dangerous," he said with an embarrassed smile.

He put the corporate card back in his wallet and switched to his own personal credit card, handing it across the desk.

Anita gave him a knowing smile as she took the card. "Perhaps a wise decision, sir."

Simon turned. "Lads, give this nice lady your names and a credit card for your incidentals on your room," he said, calling them back to the desk.

Russell swaggered over and offered his credit card in a dramatic, flourishing wave. "I expect a lot of incidents to be occurring in my room, miss."

Anita wisely avoided eye contact and kept her head down, typing while she thanked him politely. Paul was less dramatic in his presentation. As they finished up, Simon considered apologising to Anita, but he decided it probably wasn't her first encounter with an overenthusiastic arrival, and if he planned to apologise to everyone in Russell's wake, he'd have a busy holiday. He thanked her instead and received a pleasant smile in return.

With keys in hand, they followed the porter to the lift, then travelled down the third-floor hallway to where their three adjacent rooms overlooked the swimming pool and the ocean beyond. Simon thanked and tipped the porter, left his bags by the door, and strode over to the large window, sliding the net curtains aside. Before him, the sunshine glistened off the azure water of the Caribbean Sea with barely a ripple over the surface. Pale yellow sand sloped gently down beyond sprawling palm trees to meet the crystal-clear water lapping sedately up the beach.

"Bugger me!" came Russell's barely muted voice from the neighbouring room. "Look at that."

A moment later a loud knock sounded and Simon turned and noticed, with some dismay, a door between the two rooms. He walked over as the furious knocking continued and unlocked the adjoining door. Russell flung his side open.

"Did you see the bloody view?" he enthused as he bowled into Simon's room. "I thought, yeah right, it won't really be like the picture in the brochure. I was expecting one step up from the Butlin's in Bognor Regis." He bounded over to Simon's window and held his arms up as if a messiah stood outside on the balcony. "Look. At. This. Bloody magnificent."

As quickly as he had invaded the room, Russell turned and exited. "Shorts on, fellas, there're women in need of our presence," he shouted in his wake. "They thought the Beatles were the British Invasion – wait till they get a load of us three."

Simon sat on the edge of the opulent king-sized bed and shook his head, once again. "This is a British island, Russell, I think they're rather used to us coming here."

Russell poked his head around the doorway, clearly shirtless, and Simon could only hope he was clothed below the waist. "They've never had the likes of us, mate. We're like John, Paul, George and… Well, I guess we left Ringo at home, eh?"

"More like Monty Python, I reckon," Simon retorted as Russell disappeared from the doorway.

"I'm Eric Idle then," he heard Russell call back.

Simon heard a soft knock on what he guessed was the door from Russell's room to Paul's.

"Ta da!" Russell shouted as Simon heard a door swing open.

"Come on, Russell," came Paul's defeated voice. "Can't you put some bloody clothes on."

11

GRAND CAYMAN – SATURDAY

AJ pulled into the car park of Sunset House dive resort and parked near the hotel office. They had heatedly debated Pascal's demand for AJ to go back over to the lady on Melmac to borrow a phone book, but AJ had flatly refused to bother her anymore.

"They'll have one at the front desk here, I'll see if they'll let me borrow it. If they won't, I'll have to look up the name while I'm in there, which will take longer," AJ said, turning off the van. "You should come in with me."

She hoped he would, and that maybe the resort had a camera in the small lobby. She had no idea how this day would end, so it would be nice to have his face on record.

"Start the damn van back up and go get a phone book," he said impatiently, looking at his watch. "It's five minutes until noon. I'm calling the boat at 12 o'clock sharp. If you're back with a phone book or an address, I'll tell them all is well; if you're not you'll be hitting the singles scene again."

AJ started the van and stepped out, closing the door behind her. Pascal's refusal to be seen, except by her, continued to send off alarms in her mind. She knew human nature clung to hope, often in the face of impending doom, but she needed to be realistic and figure out a way to get her and Jackson out of this mess. If Pascal completed whatever it was he was trying to accomplish on the island, and they returned to the fishing boat, she knew the two of them were a loose end. She walked into the side door of the lobby and up to the desk where a young Caymanian woman looked up and smiled.

"Good morning, how can I help you?"

It surprised AJ anyone was manning the desk, as the only guests the hotels were catering to were locals taking a night or two away from home. They couldn't have many rooms occupied.

"Would you have a phone book I could borrow for a few minutes?" AJ asked.

The woman looked around behind the counter. "I think we do somewhere," she said, and searched the shelves. "I don't see it, let me see if there's one in the office."

The woman left the counter and walked over to a glass door across the lobby. She knocked and then walked in. AJ looked at her own watch, which read 11:58. She shuffled impatiently, waiting for the woman to return, and could hear muffled voices from the office. Finally, the woman came out of the office and AJ saw she had nothing in her hands.

"One more place to check," she said and returned to the backside of the check-in counter. Moving some things below the counter, which AJ couldn't see, the woman rummaged about.

"Hmm, I don't see it," she said, still moving things around.

AJ looked at her watch again. The hands were dangerously close to the top of the hour.

"Here it is," the woman exclaimed and placed the phone book on the counter.

AJ snatched it up. "Thank you so much, I'll bring it right back," she said hurriedly, and strode for the door.

"Ma'am, you can't leave with it. Ma'am..." she called out, but AJ was already through the door and jogging to the van, holding the phone book in the air for Pascal to see. He had his mobile to his ear and as she opened the door, she heard him speak.

"It's Pascal. Everything is good. 14."

She sat down, out of breath, and closed the door. Fourteen, she thought, that doesn't match. One plus four is five and it should have added up to twelve if she'd guessed the code right earlier. She sat there puzzled until he spoke.

"Well? Are you just going to sit there trying to figure out the code, or shall we look up the Thompsons?"

His Vulcan mind-reading crap was getting on her nerves and freaking her out a bit. She took a few deep breaths and calmed down, telling herself she was probably an easy read and besides, who wouldn't try to figure out a code? She opened the phone book and thumbed through until she found the Ts, and then the THs. There was a long list of Thompsons.

"Bloody hell, there's a few in here," she muttered.

"Thompsons? There's a lot?" he asked impatiently, looking over at the phone book he had no way of reading from the passenger seat.

"Yeah. But then, that's not surprising," she replied, scanning down the list. "There are several businesses on the island named Thompsons. Don't know if these people are related, but the family that owns the hardware store and the appliance store have been here for years. They're bound to have family all over the place."

Her finger paused on the page. "Here you go, D. Thompson, on North Side Road in Old Man Bay. I bet that's him. There's a phone number. Do you want to call him and find out before we go driving over the other side of the island?"

Pascal shook his head and rubbed his beard thoughtfully. "No, let's drive over there. Twenty miles, you said?"

AJ handed him the phone book, open to the page, and pointed at the entry she had found. "About that. But why don't you want to call them? I'm guessing because Damon Thompson doesn't want to see you as much as you want to see him."

He took the book and studied the list himself. "You don't know what you're talking about. Besides, it'll only take twenty minutes to nip over there."

She laughed. "You're not in America, with motorways running everywhere. It'll take us closer to forty minutes."

He looked up. "They're freeways, and if you start driving, we'll start getting there. Sitting here listening to you jabber on again isn't getting us any closer."

AJ put the van in reverse and backed out of the spot. Taking Pascal over to the north side put her physically closer to Jackson, presuming they had remained at Valley of the Rays, but much farther away in time as it would be an hour back to her boat. If she had an opportunity to ambush Pascal while they were over there it would be pointless as she couldn't get back in time. Although, she considered, her returning was less important than the police getting out there. That worried her even more. The Jamaicans likely had instructions to ditch Jackson if the police showed up, and they would run for International waters twelve miles offshore if they saw them approach with lights blazing. She pulled the van out onto South Church Street and drove around the south-west corner of the island with an assortment of mansions and condos blocking their view of the ocean. Occasionally they would pass by an old island cottage on the waterfront, a hold-out nestled between the opulent displays of wealth. They made AJ smile, seeing a family hanging on to their home that had likely been in their family for generations. A hundred-thousand-dollar bungalow sitting on a lot worth millions.

"We need food," Pascal blurted, putting the phone book down.

"We're going through Bodden Town in a while, there are some good places to grab a bite to go," AJ offered.

"Something quick," he responded. "A drive-through."

AJ scoffed, "You're on a Caribbean island and you want to find a fast-food drive through?"

"Don't you have them?" he asked.

AJ shrugged. "Yeah, unfortunately we have them, but why would you choose to eat that junk when there's great local places and everyone is set up for takeaway now."

"Because they're fast," he said, sounding annoyed, "and we're in a hurry."

"I'll find us a better place, trust me, you'll like it, and it will be super fast," AJ said, waving a hand at him.

"Whatever," he mumbled.

She continued along the south side of the island, South Church Road having become South Sound Road, and larger spaces opened between the homes revealing the turquoise water of the Caribbean Sea.

"How are we going to buy food?" she said. "I left my wallet in my rucksack on the boat when you took me hostage."

"I didn't take you hostage," he retorted. "Don't be so dramatic."

"That's not dramatic, it's simply a fact. You have kidnapped me and are holding me hostage," she said firmly.

"Jeez, call it what you will, I don't give a damn. But I'm hungry."

"Then you should have brought some money," she replied. "Who the hell goes on a kidnapping spree without bringing some cash along?"

He shook his head and sighed loudly. "I brought some cash, just not your stupid island Monopoly money."

"They take American dollars here, you know," she said, with a little more sarcasm than she intended.

"Really?" he reached into his pocket and pulled out a wad of bills held in a money clip.

She looked at the folded-up stack and could see the outside note at least was a twenty.

"Yeah, it's a three-to-one exchange rate, expensive island I'm afraid, but they'll take your dollars," she explained, trying not to smile. Screw this guy, she thought, if the only thing I get over on him today is ripping him off over lunch, it won't be a total loss.

She joined the bypass again at the roundabout by Hurley's market and continued east over several more roundabouts until making a right and leaving the dual carriageway for Shamrock Road. This took them along the southern coast again with a few condo buildings giving way to scattered homes and mangroves between the two-lane road and the water.

"Nothing too spicy," Pascal muttered.

"Do you eat fish?" she replied.

"Yeah, I eat fish. But not all spicy. Those damn Jamaicans make everything so it burns tracks down your throat," he complained.

"Don't worry, I'll have them make it non-spicy for your delicate gullet," she said and glanced at her watch. It was already 12:20pm.

"Nice watch," he said, looking over at her Rolex Submariner, a 30th birthday gift from her parents and close friends the year before.

"Oh, thanks. It was a gift," she said uneasily. "You're not gonna pinch my watch, are you?"

"Do I look like a petty thief?" he said, sounding offended.

"No, not really. But you don't look like an international tracker of people and kidnapper either, so it's hard to tell."

"I don't?" he said, grinning. "What do they look like then? Careful now, you might insult me."

"Right, yeah, suppose I don't know what one looks like. You might be the first I've met." She thought about that statement and, recalling some of the scrapes she had been in over the past few years, decided it wasn't true. But best not to tell Pascal.

"Do you think I'm forgettable?" he asked, still grinning.

"Well, no. It's not every day my boyfriend gets held hostage and I'm forced to run someone around the island under threat of bodily harm. So no, I can't say you're forgettable at the moment."

"Reasonable point," he conceded. "My question was more directed at whether you think my appearance is indistinct."

AJ looked him over. "Um, no, I wouldn't say indistinct."

"What would you say then?" he persisted.

"Blimey, I don't know. Distinguished, how about that? You look distinguished," she said, hoping to appease him.

"You're just making that up," he replied, shaking his head.

"Well, to be fair, you warned me not to insult you."

"I did, true. But the point I'm trying to make is that I am forgettable, and that's the idea. If I was some chisel-jawed Tom Brady type, I'd be noticed everywhere I went."

"Who?" she asked.

"Who what?" he replied, his grin exchanged for a look of confusion.

"Who is Tommy whatever you said?"

"Tom Brady? You don't know who Tom Brady is?"

"Nope. He an actor?"

"Everyone knows who Tom Brady is."

She laughed. "Except me I guess. Sorry, don't mean to bugger up your analogy there."

"He's a household name."

"Where?"

"In households," Pascal said, getting more annoyed.

"Yeah, but households where? If he was a Bollywood star, he'd be a household name in India, right?"

"What are you talking about? You mean Hollywood?"

"No, that's in America."

"I know where Hollywood is, I'm a goddamn American."

"Right, so I'm guessing Tim Grady is a popular fella in America. But you're not in America, and I'm not American, so it's a bit much to think I'd automatically know who you're talking about."

"You've managed to completely derail this conversation. I was trying to make a point."

"I got your point."

"You did?"

"Of course. You want to be boring looking so no one notices you doing the illegal and underhanded things you do."

He sighed again and slouched in the passenger seat. "I didn't say boring."

"See, you ended up getting insulted, and I was trying to be nice," AJ said as she pulled into a gravel car park in front of a shack signed 'The Grape Tree Cafe'.

12

GRAND CAYMAN – SATURDAY

It was 12:50pm when AJ made the sharp left curve where Frank Sound Road, which had carried them north across the middle of the island, became North Sound Road heading back west. Pascal chewed the last bite of his fish taco and wiped his finger on a paper napkin before unlocking his phone.

"According to this, 105 North Side Road is ahead on the left," he said, pointing out the windshield.

They passed a large sign advertising 'Crystal Caves, tours available' and AJ slowed as they both watched for house numbers. The homes were concrete block-constructed bungalows, in typical style of the islanders, and none were the same shape or design. Each sat on a half-acre lot with a dirt or limestone gravel front yard.

"There," AJ said, pulling the van over to the side in front of a well-maintained, pale blue home with the number 105 in small black numbers above the front door.

A clean looking, silver four-door car sat in the driveway and a dog barked from the fenced-in back yard. AJ looked at Pascal.

"What now?" she asked.

"Same routine," he said, looking at her sternly. "You're going to knock on the door."

"I'm going to ask the Thompsons if they're the Thompsons?" she asked. She knew she was being difficult, but Pascal talked like he was James Bond and acted like he was Mr. Bean, so she couldn't help herself. He frowned at her.

"Don't be stupid, I meant you're going to approach the house again," he said, clearly annoyed.

She gave herself another reminder that despite his bumbling ways, Jackson's life still rested in his hands, and she shouldn't antagonise him.

"Sorry," she conceded reluctantly. "But what am I asking these people?"

He thought a moment, staring back at the house. "First of all, verify it is the Thompsons that used to live on Melmac," he said, and paused again, looking down at the dashboard, as though it held all the answers. AJ stayed quiet for a minute.

"Better hurry up," AJ finally said, and nodded towards the house.

Pascal looked up to see the front door was open, and a seventy-year-old, dark-skinned man in blue trousers and a salmon-coloured golf shirt stood staring at the van.

"Ask about their daughter," Pascal blurted hurriedly. "They have a daughter, I need to know where she is."

AJ looked at him. "They have three children, I believe – which one are you looking for?"

"How do you know that?" Pascal asked impatiently.

"The nice old lady told me," AJ said cringing, as she guessed what was coming next.

"What part of tell me everything she says did you not understand?" he yelled, glaring at AJ from the passenger seat.

"I'm sorry, you said you were looking for the parents, so it didn't seem important. See, this is the trouble when you don't clearly explain yourself and what you're doing," she replied defensively.

Pascal was turning red and fought to keep his voice down. "Bullshit, this is what happens when you don't do what I say. You know what else happens?" he barked, holding up his phone and unlocking the screen again. "Your boyfriend gets to spend the rest of eternity dead."

"No, wait, I'm sorry!" AJ urged. "Daughter, you said? She gave me the name of the youngest daughter; we can find her!"

Pascal paused. "The youngest? Hell, I don't know which one, I just know they have a daughter."

AJ looked over and the man they presumed to be Damon Thompson was walking across his front yard towards the van. AJ opened the driver's door and quickly stepped out.

"Hi there, Mr. Thompson, is it?" she said nervously.

The man stopped 10 feet short of AJ. "How can I help you?" he said, eyeing the van and then AJ, still wearing bikini bottoms, flip-flops and a long-sleeved sun shirt.

AJ smiled. "I think I have the wrong address, I'm actually looking for Mr. Shaw."

"Are you now?" Thompson replied, "And you're who?" he looked at the logo on her shirt and on the door of the van. "Mermaid Divers?"

"Yeah," AJ stumbled, trying to think of something reasonable to say. "Mr. Shaw won a free dive trip with us and I've had a hard time tracking him down, the phone number he put on the raffle entry got wet and blurred," she managed. "Happens sometimes, you know, we're around water a lot." She realised she sounded like a babbling fool.

"Sam doesn't dive to the best of my knowledge," Thompson said flatly.

"Well, part of the prize is some lessons, maybe he decided to give it a try," AJ responded. "Can you give me his number, or better still, an address? I'd like to drop by and meet him, you know, figure out the details."

Thompson reached in his pocket and pulled out a mobile phone. "Suppose I can give you his number. Can't say I remember it off the top of my head. Keep everything in these things," he said waving the phone in the air. "Barely remember my own number."

AJ laughed. "He may have been thinking about gifting the lessons to someone else, perhaps someone he knows that would be interested," she suggested, trying to further reassure the man as he appeared to be believing her story.

Thompson squinted at his phone. "Could be, I suppose, might be for the kids or something. Here, here's the number."

He read off the phone number and AJ instinctively patted her backside where her mobile would normally be in her shorts pocket. Her bikini bottoms didn't have a pocket and she remembered her phone had been confiscated and resided in Pascal's cargo shorts.

"Let me grab a pen," she said and opened the door to the van. "Pass me the pad and pen in the glove box," she told Pascal, who seemed dumbfounded by the turn of events. He found the spiral-bound notepad and handed it to AJ along with a pen.

"Find out what other kids he has," he hissed at her.

AJ rolled her eyes. "Jeez, he didn't want to give out this number and you want me to ask him about his whole family?" she whispered back and closed the van door before he could respond.

"Give me that number again if you wouldn't mind, Mr. Thompson."

The man read her the number then slipped his mobile back in his pocket. AJ wrote the number in the notepad and smiled at Thompson again.

"Thank you, sir and sorry to trouble you," she said, turning back to the van.

"How come you ended up all the way out here? Sam's never lived at this address," she heard Thompson say.

AJ paused and turned back. "Mix-up with our Thompsons I think, somehow we looked up your daughter's address."

Thompson looked confused. "Ain't none of the kids ever lived here, don't know why you'd have this address for her."

AJ shrugged. "Yeah, strange, huh? Well, glad we got it sorted and we'll give Mr. Shaw a tinkle and see when he wants to do his diving," she said hurriedly and jumped back in the van. "Thanks, bye now," she called out and closed the door.

Waving out the windshield, AJ pulled away as quickly as she dare and drove down the North Side Road until she was out of sight of the house, where she finally breathed again.

"Bloody hell. This lying to all these nice people is a horrible way to spend the day."

"Whatever," Pascal replied unsympathetically. "Teach you to not follow my instructions. Now, what did he say? I couldn't hear him."

AJ pulled the van over to a narrow gravel strip on the right by the water and put it in park. She thought through what Thompson had said. She didn't have the nerve to ask him about all his children outright, but by deduction she figured out an answer for Pascal, who stared expectantly at her.

"He has one daughter, I'm pretty sure," she said. "He said none of his kids had lived at that house, but when I mentioned his daughter he said 'she' and didn't question which daughter."

AJ picked up the phone book from the floor between the front seats and thumbed through the pages, looking for the 'S' section.

"Sam Shaw is the husband's name, and that's his phone number on the notepad. Let's see if he's in here," she said, finding 'S' and continuing the search over a page until she found 'SH', and finally Shaw.

"This looks like him. Samuel Shaw, 218 Palm Heights Drive. What's the phone number he gave me?" she asked, and Pascal picked up the notepad and read it to her.

"Different number," she said quietly. "But probably means the old man gave me a mobile number and the phone book has the house phone. A lot of people still have a landline if they have a security system on the house."

AJ looked at her watch; it read 1:04pm. "Shit! You gotta call, it's gone 1 o'clock!"

Pascal looked at the time on his phone. "So it is. Guess I better call. Although your boy is probably floating face down by now, those two are keen to whack someone any chance they get," he replied, and took his time dialling the number.

After a brief pause, he spoke into the phone. "It's Pascal. Everything is good. 37."

He hung up and looked blankly at AJ whose face had lost all its colour. The edges of his mouth curled ever so slightly into a grin, and he shrugged his shoulders. "They didn't say anything, so I'm guessing they hadn't shot him yet."

AJ tried to catch her breath, her heart pounding in her chest. "You're an arsehole," she muttered and Pascal just laughed.

"So I've been told," he said, and thumbed to the maps program on his mobile. "Give me that address again."

It was just past the top of the hour and AJ wondered if a good swing with a phone book would be enough to subdue the man. She felt her muscles tense and her grip on the thick wad of paper tighten. Her anger clawed at the insides of her chest like a caged animal and she was sure if she possessed a billy club at this very moment she could swing it with all her might and worry about the consequences later. But a phone book? She gritted her teeth and sized up how she could best launch an attack across the van. All he had to do was raise an arm and however hard she flung the book at him, it would be harmlessly deflected away. Reg wouldn't need a phone book or a billy club. Each of his hands was the size of a young bulldog and with one swing Pascal would be subdued whether he put an arm up or not. What would be Reg's Plan B, she asked herself; if he couldn't use his brute strength, what would he do?

"Sooner we get moving, the sooner you and lover boy can be reunited. How about you tell me the address again?" Pascal said. His words were enough to soften her resolve and realise now was not the time to make a move. And a phone book was not an effective weapon.

"218 Palm Heights Drive," she replied.

He punched in the address and let the program map a route. He held his phone screen so she could see it.

"Know where that is?" he asked.

She took the mobile to look more closely and zoomed in, using her fingers on the screen. She realised he had allowed her to take the phone from him. The release for the guillotine hanging over Jackson's neck was now in her hands. If she stepped from the van, she could reach the ocean with an easy throw and the mobile would be dead, along with Pascal's connection to the fishing boat. She would have 50 minutes to raise the alarm and for the police to figure out a way to approach the boat without alerting the Jamaicans. She remembered her own mobile was in Pascal's pocket. She would need it to call the police and equally, he could use it to call the fishing boat. Destroying his phone did her no good without disabling the man.

"Yeah, I know where this is. Snug Harbour. It's right off the bypass back on the other side of George Town, behind Seven Mile Beach."

He took his mobile back. "Let's go then."

AJ put the van in drive and looked both ways down the road. She waited for one car to pass before swinging around to head back the way they had come down North Side Road. Though the situation hadn't changed since the moment they had left the fishing boat several hours before, AJ's sense of urgency was rising. She needed to get back to the dock, back to her boat, and back to Jackson.

13

GRAND CAYMAN – JUNE 1997

The three walked out of the sliding doors of the hotel to the pool area, and gazed out at the Caribbean Sea beyond. Russell surged ahead like a golden retriever unleashed in a field of squirrels. Paul came to an abrupt halt and squinted skyward behind his prescription sunglasses at the hot afternoon sun. Simon paused and looked back.

"Come on," he said, "let's go dip our toes in the ocean, then we'll find some shade."

Paul nodded and reluctantly followed. They made their way around the pool, which was bustling with family activity and people scattered around the concrete deck, sunbathing in loungers. Island music, laced with steel drum rhythms, played in the background. They passed by a pool bar and an outdoor cafe, then continued down wide steps to the sand. Several more rows of umbrella-shaded loungers hosted swimsuit-clad bodies of varying shapes and sizes, before the powdery beach stretched down to the water's edge. Simon kicked off his flip-flops, followed Russell into the warm ocean shallows and felt the water lapping over his ankles like a soothing massage, draining his anxiety and stress away.

"This is what I'm talking about," Russell enthused.

Two children ran into the water close by and leapt forward once the water became too deep, making a tremendous splash.

"Oy. Piss off," Russell moaned. "We're having a moment here. A little decorum if you wouldn't mind."

Simon laughed as the kids splashed away, ignoring the men. He turned and looked back towards the beach.

"Get in here, Paul, the water's amazing," he called out.

Paul shuffled out of his flip-flops and made two steps towards his friends.

"What's in there?" he asked.

Simon looked down at the sand swilling around his toes through the gin-clear water.

"What do you mean, mate? It feels fantastic."

"Yeah, but are there fish and crabs and stuff in there?" Paul asked, still hesitating at the water's edge.

Simon looked up at his bespectacled friend who wore plain brown swim trunks with a white haze of sunscreen coating his entire, pale body. Where on earth could you buy brown swim trunks, he wondered.

"Probably, but they're farther out I'm guessing. There's nothing here, just warm water and sand."

Russell bounded through the water towards Paul. "Come on, yer big girl's blouse. Walk in or I'm dragging you in."

For a moment Simon thought his timid mate was about to run back up the beach screaming, but he quickly took two more steps forward so his feet were in the water, and held up both hands to Russell.

"Stop. I'm in."

Russell slowed up and threw an arm around Paul's shoulders. "Come on then, let's get wet above the toenails."

The two of them took slow, short shuffles forward until Paul was in up to his thighs and Russell finally released him.

"See," Russell said, spreading his arms and letting himself fall backwards. "It's not so bad." He finished with a big splash.

Paul looked over at Simon and took off his glasses to wipe the water droplets away. "You know me, Simon, I'm not the adventurous type, I've never been comfortable with the outdoors. Or creatures," he said quietly. "Or people."

Simon smiled sympathetically. Paul had a brilliant mind. Of the three, he was the real genius behind their software. Simon was the visionary who could see the project in its entirety, but Paul was the brains behind the programming. In the ten years or so they had known each other, Simon could only recall one girl Paul had ever dated. They seemed to have a strange on-and-off-again, long-distance something that no one, especially Paul, could define. She was a programmer who lived and worked in Birmingham, and was a surprisingly pleasant-looking social misfit, like Paul.

"I know, mate. But it's good for us to get out of our element every now and again. You know, see what else the world has to offer."

Paul put his smeared sunglasses back on. "Why?"

Simon wasn't sure what to say, but Paul broke into a big grin, spread his arms, and fell backwards into the water accompanied by a resounding cheer from his two friends.

It took a while to find an open spot in the shade, but they luckily grabbed the chairs vacated by a family whose two children glowed red like nuclear fallout victims. The gift shop would likely be selling out of aloe vera, and anything else they carried to combat sunburn. A waiter quickly swooped in and Simon was disappointed to discover he was French, rather than a local. Russell was disappointed they were attended to by the one male waiter, rather than the four females working the pool area. Russell and Simon ordered flowery rum concoctions served in coconut halves, and Paul ordered a shandy. When the drinks arrived, they knocked them together in the air, and shouted cheers.

"I think we chose pretty well," Simon said, after taking a sip.

"Yeah, I could knock down a few of these," Russell said, sucking half the contents through the colourful curly plastic straw.

Simon laughed. "Yeah, the drinks are alright, but I meant the resort here. And the island. I know the brochures love to say 'paradise' about all these places, but this might actually be."

Russell watched a pretty young woman walk by in a bright pink bikini. "Paradise indeed." He grinned.

"I think we should make sure to get out of the hotel, for at least some of the week. You know, see the island itself," Simon said thoughtfully. "We could have flown to Spain, and spent a lot less money if we just wanted to sit by a pool in the sun. This is a chance to see what a Caribbean island is really like."

"Is it safe?" Paul asked, sipping his shandy.

"Oh yeah," Russell answered. "Supposed to be one of the safest places in the Caribbean."

"Is that like saying it's less bad than the others, or actually safe?" Paul questioned.

"It's really safe," Simon assured him. "They said there's no problem walking around at night. Crime here is almost non-existent."

Paul seemed appeased. "What are you thinking? Should we rent a car? I don't know about driving in a foreign country."

"They drive on the same side as we do," Russell exclaimed. "It couldn't be easier."

"Yeah, but they probably do it differently here," Paul countered.

Russell threw his arms up. "How can they do it differently? They drive in cars, on the same side of the road. Did you see lots of cars driving in reverse on the van ride over? I didn't see any people heading to the supermarket in tanks or submarines. What exactly would be different here?"

Paul shook his head. "I don't know. Foreign."

Simon interjected. "No, I wasn't thinking we'd get a car, we don't need the hassle. We're here to relax and have a drink whenever we want. But there's bound to be excursions to places; that's what we need to do."

"I'm not giving this up to spend half a bloody day sitting on a bus with chickens and luggage strapped to the roof. I did that in Greece once. Never again," Russell said, waving a hand in the air.

Simon stood up. "I'm going to find out what sort of things there are to do on Grand Cayman. I promise I won't sign us up for a chicken-covered bus trip anywhere, but we're going to see more of the island than just the hotel."

He looked around and spotted a small hut amongst the palm trees at the far side of the pool, signed 'Activities'. He headed that way, leaving Russell mumbling.

"Already saw the whole island from the window of the plane."

Simon looked at the array of pictures and descriptions surrounding the window to the activities booth.

"Can I help you with anything?" a young, dark-skinned girl asked from inside the hut.

Simon peered inside and found himself tongue tied for a moment. The young woman was slender, above average height, with an abundance of dark, curly hair and a pretty smile. He struggled to guess her age, as she could be anywhere in her twenties, perhaps even younger. Her confident smile and firm voice with her musical island accent suggested older. Simon had never lacked confidence around women. He had discovered early that appearing relaxed, even when he wasn't, was the key to opening dialogue, and had enjoyed an active dating schedule when his time allowed. The past few years had been thin in that department as their business had consumed him. Still, he couldn't remember the last time a woman left him searching for words.

"Oh, yes. Well, I'm here with some friends and I thought we should see some of your lovely island," he managed. "It is your lovely island I'm assuming?"

She laughed. A natural, easy laugh, which made her brown eyes sparkle. "I'm from Cayman, if that's what you mean, but no, I don't own the whole island."

Simon laughed with her, realising his poor choice of words. "Right," he said, and gathered his wits back up. "Is that how I should be pronouncing the name of the island? Cay-marn?" he repeated with the emphasis on the second part of the word.

"That's how we say it, yes. You're English by the sound of it?"

she asked, to which he nodded. "The English tend to say Cay-men, but it should be Cay-marn with a big rolling 'a'."

"Cay-marn," he repeated.

"There, you have it," she said with a smile. "So, what type of excursion or activity would you like to try?"

"I really don't know. I suppose I should have done a bit of research before I came, but it was a bit hectic leading up to the trip," he replied. "I'd rather get a taste of the local sites, learn about the culture and history. But we'd like to have some fun too," he added, thinking of how he would lure the others into his plans.

The woman picked up a few laminated sheets from behind the desk and laid them on the counter. "Stingray City is one of Cayman's iconic spots, so that should be on your list. It's a fun boat trip across the North Sound, that's the large lagoon looking area over here," she said, pointing to a map of the island underneath the Perspex cover of the counter. "You can swim and snorkel with the stingrays. It's waist-deep water at the sandbar and they'll come and take food right out of your hand."

"That sounds brilliant. When could we do that?" he asked.

"How many in your group?" she questioned.

Simon thought about it a little more. How on earth could he get Paul to agree to this, he wondered.

"What if someone wants to go out there, but not get in the water?" he asked, hesitantly.

"We throw them in and let them figure it out on their own," she replied without missing a beat.

Simon frowned until he saw the smile creep back to the woman's face, and they both laughed.

"Same price either way, but if you'd rather hang out on the boat, that's up to you. It's a big catamaran as you can see in the picture, and the trip comes with some rum drinks so the boat trip is fun in itself."

"Yeah, I want to meet your stingray friends, it's one of the blokes with me that might not be so keen. There'll be three of us," Simon clarified.

"There's room tomorrow morning for three," she said cheerily. "Want me to sign you up?"

"Yeah, let's do that," he said, and gave her his room number and their names.

"Okay, I have you down for tomorrow morning. The shuttle bus will be out front at 8am. I hope you enjoy the trip," she said. "Just give the driver your names."

"Brilliant, thank you for all your help."

"You're welcome. Any other trips you'd like to book?" she asked.

He chuckled. "No, well, yes, but let's see how tomorrow goes first. We might lose a participant or two on future adventures. Thank you again."

Simon started to walk away from the booth, but paused and turned around. "Do you go out on the boat trips, by any chance?"

"I do," she replied, showing a hint of shyness for the first time. "I work the booth in the afternoons and boats in the mornings. I'll be on your trip tomorrow."

He nodded and tried not to smile too widely. "Oh, good. You know, in case my friend needs to be thrown in, I'll know he's in good hands."

He walked away with a spring in his step, to the sound of her laughing once more.

"We're doing what?" Paul asked incredulously, sitting up in his lounger. "No bloody way."

"It'll be fun, don't be such a wet blanket," Russell scolded. "Why don't you want to go?"

"Sting. Rays," Paul said, looking at Simon as if he were mad, "Rays with things that sting. Why would you ever want to get in the water with a fish that can kill you at any moment?"

"Don't be silly," Simon replied calmly. "They'd hardly make a business work if they killed a customer every other day, would they?"

"Suppose not. How long have they been doing this?" Paul asked, his voice settling down.

Simon managed to keep a straight face. "I think she said this is their second week."

Russell and Simon burst out laughing, and Paul slumped back in his lounger.

"When do we do this?" Russell asked, once he could speak again.

"8am tomorrow. We leave from the lobby," Simon answered.

"What? Eight o bloody clock in the morning?" Russell moaned. "I thought we were supposed to be on holiday? I'll still be pissed at that hour. Couldn't you book the afternoon?"

Simon grinned. "I could have. But the morning's better."

14

GRAND CAYMAN – SATURDAY

AJ headed south out of Old Man Bay on Frank Sound Road, taking them back across the middle of the island. They rode in silence while AJ once again thought through her predicament and wondered how Jackson was faring. Her mind tried to play out the scenario where half of the witnesses were already taken care of, but she pushed the thought away with a lump in her throat. She glanced down at the dashboard of the van and noticed the petrol gauge read below a quarter of a tank. She knew the light would come on before the gauge read one eighth, and she also knew the van would run for ages with the light on. She had pushed her luck on more than one occasion. But Pascal didn't know that. In a variety of vehicles across her lifetime, AJ had often dreaded the fuel light coming on, but this was the first time she had ever willed it to glow its bright amber warning.

"What's out there?" Pascal said, surprising AJ from her thoughts.

"Out where?" she asked, looking around.

"Beyond all these bushes," Pascal elaborated.

Frank Sound Road had a few scattered homes along the way, but was mainly mangroves lining the two-lane road.

"They're mangroves," AJ replied.

Pascal looked around. "What's a mangrove? Looks like bushes to me."

"They are bushes and trees but they're called mangroves because they grow in the water's edge. Their roots are what hold a lot of the low-lying land together," AJ explained. "The whole middle section of the island is pretty much mangroves and low-lying land."

Pascal didn't look impressed. "Pour some concrete and you could have good development land here."

AJ groaned. "They're part of the ecology of the island, they're a vital part of maintaining the environmental balance. You can't just concrete over all this, it'll ruin the land and upset the balance. Just ask Florida."

He laughed. "Florida's a mosquito-infested sweat hole, I'd be fine with them concreting over the entire state."

AJ shook her head. "People don't realise the oceans are a key part of our planet. Without the reefs and the mangroves and the natural systems that have evolved over millions of years, our planet changes. Our atmosphere, the air we breathe, the temperature of the water and the land."

"Don't start with all that Greenpeace, tree-hugging, save the whales nonsense. You and I will be long gone before any of that matters," he said, waving a hand in the air dismissively.

"That's not true," AJ retorted firmly. "People argue that the planet has always warmed and frozen across time, which is true, but man's influence over the past hundred years is greatly accelerating the current warming. The world's population has nearly tripled since 1950 and along with it a massive increase in pollution. Our planet is changing before our eyes, and if we don't do a lot more, a lot sooner, your kids will be paying the price in their lifetime."

"Well I don't plan on having kids," he said with another wave.

"That's the best news I've heard all day," she replied, and the conversation ended with a grunt from the passenger seat.

AJ turned right on Bodden Town Road and they rode in tense silence for 10 minutes until they were through Bodden Town and back on Shamrock Road. She couldn't help getting riled over some people's cavalier approach to the environment, but she knew arguing with the man would not get her any more information, and she needed to keep him talking.

"Be about half an hour from here," she said, trying to re-break the ice.

Pascal nodded and stared out of the windshield.

"This is where much of the island's workforce lives," AJ said, trying again. "It's too expensive to live near Seven Mile Beach, so many of the locals are out here and commute every day. It doesn't seem far, but when things are normal and all the tourists are here, it's a traffic jam from here into George Town every morning."

"Hmmm, you don't think of tropical islands having traffic jams," he said, to her relief.

"Yeah, shame really," she replied and stopped herself saying anything more before she ranted on about too many cruise ships for the size of the island.

They entered a small town and the road briefly split.

"This is Savannah," she said. "Over on the coast from here is Pedro St. James. It's an old plantation house from the 1700s they've restored. You can take a tour. It's really interesting."

"There were plantations here? Like cotton plantations and slaves?" he asked, appearing to be more relaxed.

"Yup. Not as big as Jamaica, but we had a small cotton industry here. Soil isn't great for it, and they all went away when the mills in America took off."

They left Savannah, and the homes thinned along the roadside as they picked up a peek of the ocean on their left.

"Why are you looking for their daughter?" she asked, hoping he wouldn't ignore her.

"Because someone paid me to," he replied flatly.

"Why are whoever paid you looking for her?"

"Because they have a problem," he said, playing along so far.

"And you're a problem solver," she said, letting him know she had listened to what he had told her.

"Bingo," he replied, pointing a finger in the air.

"So, what is their problem?" she asked.

"I don't care," he said with a slight chuckle.

"But how can you solve a problem if you don't know what it is?"

"Because I know how they would like their problem resolved," he said, somewhat smugly.

AJ paused and tried to talk herself out of responding, but then her mouth opened. "Then you're not solving anything really, are you? You're just carrying out a demand, or a request, or whatever. They did the solving."

He grunted. "You don't know what you're talking about."

"I'm just saying, from an outsider's perspective, I'm not sure you should call yourself a solver," she said and thought for a second. "Maybe a problem resolver. No, that still implies you came up with the solution. You're just a hired hand, doing what they say. An employee, or contract labour. Are you self-employed?"

"Please be quiet," he moaned.

"Are you going to hurt her?" AJ asked.

"Who?" he responded absentmindedly.

"Mrs. Shaw, the Thompsons' daughter. Are you going to hurt her?"

Pascal sat back and looked across at AJ. "If I give you an honest answer, will you shut the hell up?"

"How will I know you're being honest?" she answered, keeping her eyes on the road.

"Because I'm damn well telling you I'm being honest, and that'll have to be good enough."

She shrugged her shoulders. "Okay. So, are you? Going to hurt her?"

He twisted in his seat and she looked over to meet his gaze. "I can truthfully tell you I have no intention of hurting Mrs. Shaw. That is not my objective."

"Hurting would include kidnapping in my mind, that would be hurtful," she said, wondering if he was trying a play on words.

"I'm not planning on kidnapping anyone," he replied.

"Epic fail there, then. You already did," she pointed out.

He laughed. "I borrowed you, and unless you refuse to shut the hell up and I strangle you to stop you annoying me, my intention is to return you."

"What about Jackson?"

"Who?" he said, turning back to the front.

"My boyfriend. His name is Jackson. What about him?"

"Oh, right. Same. Reunited in blissful happiness on your stinking hot and muggy little island," he said flippantly.

AJ felt a tightening in the pit of her stomach. She had sensed he was truly being honest about the woman she didn't know. But she didn't share that same confidence in his response about herself, or Jackson. She wondered how Jackson was doing. She pictured him tied up below deck, out of sight. Would he escape if given the opportunity? She guessed not. It would worry him the phone call would go the other way and they would make her suffer. With minimal effort they had taken the pair of them, and by splitting them up under a threat of violence to the other, debilitated them both. She couldn't believe the two of them were finally together after so much time apart in their relationship, only to be wrenched apart again, mere weeks after he arrived. Her anger began to rise once more as she thought about the man she loved. The past few weeks had possibly been the happiest days of her life. She felt guilty feeling that way during a worldwide pandemic when so many were suffering in countless ways, but she couldn't remember ever feeling this full of joy and contentment. Since she was a child at least. But you couldn't compare the happiness of a child to that of an adult, she had decided. The uncomplicated, unburdened, worry-free existence that was free to be jubilant over something as simple as an ice cream, or a game. Adulthood brought responsibility, commitments and a distinct set of emotional obligations that quickly cluttered every thought and feeling, dampening the free spirit if allowed. Being with Jackson was the closest she could ever recall to returning to that childlike place where nothing mattered except that very moment. The financial and emotional strain of the lockdown evaporated, and she was free to exist in the joy of each passing second in his warm, humorous, and loving presence. AJ glanced over at Pascal, sitting comfortably in the passenger seat of her van, and she wished with all her heart she had a tyre iron.

"So, where are you from? Isn't it hot where you're from? You said you don't like the heat here. I found most of America was really hot in the summer," she asked, focusing hard on sounding pleasant.

He looked over at her again. "Apparently you're unclear on how a deal works. Two sides agree on terms. One side supplies their agreed upon service. In this case I gave you an honest answer," he said and held up a finger, waggling it at her annoyingly. "And in fact, I gave you bonus answers not previously agreed to in the deal. I've supplied far more than our contract required. Now, you, as the second entity in the agreement, must fulfil your side of the deal. Which, in this case, is to shut the hell up."

AJ complied and didn't say a word. She had confirmed she had her way to distract the man, to take his thoughts off the moment and leave him vulnerable. Now, she just needed something more effective than an island phone book to make her move. After another five minutes of driving, AJ took the second turn off the roundabout by Hurleys supermarket in Grand Harbour to stay on the bypass, and she heard a ding from the dashboard. She looked down at the wonderful amber light, shining up at her like a beacon of hope.

"Fuel light's on, I'll need to stop soon," she said.

Pascal leaned across and looked at the dash. "It looks like it has plenty in there," he said and sat back up in his seat.

"Okay, but I can tell you the gauge isn't very accurate," she said, tapping the dash screen, "I've run out not long after the light has come on before. I usually never let it get this low."

"We're nearly there, aren't we?" he barked.

"Ten minutes or so. But then back to the dock as well." She shrugged. "Up to you. If you're okay running out of petrol this afternoon, then we can risk it. No matter to me."

"Whatever," he mumbled. "Stop and get some gas." He held his mobile up and waved it in her face. "Just remember, you're already trying my patience."

15

GRAND CAYMAN – SATURDAY

AJ stayed on Crew Road and ran alongside the one and only runway of Owen Roberts International Airport. She frantically mulled over which petrol station offered her the best opportunity, and what that opportunity might entail. She turned right at the traffic lights, putting her back on the bypass, and drove past the cricket field towards town. She decided the petrol station at the corner of Sheddon Road would work as well as any other and she carefully indicated, slowed and pulled into the forecourt. She parked at the farthest pump from the cashier's building, hoping to make it difficult for Pascal to see inside. She held out her hand towards him and shut the engine off.

"What?" he asked, looking at her.

"They insist on getting paid for petrol in the Cayman Islands, and seeing as you kidnapped me without my wallet, you'd better cough up some cash," she demanded.

He grumbled and complained under his breath as he dug out his wad of cash and peeled off another twenty-dollar bill. He held it up and glared at AJ.

"Here. And get me a Dr. Pepper and a bag of chips."

AJ took the twenty and held her hand back out. "This is an

island in the middle of the Caribbean. Petrol is over four dollars a gallon."

"You're kidding me?" he said, but peeled off another twenty and handed it to her. "Get me barbecue chips," he added as she opened the door.

"Crisps," she replied as she got out.

"What?" he said, frowning.

AJ looked back in the van. "They're called crisps here. I'll see if they have barbecue flavour, but you might have to have salt and vinegar or cheese and onion."

"Why the hell do you people have to call everything by a different name?" he said putting his money away in his pocket and picking his mobile back up.

"You call it a different name. We invented them," she retorted, and immediately wished she had let it go.

Pascal threw his hands up. "The hell you invented chips."

"We invented them too," she said and started to close the door.

"Wait up," he barked, and waggled a finger at her. "Nice try. Give me the damn keys."

AJ tossed him the keys, and berated herself for getting drawn into a verbal sparring instead of sneaking away, leaving him cooking in the hot van.

He caught the keys and leaned over to put them back in the ignition and start the engine.

"Remember," he reminded her. "I'm watching you. Anything suspicious and I'm making the call. I've had it with you and your 'we invented everything' bullshit."

AJ paused. "William Kitchiner invented crisps. Google him, he was English," she said and slammed the driver's door closed.

She walked towards the building, leaving behind the muffled sound of Pascal cursing her.

The cashiers building contained the usual assortment of snack foods, beverages and knick-knacks arranged in several aisles of chest high displays and two walls of chilled, glass-fronted cabinets. She quickly found Dr. Pepper cans and spotted Mr. Pibb just below it. Having lived in Florida for several years, she knew the difference, and that anyone asking for Dr. Pepper would never consider Mr. Pibb an acceptable alternative. She took the can of Mr. Pibb and smiled to herself. Crisps, nuts and a dizzying cornucopia of other snacks in a bag occupied a whole aisle, but AJ swiftly zeroed in on the English Walkers brand. She almost squealed in delight when she spotted their Marmite-flavoured option, grabbed the small bag and ignored the multiple options of American barbecue-flavoured family-size packages nearby. She looked back over at the drinks cabinets and surveyed the options until she found what she was looking for. She opened the cabinet door and took a can of coffee-flavoured energy drink. She clutched it in her hand and made sure her fingers wrapped all the way around the small can.

AJ hurried over and paid for the snacks and asked for the balance of the forty dollars be used for petrol and gave the young woman behind the register the pump number. She declined the plastic bag, headed out of the shop, across the forecourt and opened the driver's side door of the van.

"Here you go," she said, handing Pascal the soda and the bag of crisps. "They didn't have a choice, I'm afraid." She dropped her energy drink in the driver's seat and closed the door again to another stream of obscenities, only slightly dampened by the glass and metal of the van.

AJ pumped the petrol and after closing the petrol cap, she checked her watch. It was 1:50pm. She hopped back into the van and put her can of drink in the cup holder moulded into the door panel. She could feel Pascal seething a few feet away from her, and once she had pulled back out onto the bypass, he couldn't hold himself back.

"I don't think you're taking me seriously," he said, more calmly than she was expecting.

"I don't know what you mean," she replied. "You're the one holding all the cards here, why wouldn't I take you seriously?"

He rocked in his seat, obviously agitated, and she wondered if she had pushed him too far. She wanted to get him annoyed, as he seemed to lose focus when he was wound up, but she couldn't afford to make him unpredictable.

"I ask for two simple things and you bring me back neither one," he growled, and she could tell he was struggling not to lose his cool and start yelling.

"I'm really sorry," she said, as sincerely as she could manage. "They didn't have much to choose from. I asked someone in there if they knew a drink like Dr. Pepper, and that's what they said. I really apologise if it's not what you wanted. The crisps were a flavour I thought you might like to try."

He seemed slightly taken aback, undoubtedly expecting more debate rather than an apology. He held the bag of crisps up as though it were a dead mouse dangling by its tail.

"What the hell is Marmite?" he asked in a civil tone.

"It's a spread you put on sandwiches," she answered, glad he had calmed down. "It has a punchy flavour – give them a try."

AJ continued north, passing Thompson's hardware store, the largest on the island, and wondering if there was any relationship to the Thompson she had spoken with. Pascal opened the bag and tentatively tried one of the crisps. His face began to screw up in distaste, but then he chewed some more and actually took another crisp from the bag and popped it in his mouth.

"That is the weirdest thing I've ever tasted, but it's not that bad," he muttered.

His Mr. Pibb remained unopened, but he quickly polished off the bag of crisps, then licked his fingers and wiped his hands on his cargo shorts. AJ wondered if there was a Mrs. Pascal sitting at home, ready to do his laundry when he returned. Where would he say he had been? The concept that a kidnapper, and self-proclaimed illicit problem solver, might have some version of a normal life, somewhere in American suburbia, seemed baffling. Did he have neighbours he chatted to? "Hey mate, how's the weather been while I was away, ruining other people's lives?" AJ could feel her blood pressure rising. But that was okay, she decided, she needed to have some adrenaline pumping to do what she needed to do.

They passed by Mount Trashmore and then Camana Bay, staying straight over several roundabouts before AJ slowed and indicated right to turn into Snug Harbour.

"Go right and follow Andrew Drive down until you see another right which will take us to Palm Heights Drive," Pascal said, looking at the map on his mobile.

AJ followed the directions and paused at the T-junction to Palm Heights.

"Right or left?" she asked.

"Left. 218 is about a block up on the right. Stop short of it on this side," he replied, pointing to the left side of the road.

She drove slowly up the narrow street and could see the homes and small condos on their right fronted a canal, as many of the neighbourhoods on the east side of Seven Mile Corridor did. She spotted 218 over the front door of a newer-looking two-storey home and stopped on the left as instructed. She parked between two homes, so she didn't block either driveway, and they both stared at number 218.

Pascal took his mobile from his pocket, unlocked it and dialled a number.

"This is Pascal. Everything is good. 81."

She had tried to figure out what the codes meant, but she couldn't make sense of them. She prayed that these calls weren't just for show, and Jackson remained unharmed. Either way, the call was what she had been waiting for. AJ nervously fidgeted and felt her hands getting clammy. In the past, any altercations she had been involved with had been reactionary situations she had been thrust into, and instinct kicked in. To sit here and contemplate a physically unprovoked attack was foreign territory. But it wasn't unprovoked, she told herself, this man was holding the love of her life hostage and had forced her, under threat of harm to them both, to help him run around their peaceful island to commit whatever crimes he was attempting to commit. Her pulse quickened and her anger grew. It was time, and she summoned her inner Reg.

"So, are we going to sit here like perverts watching a school yard all afternoon, or what?" she said sarcastically. "Or you going to make me knock on another stranger's door and lie to them?"

"Jeez," he growled and looked away from her as though he was annoyed by the very sight of her presence.

AJ picked up the unopened can of energy drink and wrapped her fingers around it. She had small hands, but the weight and solidity of the can added mass and strength to the punch as she swung at Pascal with all her might, pushing through the target as Reg had taught her.

Everything happened so fast she was unclear exactly how it unfolded, but she guessed her first mistake was closing her eyes as she threw the punch. The punch that never landed. Pascal moved with deceptive speed and glanced the blow away with his left arm before surging across the space between them and meeting her throat with the blade of a knife as her momentum took her in his direction. She instantly froze as she felt the steel against her bare skin and held her breath, waiting for the pain and the gory death she had led herself into. Where on earth did the knife come from? She had no idea where it had been, or how he had hidden the six-inch blade. She looked into his eyes and saw the difference between them. Pascal was ready to take her life. She could see the callousness and indifference, the determination and intent. One glance into the man's eyes told her how badly she had underestimated Pascal the problem solver.

He held the flat of the blade against her throat, rather than the edge, pushing firmly, and articulated clearly in a venomous whisper.

"I warned you. I never warn people, but I gave you the privilege of being warned. You contemplated trying this with that phone book back at Thompson's, but at least you were smart enough not to do it then. There was nobody around out there. I could have sliced you into pieces and tossed the parts into the water. Here, I'll have to cut your throat and throw you under the seats in the back, where I'll watch you bleed out," he said, pressing the blade even harder against her throat. "I doubt you'll ever have this chance again, but just a piece of advice. If you're going to attack someone, don't be so obvious, and don't hesitate."

Pascal shoved her back into the driver's seat and slipped the knife away inside his shirt as quickly as he must have produced it. AJ sat back and tried to catch her breath. She had been sure she was about to die. Her hands shook uncontrollably, and the adrenaline made every nerve ending in her body twitch. She felt defeated and stupid. His appearance wasn't threatening at all. He looked more like an insurance salesman who had overspent in the Margaritaville gift shop and ate at the all-you-can-eat buffet whenever he could. He had warned her, and she had dismissed him as a bumbling fool that she could handle. She had come across evil people before, but none so well disguised as Pascal. In those eyes she had seen what lay within his harmless appearance. Taking her life would mean nothing more than a logistical challenge to him.

Her foolishness had nearly cost her own life, but what scared her more was the idea that she may have cost Jackson his. They sat in silence and stared at number 218 Palm Heights Drive.

16

GRAND CAYMAN – JUNE 1997

Simon and Paul sat in the second-row seats of the shuttle van and stared at the lobby doors of the hotel. Simon looked at his watch. Again. It read 8:12am. Six other guests, who were crammed in the two rows of seats behind them, mumbled and complained under their breath. The driver, the same local man who had collected them from the airport, slid his baseball cap back on his head and turned to Simon.

"I'm sorry, sir, but I have to leave. I'm only allowed to wait five minutes, and it's been much more than that by now."

"Maybe we should cancel and just do this another time," Paul said, looking at the floor.

"No, we're going." Simon urged. "I am sorry to hold everyone up. I swear he was awake and said he'd be right behind us."

The driver turned to the front and put the van in drive. "I'm sorry, I have to leave."

"Wait," Simon said, as the lobby door opened. "Here he is."

Russell plodded towards the van, his eyes squinting against the daylight and coffee spilling over the paper cup in his hand. The driver leaned over and opened the passenger door.

"Please, sir, sit up front, we must be going."

"Yeah, yeah, sorry everyone," Russell burbled as he stumbled into the passenger seat and waved to the people in the back. "Bit bloody early all this, isn't it?"

The driver pulled away with more groans and whispered comments from the other passengers. Russell attempted to sip his coffee, but most of it spilt down the front of his tee-shirt, which he was wearing inside out.

"Shit," he complained, and wiped the coffee with his hand. Giving up, he turned to look at Simon and Paul, who both stared back in wonderment. "How's everybody doing this morning, then?"

Paul shook his head and looked back down at the floor of the van. Simon grinned. "I'd rather be me than you, I guarantee that."

Russell waved a hand at his friend, spilling more coffee from the cup in his other hand. "Nonsense, I'm tip-top, mate, never better."

Simon looked at his ruffled, uncombed hair with a strange flat area on the side of his head where presumably he had lain on the pillow. His eyes were bleary, his face unshaven, and he kept licking his lips, as though consciousness had an unpleasant taste. Simon was glad he wasn't close enough to smell his breath.

"You do look like an adventurer prepared for an exciting day," Simon replied.

Russell turned back to the front and wriggled around until he produced a crumpled croissant from his shorts pocket, holding it up like a trophy.

"Here we go," he said, showing the pastry to the driver.

"Very nice, sir," the driver replied, leaning away from Russell's outstretched hand. "Would you please put your seatbelt on, sir."

Russell took a bite of the croissant, then handed the rest to the driver. "Oh yeah, safety first and all that. Here, hold this a minute, mate."

The driver reluctantly held the croissant between two fingers while Russell wrestled one handed with the seatbelt, spilling more coffee in the process.

The boat was the same large white catamaran Simon had been

shown in the pictures, but he was disappointed to see a crowd of other passengers already waiting on board when they arrived. He had assumed it would just be the people from their hotel, but the boat was clearly operated by a contracted company, and they filled it with guests from multiple hotels. As they boarded the boat he was pleased to see the young woman from the activities hut was checking people in.

"Hello again," he greeted her and was met with a smile.

"Hi. You guys made it. We were getting worried," she said, and he noticed she checked his name off without having to ask.

"These are my friends, Russell and Paul," he explained, pointing a thumb behind him. "Russell is the one that looks like a uni student on a Saturday morning, and Paul is the one that dipped himself in sunscreen before leaving the hotel."

She laughed, and looked the two of them over. "Welcome aboard," she said, and then whispered quietly to Simon. "I'm guessing Paul's the one that might be tentative getting in the water?"

Simon grinned. "Yup. The other one will probably fall in a few times before we get there."

She pointed to an open space on the broad deck of the catamaran, and Simon beckoned his friends to follow him. He turned back to the woman who was checking the other Westin guests aboard.

"Excuse me, I was rude and didn't ask your name yesterday."

She looked up from her clipboard and he decided it would take an eternity to tire of her smile.

"Renee, Renee Thompson," she said.

Simon nodded. "Lovely. Nice to meet you again, Renee."

She held his gaze a few moments longer before he tore himself away so she could finish boarding the customers. He sat down on the deck next to Russell, who gave him an unsubtle nudge.

"She's a bit of alright, ain't she?" he said, louder than Simon would have preferred. "You putting the moves on that then?"

"Her name is Renee, if you must know, and I doubt she's interested in the likes of us," Simon answered, but was pretty sure she was showing interest in one of them.

The crew performed their safety briefing as they pulled away from the dock and the boat made its way through a short mangrove-lined channel out into the wide expanse of the North Sound. The sail remained wrapped, and the boat cruised on its motors, the sound of which was quickly drowned out with loud music over the speakers. Renee and another crew member circulated with trays of rum punches, followed by the distribution of masks and snorkels. Paul declined the rum punch and then attempted to decline the mask and snorkel, but Russell overrode him and insisted he take one.

"When I hold your head underwater, you'll be glad you have a snorkel, mate," he told him.

Paul looked at him with a mixture of humour and concern. Mainly concern.

Fifteen minutes later the boat slowed, and they all looked over the side. The water was flat calm beyond the wake from the catamaran, and they could see the sandy bottom which appeared to be a few feet below them through the twinkling turquoise water. Dark, brownish grey shadows began approaching the boat as it slowed, and everyone gathered along the rope railing, pointing at the stingrays as they circled. They varied in size from a few feet across to over four feet, and their long, thin tails trailed behind them as they glided by. The boat captain, a dark-skinned local man, dropped the anchor in the sand and shut the motors down. He stepped from the covered wheelhouse and called out loudly for everyone's attention. He went on to explain some basic procedures of getting in and out of the water and asked everyone to follow the directions of the crew who would be in the water with them. He made special note of reminding everyone to avoid stepping on the rays and to leave their tails alone as the top of the tail, just behind their body, contained the stinger.

"Ready?" Renee's voice came from behind Simon, and he turned around. She was wearing a red one-piece swimsuit with the boat logo emblazoned on her chest and he struggled to keep his eyes on hers.

"Absolutely. Let's give it a go," he said, carrying his mask and snorkel as he followed her, with Russell tagging along. Paul watched them head to the steps down the back of the boat.

"I'll watch from here," he said quietly and peered over the side at the stingrays converging on the people as they got in the water.

Renee ushered several more people into the sound along with Simon and Russell. They shuffled across the waist-deep water until they were well clear of the boat, and she asked them to form a wide circle. Several stingrays effortlessly swam between the people and rubbed along Renee's legs with their soft portobello mushroom-shaped bodies. She pulled a piece of squid from a large plastic bag and shook it in the water, warning everyone to watch carefully and not to make any sudden moves. A large stingray immediately swept into their circle and swam straight over to Renee who stretched her arms out in front of her, just below the water. The creature settled in her arms to the amazement of the crowd, and when she reached underneath, the squid vanished from her hand.

"Stingrays are a cartilaginous fish, related to sharks, and throughout most of history they've been feared and considered dangerous. It is only recently that we've begun to interact with them more and realised what gentle and non-threatening creatures they are," Renee explained as she fed the ray another snack. "A couple of dive masters here on the island began scuba diving with them at a spot not far from here, which they named Valley of the Rays. The name came from the large numbers of stingrays that would gather there because the returning fishermen would clean their catch and throw the waste over the side of the boats. Stingrays are intelligent fish and they quickly figured out that there was a free meal to be had every day, hence the gathering. The two divers began bringing other divers out to experience the rays, and while on a visit, a journalist from Los Angeles went out with them one day. She was so enthralled with the experience, she wrote an article when she returned home, including underwater photographs she took. In the article she talked about the 'City of Stingrays' and that's how the spot got the name we use today."

"They were diving in this shallow water?" Russell asked.

"No, Valley of the Rays is deeper than this and it's over there by the outer reef that divides the sound from the ocean," Renee explained, pointing north. "When the tour operators began bringing more people out they moved to the sandbar so it was safer for children and people less comfortable in the water. The fishermen don't clean their catch out there anymore, so the stingrays happily moved over here."

She washed water over the top of the ray, still hanging in her arms. "Here," she said, and looked over at Simon. "Come over and hold her."

Simon moved next to Renee, and stretched out his arms as she had done. She slid the stingray over to his arms and he felt the slightly coarse texture of the ray rub his skin. Renee took out another piece of squid and handed it to Simon. He took his right arm out from under the ray, who gently fluttered her body to stay in place, and Simon took the squid from Renee.

"Okay, keep your hand flat and your fingers together, like you're feeding a horse, and bring the squid up to her mouth. She won't bite, she'll suck the squid up, but they're powerful."

Simon did as instructed and felt the squid shoot from his hand which pulled up against the ray's mouth and he felt it searching his palm for more. He pulled his hand away, and the ray squirmed from their arms and swam away in a circle as two more came into the crowd for their turn. They continued feeding the rays for half an hour with Renee making sure everyone had a turn. Simon put on his mask and snorkel, swimming around and watching the amazing and gentle creatures as they comfortably glided around the clumsy humans. He noticed a pair of pale legs and brown swim shorts standing in the water near the boat, and he stood up.

"Bloody brilliant, mate," he said, his voice sounding strange with his nose inside the dive mask. "Come on over and take a look."

Paul slowly shuffled over in Simon's direction but stopped well short of the circle of people where the rays were manoeuvring to get the next treat.

"Put your mask on and duck under, it's wonderful to watch," Simon encouraged.

To his surprise, Paul slipped the mask over his head and stuck the snorkel in his mouth, making huffing and panting noises as he tested his breathing through the plastic tube. Simon sank to his knees, so his face dropped below the surface, and after a few moments his friend did the same and they stared at each other through their clear plastic lenses. Paul's eyes got wider as a stingray cruised their way and swam between the two men, but he stayed put and watched it go by. Simon gave him an enthusiast thumbs up and got a subtle nod in return.

They swam around and played with the stingrays for another hour, until the captain called for everyone to return to the boat. Paul stayed in the water the whole time and while he never ventured to touch a stingray, he seemed to become a lot more comfortable and enjoyed himself. As they stepped up the ladder, Simon notice Paul's shoulders were glowing red and wondered how he could possibly burn with the industrial quantity of sunscreen he had applied. More rum drinks were served for the trip back in and once Renee had attended to everyone, she wandered over to where Simon stood at the railing, enjoying the cool breeze rushing over his face. She had changed back into her golf shirt and shorts, and her mass of wet hair was bundled back in a bun, the sleek look making her appear younger.

"Brilliant suggestion this. Thank you," he said, wondering exactly how old she was.

"It's the most popular trip, so it's always a winner," she replied.

"So, what's next on our week of adventure?" he asked with a grin. "Now you have to come up with something to top that."

She laughed. "That's easy. Ever been scuba diving?"

He looked thoughtful. "Hmmm, let me think. I sky dived into a Nicaraguan jungle last year. Two years ago Paul and I hang-glided off the Matterhorn, but no, I don't think I've ever got around to scuba diving."

"Very funny," she said, nudging his arm. "It's not a crazy sport. It's really safe, and you can do a resort dive, which is where they give you some safety training, then guide you on a shallow dive. You don't have to do the whole certification course to try it out. If you liked this, you'll love scuba diving."

"What do you think the chances of getting Paul to scuba dive are?" he said, looking back at his friend, wrapped up in two towels to hide every inch of his flesh from the burning sun.

She chuckled. "Maybe not Paul." She nodded towards Russell, who was passed out asleep with a cup of rum punch spilled across his lap. "And that one you'll have to bring sober or they won't take him."

"Might just be me then," Simon said with amusement.

They turned back and looked ahead at the approaching coastline. "Are you on that boat too?" he asked.

"I'm afraid not, we use a small operation on the west side. They'll pick you up from the beach," she replied, and maybe it was wishful thinking, but Simon swore she sounded as disappointed as he was.

"Okay, so sign Russell and me up for diving, and I'll try my best to keep him sober, but what about something more uniquely local?" he asked, more seriously. "These are fun and exciting, but I want to know what your island is truly about."

She thought for a moment. "Hell is popular."

"You want to send me to hell?" he asked with a laugh.

She giggled. "Not really, it's this ancient limestone formation in West Bay they call Hell. There's even a tiny post office there where you can send a letter postmarked from Hell." She leaned in closer and whispered. "It's a waste of time if you ask me."

"Good," he whispered back. "I may end up in Hell, but I'm not ready to go yet."

She stayed leaning against his shoulder and continued quietly.

"To be honest, everything we offer is just touristy stuff. I mean, we are a hotel offering trips to the tourists, right?"

"Exactly," he agreed, "So what I need, Renee Thompson, is the secret local spot that the average tourist misses."

She looked at him and smiled, her big brown eyes full of youthful exuberance, mixed with an old soul. He was sure she was quite a lot younger than he was, but she had a maturity and confidence that made the gap seem inconsequential.

"Let me think about that," she said softly, leaving him with a heart full of hope, and a light sprinkle of concern she was dismissing him politely.

17

GRAND CAYMAN – SATURDAY

AJ had finally stopped shaking, but her feeling of defeat and inadequacy would not go away so easily. They sat in silence and Pascal only took his eyes from the house when he occasionally scanned the street, or noticed a neighbour coming or going. Snug Harbour was an older, well-established and sought-after area. The homes on the south side of Palm Heights Drive fronted Britannia Canal, which ran directly into the North Sound. The other streets weren't on the water but were mere steps away, and a mixture of surviving older, smaller homes were sprinkled amongst the larger modern houses that had replaced many of them. Most were owned by full-time residents, but many of the houses and condos along the canal were seasonal rentals which sat empty during the border and travel restrictions.

AJ hated the sitting and waiting. If she ever considered a career in MI5 – which she hadn't – surveillance would be the deal breaker. It was also killing her not knowing Pascal's intentions. She had obviously been worried before, but since her failed attempt at escape, and his display of ferocity, it now burned in her conscience. She would rather he slit her throat than her actions enable him to do the same to someone else. She simply couldn't live with the guilt. She had believed him when he told her he meant no harm to the Shaw woman, but then why was he going to so much trouble? He had illegally entered the island; he had certainly broken several laws in holding her and Jackson hostage; his crew were in possession of a firearm and he'd threatened her with a knife. That added up to a lot of jail time in the Cayman Islands, and he was yet to achieve his main objective. Whatever that was. Snug Harbour was an affluent neighbourhood, and the house they were watching was certainly nice, but if this was financially motivated there were certainly far richer targets to be had on this island. They could have filmed 'Lifestyles of the Rich and Famous' on Grand Cayman exclusively and filled plenty of seasons. Of course, during the pandemic, none of the foreign celebrities were able to visit their mansions, but the island had plenty of resident multi-millionaires.

What would Reg do now? Her first response to her own question was to berate herself, as Reg wouldn't have screwed up the attack on Pascal. She scolded herself for being so hard on herself, and just managed to stop from chuckling at her own ridiculousness. AJ had an inner confidence that took over when she didn't have time to think, but when left to ponder or second guess herself, doubt was quick to attack. Self-deprecation and humour were very English traits when it came to compliments, from others or herself, but she would rather be modest than pompous and egotistical. In a world where arrogance was commonly mistaken for confidence, her goal was humble. AJ considered her options, which didn't appear to be anything except continue to play along at this point. She needed more information, and another opportunity. The more she could learn about Pascal's mission, the better she could understand her circumstances. As for opportunity, she now had a clearer understanding of what she was up against, and wouldn't underestimate her nemesis again. This would take more than an opportunistic swing. She needed to get them back to the dock, and hopefully before Pascal could do any harm to the family who now turned into the driveway and parked in front of 218 Palm Heights Drive.

AJ noticed Pascal stayed remarkably relaxed, slumped in the passenger seat, but his eyes were sharply focused and watched every move. A family of four got out of a BMW four-door saloon. The parents appeared to be in their forties; she was dark skinned, slim, with a wild shrub of frizzy hair and wore a form-fitting sundress. Her husband was white, tall, and dressed as though he was heading for a golf course. From the back seat a teenage boy emerged, headphones in place and phone in hand, wearing board shorts and a tee-shirt. The daughter stood tall, looked older than the boy, although how old was hard to tell from across the road, and shared her mother's build and hair. She wore capri-length leggings and a tank top. They seemed happy, chatting and laughing as the father unlocked the front door to the house and they all entered, greeted by an enthusiastic golden retriever.

The street fell strangely silent again after the door closed. Pascal didn't move.

"Is that who you're looking for?" AJ asked.

"I'd say so, yes," Pascal replied quietly as he texted someone on his mobile.

"So, what happens now? Do you need to speak to her?" AJ continued, surprised he had responded.

"We wait for a while," he said, looking at his watch.

AJ checked her own timepiece. It was 2:25pm.

"Someone is going to a lot of trouble, and I assume expense, to find this woman. They look like a regular family, it's hard to imagine what it is your client wants from them," she said, trying a slightly different tack.

"Maybe they don't want anything from them," he replied.

"They must want something otherwise you wouldn't be sitting here," AJ said, but was careful to keep her voice pleasant.

"There's a purpose, that's for sure," he said quietly. "But are you sure you want to know the details of what's really going on?" he added, looking over at AJ. "Think about that for a minute. What does this knowledge do for you? Huh? Besides, satisfy your curiosity."

AJ thought about the question. "It could help me be of more use to you. If I knew what the goal was, I might have some local knowledge to help speed things up. Looking for this lady rather than her parents being a case in point."

He waggled a finger in the air. "That delay, and subsequent trip halfway around this island, was because you ignored my instructions. As I've said from the beginning, follow my requests and everything will be fine."

"I did apologise for that," she said with little conviction.

"You want to know what's going on so you can drum up another way to intervene or stop me," he said, still looking her way. "But I think I've proven to you that you're wasting your time. Just sit back, chill out, and this will all be behind you soon enough."

The part she felt he implied, but didn't expand on, was that more incriminating knowledge meant she was more of a liability. He couldn't tell her she was going to be a loose end by sundown that required dealing with, or she would never comply to do anything. But he was still keeping her around for something. If he had tipped the blade edge, she would no longer be a distraction, or an annoyance. She would be a messy corpse to clean up. Or not. He could drive himself to the marina, take her boat back across the North Sound, and leave on the fishing boat before anyone discovered her body. The maps on his phone would guide him through all of it. His biggest challenge would be starting and piloting the RIB, as he obviously didn't know the bilge from the stern when it came to boats. He still needed her for something, she concluded, but what that was she was no closer to understanding.

AJ stayed quiet, and they sat watching the house to the sound of the air conditioning fan. She was thirsty and idly sitting there was making her sleepy, so she picked up the can of energy drink off the floor. He looked at her and she hesitated.

"I was going to drink it, if that's okay?"

He smirked. "There's a Mr. Pibb over here if you'd prefer."

She shook her head. "Those things taste like medicine to me."

"Me too, that's why I drink Dr. Pepper," he countered, but kept grinning.

"Sorry about that too," she said and opened the can.

She usually avoided the chemically charged energy drinks and sodas, preferring water, but unspoilt for choice, she was pleasantly surprised by the taste. It was coffee flavoured and her caffeine fix of choice was definitely coffee. Her co-worker Thomas, a young Caymanian who was permanently upbeat and smiling, knew to give her a wide berth until she'd had her first coffee of the day. That reminded her, she was supposed to meet Thomas and his girlfriend that evening for drinks. He had probably tried reaching her to set up a time. She wondered who else had found her phone going straight to voicemail, turned off in Pascal's pocket.

The front door opened, and the wife stepped out of the house, still wearing the bright blue and yellow sundress. AJ could see her face more clearly as she walked to the car. The woman was pretty, with a slender figure and long legs. She glanced across the road towards the van before opening the driver's door and getting into the BMW. If the strange vehicle bothered her, she showed no outward sign. The car reversed out of the short driveway, onto Palm Heights Drive before pulling past the van and heading down the street. AJ put the van in drive and was ready to turn around, but Pascal stopped her.

"We're staying here," he said, holding up a hand.

AJ put the van back in park, more confused than ever.

"I thought you were looking for Mrs. Shaw? Pretty certain that's her that just left."

"We're fine, she'll be back," he said calmly.

AJ thought for a minute. "Wait a second. It's not her, is it? It's Mr. Shaw. What was his name in the phone book? Samuel? Is it Sam Shaw you're here for?"

Pascal shook his head slowly, but carried a wry smile. "Quite the Sherlock Holmes, aren't you?"

"Can't say I've solved anything today," she replied, puzzling over the turn of events.

She checked her watch. 2:58pm.

"It's about time for your call," she reminded him.

He kept looking at the house for a while before checking his own watch and pulling out his mobile. Once more, he hid the screen so she couldn't see the unlock code, and dialled a number.

"Hey, it's Pascal. All is well. 22."

"You changed it," AJ quickly said as he hung up.

"What do you mean?" he asked.

"You always say 'everything is good' and this time you said 'all is well'," she said nervously. "You changed it."

"I also give a different number every time," he said, putting the mobile back in his pocket.

"Yeah, but that's a meaningless code," she said, committing to a hunch. "But you've been consistent with the 'everything is good' part. Until now."

"Oops," he said and shrugged his shoulders. "I hope I didn't screw up. Maybe they're blowing your boyfriend's brains out right now. Should I call them back?" he said with more than a hint of cynicism.

AJ stopped herself from biting on the lure. Her blood was boiling, but she wouldn't give him the pleasure of seeing her tear herself apart. He hadn't contradicted her about the code though, so she figured she was right about that. Her guess was they had a keyword if things were not well on his end, and as long as he didn't use the keyword, then they knew he was fine. It was likely to be something similar in phrasing, so whoever had him compromised would hear him say all was okay, but the keyword revealed the opposite. His change in phrasing on the last call threw up her radar, but he had no reason she could think of to call in an alarm. Two things she quickly concluded from all this, as they fell back into silently sitting and watching. One, she shouldn't consume energy drinks because she was all jittery and her mind was bouncing off the walls. Two, she was no MI5 agent, or Sherlock Holmes; Pascal had her baffled on every subject.

18

GRAND CAYMAN – SATURDAY

Jackson thought about throwing the next game of backgammon, but he wasn't sure how he could do that, short of making obviously poor moves. He had beaten them both twice, although the last game with Fatty came down to a tight finish where he was fortunate to roll a double at the end. After Ganjaman's second defeat, the Jamaican had flipped the board over and stomped around the deck for five minutes, finally declaring his retirement from the internationally recognised game of backgammon. During Ganjaman's ninety minutes of retirement, Fatty disappeared in the cabin for a while, and returned with an array of fruit for lunch. He also brought two Red Stripes which the Jamaicans drank cautiously, keeping an eye on the cabin door. Jackson now sat opposite Ganjaman, with the board once more between them, and his determined-looking opponent mumbling good luck chants in patois. Or perhaps curses on Jackson and his family – he had no way of knowing.

"I'm honoured you chose me to face on your return from retirement," Jackson said, managing to keep a straight face.

"Keep up yah clever talk dere lucky white boy, Ganjaman's

bringing his top game this time," he replied, taking an extraordinarily long time to shake the dice before rolling a double five.

"Hah!" he exclaimed, jumping up and pointing at the dice, "See dat?" he looked over at Fatty. "See dat, mon? Dat's the power of dah spirits I be conjuring up during my retirement from dah sport."

Fatty shook his head. "Yah rolling to see who is to be going first."

"Nah, nah, not dis time," Ganjaman said, waggling a finger, "That roll right there mean I'm going first. Dah dice has spoken."

Jackson started to say something, but Ganjaman plonked back down on his crate and glared at him.

"You not be tinking about crossing the dice now, are you mon?"

Jackson held up both hands in surrender. "Wouldn't dream of it, please carry on."

Ganjaman made his move and rubbed his hands together in glee. "Winna of dis game take the whole tournament, agreed?"

Jackson rolled the dice, which came up double six, and looked back up at his adversary. "Agreed."

Ganjaman stared at him blankly, then turned to Fatty and held out his hand. "Give me dat gun."

Fatty laughed. "Teach yah for cheatin', see, now you gotta finish dah game for the tournament, like yah was crowin' about just den."

"I swear, I'm eider shootin' him, or I'm shootin' me, but we can't both be stayin' in dis game, I tell yah," Ganjaman announced.

"Quit yah whinin' and play dah man already, den yah can retire again," Fatty managed to say between laughs.

Twenty minutes later, with the board laying on the deck again, the three sat with their backs to the wheelhouse under the shade of the overhang. Jackson sipped a bottle of water and tried to think through any moves he could make. He felt hopelessly trapped. The mysterious fourth man made any attempt at escape futile, and likely harmful to AJ. Fatty's mobile had rung every hour on the hour since the man had left with AJ in the RIB. Fatty never said a word over the phone, he just listened. Jackson presumed it was an hourly check-in, where either party could warn the other if needed. If a check-in was missed or the phone not answered, they would know something had gone awry. He couldn't believe he had only been on the island a few weeks, after having to wait so long, and now this. It didn't appear they had been targeted; the men showed no signs of knowing who they had held at gunpoint, which meant they had just been that unlucky. He wanted to believe that AJ would be returned unharmed, and they would both be released as promised, but that seemed implausible. They were witnesses to whatever no good the man was up to on the island, beyond the kidnapping, gun threats and other crimes. It was much more likely they were destined for a one-way trip off the island when this was over with.

"When do you expect your friend to return?" he asked casually.

When there was no response, he looked at the two Jamaicans, and saw they both had their eyes closed. Fatty groaned and stretched, finally opening his eyes and looking back over at Jackson.

"When he come back," he replied. "Believe me, mon, we want gone as much as you want us gone."

"Gotta be slow going in this thing," Jackson said, looking around the deck of the boat, trying to keep him talking.

"She old and slow, but she get there," Fatty said, closing his eyes once more.

Jackson looked at the well-worn wooden deck and the chipped and worn paint on the gunwales. The boat was ancient, but appeared sturdy, albeit in need of some attention and care.

"You two fishermen back home?" he persisted.

Fatty sighed, but didn't open his eyes. "Nah. Boat was ma Papa's. He dead and gone, so it came to me. He did dah fishing. Not me, mon, that a fool way to make a livin', stinkin' o' fish every day. Ganjaman and me run uder tings wit dah boat, make us more money and less of dah stinkin'."

"Other things like this?" Jackson asked, still unsure what 'this' was.

Fatty chuckled. "Nah, mon. Dis dah craziest ting we ever do." He opened one eye. "Best money we ever make, and all."

Jackson let that sit for a moment before asking his next question.

"Are you confident you're going to get that money they promised you?"

Fatty opened both eyes. "Already got more dan I tink we ever get. Rest comin' when we get home." He nodded knowingly. "And I got dah gun, right?"

Jackson had only seen the MMA-looking guy for less than a minute, but he guessed these two were no match for that man, with or without a gun.

"That's true," he said. "And I'm sure they're cutting you two in on whatever they're making on this job. Has to be huge money to warrant all this risk and trouble."

Fatty stared at him blankly. "I don't know what dey be doing, and I don't want to know what dey be doing. Me and Ganjaman make our piece and we can take dah next few months plenty easy."

"That does sound like a good deal," Jackson said, settling back and closing his own eyes. "Unless it goes to shit, of course."

"It ain't goin' to shit," he heard the man retort.

Jackson opened his eyes and glanced at his watch. It was nearly 4:00pm. "Been gone an awful long time. Hope it hasn't gone to shit."

"He called every hour, ain't nutin' gone ta shit," Fatty replied, getting annoyed. "I told yah before, don't matter ta me weder yah breathin' or not, so best yah stop aggravatin' me."

"I'm sorry dude," Jackson said calmly. "I'm not trying to aggravate you. It's just if things go to shit and you guys and those two get into some kind of beef, I figure it'll be bad for AJ and I."

"Dat's right," Fatty grunted.

"So, I'm just making sure you two are covered in this deal," Jackson continued carefully. "You seem like decent guys, I'd hate to see you taken advantage of."

"Dis ain't our first shimmy up da palm tree mister," Fatty said defensively. "We'll handle dose two we need to, don't yah worry none."

Jackson heard Fatty's mobile buzzing in his pocket and the man dug it out and took the call. He looked at Jackson with a smirk, listening for a few moments before hanging up.

"See. Every ting just fine. Yah need ta quit aggravating me and hush up now."

"Fair enough," Jackson said quietly. He waited a few beats before speaking again. "Be getting dark soon."

"Happen every day, weder we likes it or not," Fatty snapped back.

"Not everywhere," Jackson pointed out.

"What dah hell yah mean? Course it do."

"Not at the North and South Poles. They have a day every year when it never gets dark," he corrected him.

"For real?" Fatty said, clearly unsure whether he was being deceived or not.

"For real. You live not far from the equator, so your days stay relatively even all year round, between day and night. Farther you get away from the equator towards the earth's axis at the poles, the bigger swing they have. They both get one day each year of total darkness, and one day each year with nothing but daylight," Jackson explained patiently.

"Damn. Don't see I'd like da whole day being night," Fatty said, looking thoughtful. "Bet da rooster confused on dat day, huh?"

Jackson smiled. "I expect he would be, but I'm not sure there are too many roosters at the South Pole. Maybe a penguin."

"Hah," Fatty chuckled. "Dem funny dose penguins. I saw dat movie now, wit dah penguins. Funny as shit."

Jackson wondered if the Jamaican had found *March of the Penguins* amusing, or whether he was referring to the *Madagascar* animated children's films. He decided not to enquire.

"Anyway, I'm sure you want to be on your way before dark, and it'll be getting dark pretty soon."

"Don't make no matter ta me, mon," Fatty replied. "Why should I care 'bout dat?"

Ganjaman snored loudly and stirred but didn't wake. Jackson waited for him to go quiet again.

"Well, if things are going to go to shit, I'd say after dark is when they'll choose to do it."

Fatty didn't say anything, but Jackson could hear the gears turning in his mind.

19

GRAND CAYMAN – JUNE 1997

Simon hadn't managed to keep Russell entirely sober the night before, but he had made sure to drag him away from the bar by 10 o'clock, so at least he was coherent and surprisingly rejuvenated by morning. They stood on the sand and watched the small dive boat approach as the captain swung it around and reversed towards the beach. Paul had come down with them to see them off, having reaffirmed Simon's guess that he in no way wanted to participate in the deadly sport of scuba diving.

A burly man with a goatee piloted the boat from the small, covered helm and a blonde woman waved to them from the deck, before jumping into the knee-deep water, once the man had cut the motor. Neptune's Divers was the name across the stern of the boat and emblazoned on the woman's tee-shirt.

"Good morning, ready to go diving?" the woman said enthusiastically with an American accent.

Simon walked into the ocean and shook the woman's hand. "Yeah, can't wait. I'm Simon and this is Russell."

She shook hands with them both. "I'm Casey," she said, and pointed back towards the boat, "and this is Keith."

She peered around them at Paul, who remained on dry land. "I was told it was two of you, but we can take three. You're the only ones on the boat this morning."

Simon looked back at Paul, who was wearing the same brown swim trunks as the day before and a newly acquired wide-brimmed straw hat. All exposed flesh was once again lathered in a white haze of sunscreen, but the red glow of sunburn still radiated through the liberal coating of SPF50.

"Last chance Paul, why don't you come along?"

"I have acceptable ways of leaving this world and eaten by sharks doesn't make the list," Paul said flatly.

"You're welcome to ride along and just hang out," Casey offered. "There's shade on the boat. Maybe you'll decide you'd like to try it, or you can snorkel if you want."

Paul stared back as though he had just been asked to step off a cliff.

"Come on mate," Russell called out, splashing back to the beach. "What's the difference whether you hang out on the boat, or hang out by the pool? This way you'll be with us. It'll be a laugh."

Paul shuffled nervously as Russell reached him. "The difference is, I can see there's nothing in the pool that wants to eat me."

"I wouldn't be so sure, mate, that rather large lady from New York who didn't quite fit in her swimsuit looked like she might want to take a bite out of you," Russell said, laughing. "Come on, let's go. You turned out to be a regular Jacques Cousteau yesterday, maybe you'll enjoy this too."

Paul relented and trudged into the water with Russell and Simon applauding.

"Three it is then," Casey said, and helped them clamber onto the swim step and over the transom onto the deck.

As they motored away from the shore in the calm water of Cayman's west side. Casey had them all sign waivers, which didn't help Paul's disposition, and then began bringing up dive gear from the cabin below. Keith turned from the helm and looked at the three friends with a grin. He had a deep tan, a barrel chest that filled out his Neptune's Divers tank top, and wore an old Spanish coin on a gold chain around his neck. He had a deep voice and also spoke with an American accent. Simon wondered if the lovely lady was the lure before the intimidating captain used them for chum.

"You're in good hands, don't worry," Keith said in a surprisingly amiable tone, and looked at Paul. "You can do as little or as much as you like. Main thing is to have fun. Don't worry, we'll keep you perfectly safe."

Simon chuckled to himself for thinking the man might be anything but friendly and professional, and looked at his two friends trying on masks to find one that fitted their faces. It was starting to sink in how fortunate he was to be in a position to take this trip, and to do it with people he cared very much about. He had been so determined and focused to build the company, the idea of time for anything outside of the office never occurred to him. If the three hadn't made the agreement over late night takeaway food at the office, they wouldn't be here now. It had been a silly deal they had made, something to spur them on to keep grinding away, and he was surprised they had even remembered the conversation. But all three had, and he was glad of it. He vowed to make sure he allowed time in his future for more trips like this. He was thirty-three years old. At some point, if he wanted a family, he would need to allow himself the time to make that happen.

"Try this BCD on, Simon," Casey said, holding out a technical-looking vest that he saw would be the device the scuba tank strapped to.

He took the BCD from Casey and grinned at his two friends. The cooling breeze brushed over them as the boat motored across the turquoise water on a beautiful clear, sunny day. A day on which they were about to try something else none of them had ever dreamed of doing.

"I'm really glad we did this, chaps," Simon said warmly.

"In a million years I never thought I'd go scuba diving," Russell agreed, shaking his head.

"Yeah, this, but I mean the whole trip, mate. I'm really glad we stopped and made it happen," Simon clarified.

Russell stopped fussing with his own BCD and smiled broadly at Simon. "Bloody right, this shouldn't be the last time we do this sort of thing. I mean, what's the point of all the work and bullshit if we don't get to enjoy something at the end of it, right?"

Simon nodded. "Exactly."

They both looked at Paul, who stared back at them through the lens of his scuba mask.

"I think this whole thing is a plot to kill me and take my share of the company," he said. And then broke into a huge grin.

Keith tied the boat to a mooring ball, and then he and Casey began explaining the basics they needed to know to dive safely. After the instruction, they donned their BCDs for the first time with the tanks attached, and stepped off the back of the boat into the Caribbean Sea. Paul watched them go. He had paid attention throughout the class, and Simon had hoped he would join them in the water, but he politely declined when it came time to gear up. Casey led Simon and Russell to the bow of the boat with their BCDs inflated with air to keep them bobbing on the surface. From the bow, the tie line ran to the buoy that was moored to the reef, easily visible 30 feet below them. One by one she had them deflate their BCDs and slowly descend, using the mooring line as a guide they could hang on to. She made sure they each equalised their air passages by pinching their nose through the skirt of the mask and blowing air down their throat. Once they were all halfway down, Casey had them practice flooding and then clearing their masks, so they would be comfortable doing that during the dive should their masks leak in any sea water.

Simon focused on the exercises, especially when he felt the pressure in his ears build quickly by only descending a few feet, but it was easy to be distracted by the surrounding scenery. Colourful fish were everywhere, and the reef itself was a magical swaying garden of strange plants and coral growths. When Casey was finally happy they were both equalising properly and had their buoyancy sorted with the air in their BCDs, she ushered them away from the line and they kicked their fins into another world.

Simon tried to remember all the instructions they had been given as he felt himself starting to float up and realised he was holding his breath. After he exhaled, he began to sink again, and for a moment felt panicked he would drop onto the reef – something Casey and Keith had gone to great lengths to explain could cause years of damage to the coral – but once he had evened out his breaths, he found a gentle rhythm to the subtle rise and falls. He desperately wanted to ask what every fish was called, but short of pointing, he had no way of asking, and as pointing usually meant he was drawing attention to at least twenty different types of fish, he decided to relax and enjoy the view. Russell looked to be lost in the same wonderment as they gently finned along behind Casey, who appeared to be one of the fishes herself, easily gliding along with barely any movement. She dropped over the edge of the reef to a large sandy area where a hulk began to appear from the edge of visibility. As they descended towards the sand, Simon felt himself dropping quickly again and remembered he needed to adjust the air in his BCD as he went deeper. He pressed the red inflater button and heard a rush of air shoot from his tank into the bladder of his BCD, and his descent was halted. He was gaining confidence, but noticed Casey hadn't touched her controls once that he'd seen since they left the line, and wondered how she was always perfectly buoyant. He looked over at Russell and saw him crashing into the sand as he fumbled for his inflation button. Simon couldn't help but laugh, wrinkling his cheeks, which broke the seal on his mask. The mask quickly filled with sea water and he inadvertently held his breath again. He immediately sensed he was rising, although he couldn't see a thing through his flooded mask, with salty water stinging his eyes. He fumbled for his own deflation button, holding it above his head to release a little air, but hit the inflation button instead and felt himself rapidly ascend. Damn it, he thought, Paul was right, I might die doing this. Number one on the list of things not to do, according to Casey and Keith, even worse than harming the reef, was to shoot to the surface. This, apparently, was how you got 'the bends', which could kill you.

Simon felt a firm hand on his ankle as he finally found the deflation button and released a slug of air in a burbling rush from his BCD. As he thwarted his uncontrolled ascent, with an assist from Casey, he managed to purge his mask and get his vision back, which calmed his breathing down. He looked around and saw Russell staring off in the direction they had been swimming. He turned and gasped. The hulk they had seen was the bow of a shipwreck looming ahead of them with large chunks of steel wreckage scattered about the sandy flats. They had been told they were diving the Oro Verde wreck, but Simon's mind had been too busy remembering their instructions to think about what that may entail. Seeing the 130-foot-long ship broken apart on the sea floor before them was an awesome sight. Casey signalled for them to stay well above the sandy bottom, as it deepened towards the wreck, and Simon looked at his depth gauge. It read 45 feet and he carefully moved up to the 40 feet, which was supposed to be their maximum depth for a resort dive. He laughed to himself, as he envisioned a police submarine showing up with sirens blaring to write a ticket for a depth violation by a new diver.

The wreck was covered in coral growth, and through the twisted opening where the bow had separated from the rest of the ship, Simon could see a million small fish swirling around the dim interior. Casey let them explore for several minutes, pointing out a large green eel poking his head out from a pile of steel debris below them. Larger fish circled above the wreck and several long thin silvery fish, which Simon presumed were barracuda by their mouths full of sharp teeth, coasted curiously by to investigate the divers. They made their way back towards the reef and Simon realised he had no idea which direction they had approached from. Looking through the mask seemed to distort his view, and looking at his own hand, he noticed everything appeared larger than it would above water. He was happy Casey knew where she was going as the hull of the dive boat came into view ahead of them. Simon reached over and shook Russell's arm, pointing towards the buoy line. There, holding the line just above the reef, was Paul.

Keith was next to him, calmly demonstrating a mask flood and clearing.

Casey checked up, and the three hung back and watched as Paul flooded and proficiently cleared his own mask. Simon couldn't believe his eyes when Paul let go of the line and followed Keith away from the dive boat and over the vibrant reef. Casey followed them at a comfortable distance, with Simon and Russell excitedly trailing her, watching their friend do the most adventurous thing he had ever tried in his life. As if on cue, a sea turtle appeared from the deeper water, and nonchalantly swam by Paul, who watched in amazement. They were twenty feet below the surface, less than 500 yards from the beach, yet for Simon, and undoubtedly for his two friends, they could have been on another planet.

20

GRAND CAYMAN – SATURDAY

At 4pm Pascal had made his call, unprompted. He was back to saying, 'everything is good' and the new code was 79. AJ couldn't be sure, but was building confidence in her theory that the code meant nothing except he must say two numbers, and the distress call involved an unknown keyword. Or maybe it's a specific number, she thought, as they continued their boring surveillance of 218 Palm Heights Drive. Perhaps number 50, or whatever they chose, was the signal. The mother was yet to return, and for the past hour and fifteen minutes since she had left, there had been no external movement at the house. The late afternoon sun was beginning its descent from overhead towards the western horizon, and the intensity of its rays were weakening as they moved from the roof of the van to the rear doors and windows. Pascal still insisted on blasting the air conditioning fan at warp speed, and despite closing all the vents on her side, AJ was still freezing cold. Her bathing suit had dried hours ago from her morning dive, but her Mermaid Divers long-sleeved polyester sun shirt offered little protection from the arctic conditions the man seemed to prefer.

She was used to spending her days in a bathing suit with a shirt thrown over for sun protection, but enduring hours held captive in her own van with a kidnapper made her feel uncomfortably under-dressed. Pascal hadn't given her cause to feel threatened in a sexual way, and his eyes had been surprisingly respectful since the first time he looked her over, but she would still prefer to be wearing a pair of jeans. She was also in sandals, her daily footwear, which would prove compromising if she found herself in a foot race.

"I don't know how you do this," AJ said, thinking how strange it was to be in the middle of a kidnapping, yet bored out of her mind.

"Do what?" he asked.

"This stakeout business, or whatever it's called. It's tedious," she replied, wondering what exactly she would like to see happen instead.

"It's part of it," he said. "It's not all glitz and glamour."

She looked over, and he was grinning, but his eyes never left the house.

"Part of what, is the question," she said, knowing veiling her question was pointless.

He ignored her, and she noticed his focus had intensified so she turned back to the house. The front door was open, and the daughter stepped outside. She was wearing matching purple sports bra and compression leggings plus bright green trainers and her mop of frizzy dark hair was pulled back in a ponytail. The golden retriever followed her out of the door, excitedly carrying his own lead in his mouth. The girl closed the door and began stretching her long legs, clutching a foot behind her, one at a time. The dog bounced and scurried around her in circles, and AJ could see the girl was talking to him and getting spirited tail wags in return. As the young woman continued her stretching routine, AJ had a better look at her face. She guessed her to be late teens or early twenties, but that age range was always hard to pinpoint. She noted she had wireless earbuds and a small MP3 player attached to her sports bra strap. By her toned figure and those long, lean legs, AJ guessed the young woman was a regular runner. AJ herself ran most days, usually logging five miles from her small apartment at the north end of Seven Mile Beach, down the sandy beach towards the hotels lining the shorefront and back. She was a decent runner but doubted she could keep pace with this young lady. She smiled as she wondered if the golden retriever could keep up with the girl.

Stretches complete, the dark-skinned girl took the lead from her dog, who found another gear of enthusiasm, and turned right from her house along Palm Heights Drive, breaking into an easy jog.

"Switch seats," Pascal said, surprising AJ.

"What?"

"Switch seats," he repeated impatiently.

"What are we doing?" she asked.

"We're switching seats, and we're doing it now, so move," he said, glaring at her.

AJ stepped back between the two front seats to allow room for Pascal to shuffle his bulky form across and take the driver's seat. She then took the passenger seat while he selected drive and slowly pulled the van away from the side of the street.

"Why do you care about her?" AJ asked.

Pascal ignored her and, looking at the map on his mobile, turned left on an unmarked cut-through from Palm Heights Drive to Andrew Drive, the next street over. The Shaws' daughter had stayed on Palm Heights Drive and was running down the right-hand side of the narrow road with the dog gamely keeping pace. At Andrew, Pascal waited, glancing between his mobile and the far end of the street where AJ assumed the woman would pass by after reaching the end of her own street and turning left. She did, and turned left again, turning towards them up Andrew Drive. Pascal backed the van up the short lane that connected the two streets and waited.

"I'm really confused," AJ said. "You said you were trying to track down the Shaw woman."

"No, I didn't," Pascal replied under his breath.

AJ thought for a moment. He had told her he was looking for the Thompsons, and then he had revealed it was their daughter, but he had never mentioned a granddaughter. He had only let her know the minimal information needed for each step of the search, she realised, and unless the golden retriever held a hidden secret, this young woman must be his real target. AJ's heart sank when she realised Pascal had sworn he wasn't going to hurt or kidnap Mrs. Shaw. She had been right, he wasn't lying, his ultimate target was never the Thompsons' daughter; it was their granddaughter, it appeared. His assurances were meaningless, and this girl could well be in danger.

"What do you need her for?" she asked. "You said you weren't planning on hurting anyone," She added, knowing it wasn't the case.

The woman ran by the lane, already warmed up and hitting her pace, which appeared to be as keen as AJ had suspected. The dog trotted beside her with his tongue already hanging out of his mouth in the tropical heat, but he appeared young and up for the challenge. Pascal turned to AJ. His face was stern and his eyes focused and penetrating.

"I don't want to hear a word out of you." He once again held his mobile in the air. "I have a text ready to send. If you speak, move, or interfere in any way, I hit send. One button to press, that's it, and your boyfriend is dead."

He tossed AJ's empty energy drink can into the back of the van and sat his mobile in the cup holder.

"Am I a hundred percent clear?" he barked.

AJ nodded. "Please don't hurt this girl, she's just..."

"Shut up!" he yelled, picking the mobile back up. "Am I completely understood, or not?"

AJ nodded vehemently again, and didn't say a word.

Pascal eased the van forward to the junction and looked down Andrew Drive. The young woman was halfway down. Pascal looked at his mobile again, studying what AJ guessed was the satellite map of Snug Harbour. She assumed the girl would loop up and down the three streets that made up the neighbourhood, but wasn't sure where she could go after that. Based on her fitness she guessed the girl was easily capable of 5-10 miles, but that would be a stretch for the dog in this heat. AJ had never run these streets, but judging by the length of Andrew Drive she would either have to do multiple loops or had another neighbourhood she could reach. AJ tried to remember what was north of Snug Harbour and recalled it was a very upmarket, gated community with large homes on canals.

Pascal pulled the van onto Andrew Drive, turning right to AJ's surprise. She looked back and saw the woman was making the turn at the opposite end. He drove slowly to the end of the road by the North Sound, with mansions overlooking the water, and turned left along Diamond Lane that bridged Andrew Drive and the third and final street, Jennifer Drive. He stopped at the corner and AJ could just make out the young woman running towards them from the far end of the street. Pascal had obviously guessed correctly that she wouldn't take the dog out of the neighbourhood onto the bypass, which although it had a bicycle lane would not be a safe place to run. Of course, AJ thought forlornly, this might not be very safe either.

Looking north, she could see there were more homes on another street, but it didn't seem to be connected to Snug Harbour. Jennifer Drive had a lane leading that way, but it turned again to feed a row of homes still part of this neighbourhood. The girl would either keep making loops on these three streets, or had a way to cut over to the next community on the adjacent spit of land. The whole area was once mangrove-covered limestone but as developments expanded, canals were dug in from the North Sound, the mangroves cleared, and the homes built. Waterfront property was highly desirable, so digging canals greatly expanded that opportunity.

After several more minutes running towards them, the woman reached the last available lane on her left, and turned. Pascal once more consulted the satellite map and seemed to realise he wouldn't be able to follow her that way to the next street. He turned down Jennifer Drive and slowly rolled past the lane, watching the young woman run through a small gap in the hedge at the back of the car park for a two-storey condo building. Pascal picked up the pace and drove down Jennifer Drive, left on the short lane at the end, then right to meet the bypass at the entrance they had come in through. The bypass had a central divider and no crossover lane to go north, so he turned left and sped to the next roundabout to double back, following his track on his mobile. He cussed and fretted under his breath when he realised there wasn't a turn from the northbound side onto Canal Drive, and he had to keep going to the next roundabout to loop back once again. The roundabout was only a few hundred yards up and he slowed a little once he appeared to have figured out it wasn't a big delay. He turned left on Canal Drive with mangroves on their left and Southampton Gardens Condos on their right until he came to a junction. If AJ had it worked out correctly, the woman would be coming from their right and would continue down Canal Point Drive, a gated community with opulent canal front homes on large lots. That would be a dead end so she would have to return the same way and backtrack into her own neighbourhood again. Pascal backed the van up thirty feet, parked it against the mangroves on their left, and waited.

AJ was at a loss what to do. Her level of risk was exclusively tied to Pascal's intent, which she had no way of knowing. It was possible he was simply observing the girl, but in that case, she reasoned, surely he'd have a camera and be snapping pictures. It seemed far more likely he planned to abduct her, based on the events of the day, but why this woman was of interest was a mystery. It didn't appear to be sexually related, and if he was a human trafficker, there were far easier, cheaper and less risky targets throughout the Caribbean. There had to be something about this girl of particular interest to Pascal's client. Something worth a great deal of trouble and money. If kidnapping was his plan, then they would head to the marina next, for the ride back out. If she could get everyone safely to the dock, then she had a plan. Against all natural instinct, AJ resigned herself to allowing Pascal to grab the girl. The least she interfered, the more likely everyone would be unharmed, and Jackson would stay safe. As handy as Pascal had proved to be with his knife, someone would be hurt if she tried anything again, and Jackson was a text away from a bullet.

The young woman appeared in view, sweat forming a glow on her brow and the golden retriever maintaining an impressive pace at her side.

21

GRAND CAYMAN – SATURDAY

Once the woman had passed in front of them, Pascal eased the van forward and AJ wondered how he thought he could get through the electronic gate guarding the neighbourhood ahead. On foot, the girl was able to run around the edge of the ornate, unmanned entranceway. But he turned right in the direction the woman had arrived from and slowly rolled along, looking around. To their left was a construction site fronting the canal, which appeared to be condos by the size of the foundations, and to their right were shrubs and small trees separating them from the Southampton Gardens community. Ahead was a small roundabout with a lane to the right into more new construction, and another road to the left, running down the side of the canal. Large new homes were being built on the left, fronting the canal, and Snug Harbour was to the right. This road would dead-end where the woman had found a path through the hedge. Pascal pulled around the roundabout and took the lane towards the building site on their right, where he turned around and parked the van facing back the way they had come. From there they could see the roundabout and straight down the road ahead, between Snug Harbour and the new homes on the canal. It was Saturday and, glancing at her watch, AJ noticed it was ten to five, so the construction sites were unsurprisingly silent. Whatever was about to happen was going to be taking place at the top of the hour, just when Pascal should be making his phone call, keeping Jackson safe. She hoped.

Five minutes passed by, which felt like a day. Time had become an uphill hike through molasses, and between the nerves and the energy drink, she needed to pee. AJ focused on stopping her legs shaking, which made them shake more. Pascal startled her by moving in the driver's seat. He took out his mobile and dialled a number.

"It's Pascal. Everything is good. 61."

Well, she thought, that's one concern put to bed, and her legs calmed for a few moments. But it was a brief respite. The young woman came into view along the road and stayed to the left through the roundabout. Pascal put the van in drive. AJ's legs twitched again in nervous anticipation, and her mouth went dry. How would he do this? Pull up alongside and ask for directions? Swerve in front of her? Somehow, he had to get from the driver's seat on the right, to her side of the road on the left, then hustle her into the sliding door on the passenger side. The logistics seemed incredibly awkward without an accomplice. It dawned on her at the same time Pascal spoke.

"You're going to tell her you're lost and you need to find Snug Harbour. Keep her talking. I'll be getting out of the van. If you do anything to interfere, the girl, you and your boyfriend die. That clear?"

Every nerve ending resounded throughout AJ's body and she felt instantly nauseous. She was now to be his accomplice. It was one thing staying passive while the abduction took place – give up the battle to win the war and all that – but to have an active part in a kidnapping was altogether different.

"I need you to acknowledge and agree, right now, or I make another call," Pascal snapped.

She could barely speak. They had been sitting around for hours and now it was all happening too fast. What choice did she have?

Help him, and maybe there's a way everyone gets out of this mess, or refuse and everyone dies now.

"Yes," she managed to shakily utter, nodding her head.

Pascal pulled away and drove around the roundabout. The woman was a hundred feet ahead, maintaining her same pace, with the dog trotting by her left side at the edge of the road. Pascal picked up speed in the van to what felt like 50mph to AJ as everything continued to unfold at an alarming rate, but was likely a lot less.

"Ready?" he asked calmly.

"Yes," she replied, despite being the furthest thing from ready for anything like this.

Pascal accelerated again and the van really sped up. He swung out to the right, then floored the throttle and turned the van back left, aiming straight at the oblivious young woman and her startled golden retriever. AJ reacted. The realisation of what was actually taking place surged through her muddled mind, but she had no recollection of making any decisions. She simply reacted. Lurching across the van, she dived for the wheel and felt the van lurch as she heard a dog bark over the screaming note of the engine. There was a violent bump and a hard thud from underneath the van at the same time she felt something hit her in the side of her face. The van continued to bounce with gravel and debris spitting from the tyres against the underside of the floor as AJ rolled back towards the passenger side with her head spinning. She fought to stay conscious as she careened off the dash and fell back across the passenger seat, slamming against the door. She couldn't focus her eyes, but sensed a flailing blur from the driver's seat as Pascal fought to control the van. The movement settled, the engine note changed and the front of the van dipped aggressively as Pascal braked hard, sending AJ flying forward. She felt the van reverse, stop, then accelerate forward once more. AJ shook her head and pushed herself upright in the seat, her focus returning. Pascal was swearing under his breath, his teeth gritted as he sped past a cloud of dust where they had veered off the road. Several bags of cement were strewn over the side of the road, torn open and their powdery contents scattered. As they raced away AJ looked back and could just make out a figure, straining to hold back a manic golden retriever who was barking at the van as it disappeared.

AJ was panting like a sprinter and the right side of her face ached and stung. She could feel pressure around her right eye and guessed it was swelling up. It felt tender and hot to the touch. She put her seat belt on as Pascal reached the junction to the bypass where he had no choice but to turn left. He fumbled with his mobile and AJ's heart stopped beating. This was the moment. He was about to call and tell them to shoot Jackson. The man with a beautiful soul and a loving heart that cared more about our planet than himself, was about to pay the price for making the mistake of loving her. This was her fault. She had put the life of a girl she didn't know ahead of the man she adored. Her soulmate. She wanted to plead with Pascal, scream, punch him, persuade him, anything – but she was paralysed. Completely devastated. The scene had unfolded in a few milliseconds, and while thoughts and epiphanies had flown around her frantic brain, she had subconsciously made a decision and acted. In that desperate, frenetic moment she had made a choice, and now Jackson would die.

"Where is the damn marina!" Pascal growled, and AJ realised he was looking at the map on his mobile and trying to get back to the boat.

"At the roundabout ahead, go back on the other side of the bypass," she said, her voice weak but recovering. "It's that way," she added, pointing behind them.

He slowed for the roundabout and looked over at her. "You have no idea what you've caused. You think you've saved someone? You haven't saved anybody. More people will suffer because of you."

"You lied," she spat back. "You let me think you were going to take her, then you tried to run her over. What has that girl done that she deserves to be run over? And her bloody dog! You would run over a harmless dog? You're a piece of shit."

Pascal was shaking, spittle forming at the edge of his mouth as he swung the van around the roundabout. "Grow up!" he yelled. "Believe me when I tell you I'm the nicest guy involved in this."

He swung a fist haphazardly towards her, which she easily dodged. "Sit there and shut the hell up, not one word or I'll start cutting you up," he barked. "Tongue first."

He continued, muttering under his breath as they sped north along the bypass towards the marina. AJ settled herself down; she knew she needed to think. Everybody was still alive for the moment, which meant she had bought some time. The poor girl would be reporting the incident to the police, which meant they would be looking for the van, she surmised. Of course, that's why she had been kept around. The van would be found at the marina with gory evidence of the hit and run splattered on it, and AJ along with her RIB and boyfriend would be missing. That had to be his plan. Which meant Pascal had no intention of setting her and Jackson free. He couldn't afford them talking and telling their story, however far fetched it seemed. The RIB would be towed offshore, their bodies dumped, and the police would be left scratching their heads as to why she'd run a young woman over and fled. But what now, she wondered. She and Jackson were certainly of no use to them anymore, but the job they had come here to do was still incomplete. The young woman was alive. Best she could figure, Pascal wanted to get her back to the fishing boat where it was easier to deal with them both and dispose of them. If the police were busy hunting for AJ, Pascal could slip back to the island and try again. Everything came down to the marina. Once she left shore, she was positive she and Jackson were as good as dead.

The sun was sinking in the western sky to her left. It would be getting dark within the hour. They continued down Esterly Tibbetts Highway, Pascal, seemingly confident of where he was going now he had calmed down. He was back to looking like an overweight tourist, ready for his boat ride out to Stingray City where he could stand in the waist-deep water and fondle the wild creatures. But AJ now knew better. This man was capable of cold-blooded murder.

He had been willing to mow down a young woman and her dog. He had also held a blade to her own throat, and she had no doubt he would have had no hesitation in using it. With a shiver, she imagined his intention was to do just that once they were back aboard the fishing boat.

22

GRAND CAYMAN – JUNE 1997

Simon hadn't stopped smiling from the moment they surfaced, all through lunch, right up to the moment he walked up to the activities hut, to be greeted by a polite young Caymanian man. He felt the wind leave his sails, and he realised he was staring like an idiot at the poor chap who had asked if he could be of help.

"I'm sorry, is Renee not working today?" he bumbled out.

"Not today, sir. She's off today and tomorrow. But I can help you with whatever you need," the man said, beaming a big smile. "Looking to take an excursion, sir? Stingray City is our most popular trip, I can fit you on the boat tomorrow if you'd like."

"No, no, that's okay, we've already done that, thank you," Simon said quietly. "I just wanted to thank Renee. She arranged for us to go diving today, and it went really well."

Simon wondered why he felt like a rejected schoolboy; the woman was allowed a day off, and it wasn't as though they had made plans. He had always rolled with the punches when it came to dating – sometimes things worked out, sometimes they didn't, but he never let it get him down. He tended to fall in lust, rather than love, and the handful of long-term relationships he had committed to had all ended when they wanted more than he was prepared to give. He couldn't understand why this girl, whom he had just met and spent very little time with, could have such an impact on him. It must be the island, he decided. Who wouldn't want to have a holiday romance with an exotic island girl?

"I'll pass the message along," the man said, with little conviction. "But while you're here, have you had a chance to see Hell? You can't stay on Cayman without seeing Hell," he enthused.

Simon laughed, "I'll pass, thank you." He turned and started to leave, picturing Renee smiling while she told him what a waste of time she thought a trip to Hell was.

"Hold up, sir," the man said.

Simon preferred to keep walking, but he paused and looked back, not wanting to appear rude.

"I'm good, mate, I don't need to book any tours at the moment," he said, as patiently as he could muster.

The man looked at a pinboard inside the hut, then back at Simon. "Is your name Simon, by any chance? Simon Lever?"

Simon wondered what sales trick the man had up his sleeve, and guessed he was looking at the schedule for diving, where he had picked the right name. He had to give him credit for quick thinking, but he felt tired after the morning dives, and disappointed he was not having a flirtatious chat with Renee at this very moment. A cold drink by the pool and a siesta was holding great appeal.

The man pulled a piece of paper from the board and handed it over the counter. It was a folded page from a hotel notepad with his name written on the outside. He unfolded it. Written in blue ink with neat, flowing handwriting, it had a phone number followed by a short note: 'I have an idea, call me, Renee'.

"That her phone number?" the man asked incredulously, leaning over the counter.

Simon quickly refolded the paper. "Yeah, it is," he replied, trying to hide the elation he suddenly felt.

"Damn, brother, that girl don't give her number to nobody," he said, shaking his head, and Simon guessed the fellow had tried more than a few times himself.

"I owe her money," Simon said, and hastily retreated.

"Alright, that explains it then," he heard the man saying and Simon grinned as he hurried towards the lobby. Better to keep the guy's ego intact, he thought, and not get Renee in trouble for fraternising with guests – which he was sure would be frowned upon.

Back in his room, he dialled the number from the piece of paper and listened to it ring too many times. Despondency threatened to creep back in when he heard somebody answer and say something he couldn't quite understand in a heavy island accent.

"Hello, I'm sorry to bother you, I was trying to reach Renee. She gave me this number," he said politely, guessing he was speaking with her roommate – or her father, he suddenly thought with a moment of panic.

"She be here somewhere. May I ask who's calling?" the man asked, his accent softening for Simon's benefit, he presumed.

"This is Simon, I'm a work associate," he said, and groaned to himself at his half-cocked story that was probably unnecessary.

He heard the receiver being placed down and muffled voices in the background he couldn't understand. Bloody hell, he thought, with memories of dealing with suspicious fathers attempting, often unsuccessfully, to defend their daughter's chastity. Those memories were from a long time ago in Simon's world, and again he felt a pang of uneasiness about this young woman's age.

There was a clunk as someone picked up the receiver, and then he heard Renee's voice. "Hello? Simon?" His concerns instantly evaporated, and he felt his mouth draw into a smile.

"Hey, sorry to disturb your day off, but the chap at the activity hut gave me your note," he said, trying not to sound overly enthused.

"That's okay," she replied. "I was hoping you'd get the note."

Simon laughed. "If the fellow had known it was your phone number folded in the paper, I don't think I would have, and you'd be talking to him."

Renee groaned. "That's Benjamin, he thinks he's quite the ladies' man. My Papi would hang up if he called," she said and laughed.

"I didn't know what to tell your dad, so I said I was a work associate," Simon admitted.

"Don't worry, he's just over-protective like any father would be," she said.

The age issue sneaked back into his mind and he guessed if he ever had a family, he would be protective of his daughter too. Especially one as pretty as Renee, who attracted an array of suiters. He quickly steered the conversation in a different direction.

"You have an idea," he said. "According to your note."

"I do," she replied brightly. "You said you'd like to see some of our Caymanian culture. Well, there's a wonderful little museum in downtown which is often overlooked. It doesn't take long to go through, but it will show you all about the island's history, and it's in one of the oldest buildings still standing."

"That sounds perfect, when do we go?" he asked, hopefully.

She laughed again. "You said you wanted to know where to go. You didn't say anything about requiring a guide."

"I would consider you a companion more than a guide, but I'm happy to hire your services," he said, and couldn't help crossing his fingers.

"That won't be necessary," she replied, and he pictured her smiling. "Ask for the shuttle to run you into town to the museum, and I'll meet you there at 2:30."

Simon looked at his watch, it was 1:45pm. "Great, the driver will know which museum?"

She laughed. "There's only one," she said, and hung up.

As the shuttle driver dropped Simon off by the kerb in the narrow little waterfront area of George Town, he didn't know what he had been expecting, but this wasn't it. The harbour was a small, natural bay with a concrete dock built along one side for larger vessels to tie up to, and colourful shops and restaurants overlooked the water from the inland side of the road. The whole 'downtown' took place in less than 500 yards. The museum was nestled between two streets leading away from the waterfront, and appeared to be an old two-storey building, white with a red roof with a full width porch on the ground floor and a matching balcony on the second. If it wasn't for the 'National Museum' sign and the flagpoles flying the British and Caymanian colours, he would have believed it to be somebody's home.

Simon walked up the path, between the palm trees, and saw Renee standing by the front door. She was wearing a simple yellow sundress, sandals and sunglasses. She smiled, and he was glad of the short pathway to gather his thoughts.

"You found it," she said.

"Yeah, the driver took me to the Museum of Natural History first, but I straightened him out," he kidded, and she laughed.

They entered the building through an unassuming door into a small gift shop. The room was no bigger than a large bathroom, and a pleasant lady sat behind the counter at the far end.

"Good morning," she said in an island accent. "Would you like to take a tour of the museum?"

"I believe we would, yes," Simon replied and approached the counter.

The lady peered around him at Renee, who had slid her sunglasses up, nestled into her mass of curly hair.

"Dat Renee Thompson? How you been, girl? How's your Papi?" the lady said, her accent noticeably thickening.

"Aft'noon, Mrs. Ebanks, he be well, thank yah. Yah ready for summa break now?" Renee replied, her own accent turning so heavy Simon could barely follow the conversation.

The two chattered some more while Simon paid before stepping through a narrow doorway into the museum itself.

"She was one of my teachers in school," Renee whispered once they were down the hallway.

Simon nodded, and found himself relieved she used the past tense when referring to school. The hallway led them to a series of rooms and the museum indeed had the feel of walking through a house or an old office building. None of the rooms were large, but they had managed to squeeze a lot of artefacts into the building, following the timeline from Cayman's first sighting by Christopher Columbus in 1503, Sir Francis Drake visiting in 1586 and the first settlers, Watler and Bodden, making it their home in 1658 after serving in Oliver Cromwell's army in Jamaica.

Simon was fascinated in the history and enthralled with Renee's enthusiasm and knowledge of her heritage. In each room she would have an interesting anecdote or tale to add to the story presented in the descriptive texts accompanying the pictures and displays. She explained how the building itself was the oldest remaining public structure, and had been a courthouse, a jail, and a post office, amongst many other roles, before becoming the National Museum. When Simon had arrived, he would have sworn it would take no more than 30 minutes to walk through the rooms, if they dawdled. It was 5pm when Mrs. Ebanks called up from the gift shop to inform them they had to leave as she was closing for the day. The afternoon had flown by and Simon couldn't remember the last time he had experienced a day like the one he was having. He had scuba dived into another world, spent the afternoon with a beautiful, intelligent woman learning about a magical Caribbean paradise; and now what? The question hung on his mind as they thanked Mrs. Ebanks and stepped outside into the bright sunshine of the late afternoon. All the signs showed Renee was interested in him and seemed to be enjoying his company. But the next step crossed a line between enjoying someone's company and heading down a different path. Was she simply being friendly? Was the obvious age difference a deal breaker for her? He second guessed himself until they reached the pavement.

"That was brilliant, I've never enjoyed a museum so much in my life," he said, trying to sound casual. "The least I can do is buy you dinner, seeing as you declined the guide fee."

"I'd like that," Renee answered without hesitation.

23

GRAND CAYMAN – SATURDAY

Pascal looked cautiously around as he pulled the van into the car park behind the Yacht Club marina. It was 5:15pm, and a few of the boats that had been out for the afternoon were now coming back in and unloading. What had been deserted jetties when they had arrived that morning were now populated with a scattering of people and the car park housed a dozen vehicles.

"Where do you park? Which jetty is your boat on?" Pascal asked.

"The second one," AJ said, pointing to the gate leading to the second of four jetties forming the marina. "All the dive boats are on that one."

Pascal pulled up and parked in an open space between two other vans brightly adorned with dive operator logos and wraps featuring scenes of coral reefs. He left the engine running and eyed the jetty suspiciously. No one paid attention to them, but pier two was the busiest with customers leaving and crews cleaning down their boats. The borders were still restricted, but all the operations were offering great deals for residents to go diving, trying anything they could to keep cash flowing.

"Okay, straight to your boat, no bullshit. Understood?" Pascal warned.

AJ nodded. "Understood," she replied.

They exited the van and walked to the gate, with Pascal keeping the keys and omitting to lock the doors. He made AJ walk ahead, and she guessed he wanted to keep an eye on her while maintaining an option to bolt back to the van. They started down the six-foot wide pier constructed of composite deck planks and AJ took her time, casually walking at a steady, unhurried pace.

Pascal whispered in her ear, his voice disturbingly close, and she felt a nudge to the back of her leg. "First thing that happens if anything goes wrong is your popliteal artery is going to be severed. You've likely never heard of it. It's behind your knee, and you'll die before help can arrive."

For a second AJ thought her legs would buckle as a shiver ran through her entire body and the strength seemed to drain from her limbs. She swallowed hard and gritted her teeth, fighting back the fear.

"Hey AJ, you night diving?" came an Englishman's voice from one of the boats as they passed by.

She turned towards the sound and waved a hand. "Hi Drew, yeah, thought we would, nice night for it."

The man waved back and watched the two continue walking. "Not much moon tonight," he added.

AJ felt another nudge, this time in her back, and kept walking. Up ahead there was only one person between her and Arthur's Odyssey, which was moored on the left side of the jetty. The broad-shouldered man had his back to them and appeared to be in conversation with a dark-skinned young local, who stood on the deck of the boat. Neither were paying any attention to anyone on the pier.

"I'm just up here on the left," AJ said quietly and heard Pascal grunt an acknowledgement.

"AJ!" the same voice shouted from behind them. AJ stopped and turned.

Pascal glared at her. "Get rid of this guy," he growled and stepped to the side, looking out over the boats, turned away so the man couldn't see his face.

Drew was walking towards them. "I meant to tell you, we're thinking of doing a lionfish cull next week if you're interested?"

"Yeah, brilliant," she replied. "Give me a call, or shoot me a text with the day and time, alright? Gotta run, want to get this chap in at dusk."

Drew slowed and stopped, his face looking slightly surprised. "Yeah, alright then. We're thinking Wednesday, but I'll text you." He trailed off and AJ turned back to continue down the pier.

"Good," Pascal whispered harshly. "Now let's get going before…"

He never finished his sentence, and all AJ heard was a thump and a gasp as a whir of movement happened beside her. She spun around to see Pascal spilling off the pier, over the transom of a moored boat, and landing with a loud thud on the deck. He was out cold.

"Bloody hell, Reg, did you kill him?" AJ asked the broad-shouldered man with a scraggly grey beard and a mop of salt and pepper hair.

"I don't think so. He should be a bit embarrassed if he conks it on one punch from a 65-year-old bloke, don't you think?" Reg replied in his gruff London accent.

"Maybe, but he'll still be dead, won't he?" AJ said as Drew ran down the pier to join them and Thomas stepped from Reg's boat.

"Suppose," Reg grunted, stepping down to the deck and looking closely at Pascal. "Nah, he's breathing."

"What the hell just happened?" Drew asked, staring at the unconscious man.

"Reg just knocked that bloke out," AJ explained. "But don't worry, he had it coming."

Drew shrugged his shoulders. "I figured that much, Reg don't usually smack people for nothing. He not like Pearl's singing or something, Reg?"

Reg shook his head. "I don't know," he said, nudging the man with his foot. "AJ called me hours ago and said to wait here until she showed up with some bloke. Told me to take him out. Make it a surprise. Can't say I know why as yet," he added, looking up at AJ.

"Who is he?" Thomas asked, leaning over and staring at the prone man. "Looks like an insurance salesman on holiday."

"Pascal the problem solver, and outright douchebag," AJ replied.

"He don't look French?" Reg said.

"He's not, he's a Yank," AJ corrected. "Believe it or not, he's a bloody hitman. Tried killing a young girl about half an hour ago."

They all stared at Pascal, who was sporting a large red mark on his cheek and a trickle of blood from his left nostril.

"Really?" Drew said.

"I know, I made that mistake earlier. Then he held a knife to my throat when I tried to take him out. He's an evil bastard," AJ explained. "Go through his pockets, Reg, he has a knife and there should be three mobiles – two are mine and Jackson's. We need to call Whittaker asap. His mates have Jackson held on a fishing boat out at Valley of the Rays."

Reg knelt down and began rummaging through Pascal's pockets, quickly finding the military-style titanium blade in a chest holster, and the mobile phones in his cargo shorts.

AJ looked at her watch; it was 5:20pm. "Shit, we gotta move quick. He calls the fishing boat at the top of every hour with a code; if he doesn't, they shoot Jackson."

"Bloody hell," Drew exclaimed. "This is nuts."

Reg threw AJ's mobile up to her, and she held down the power button. "Yeah, started off a lovely day too," she said, impatiently waiting for the phone to boot up. "We have to get out to the fishing boat, but we can't go in all fire and brimstone or they'll likely shoot Jackson and make a run for it."

"Best let the police deal with that, surely," Drew said, standing back and watching the other three carrying on like this happened every day.

"We need to be there," AJ replied firmly. "There's not enough time to organise the police and they can't approach with one of their boats as they'll be spotted a mile away. I have a plan," she said as she started walking away towards the end of the jetty. "If they'll go along with it of course," she added under her breath.

"Thomas, help me get this lump up to the pier," Reg said, "We better tie him up before he comes to."

"Can I do anything?" Drew asked, looking bewildered.

"Grab some zip ties if you wouldn't mind. Look in the toolbox on my boat over there. Red metal toolbox down in the cabin on the right," Reg replied as Thomas stepped down to help him heave Pascal's weighty body towards the jetty.

"Lord now, this fella's a lump I tell you," Thomas complained as they hauled the limp body across the transom and plopped him down on the pier.

AJ's mobile finally came to life, and she hurriedly found Detective Whittaker's number in her contacts. They had become friends over the past few years as their paths had crossed on several police cases. The Cayman Islands were one of the safest places in the Caribbean, but AJ and Reg had found themselves involved in a couple of the more interesting incidents the island had seen. Reg had known the man longer than AJ, from helping the police department when an experienced or technical diver was needed during an investigation. Roy Whittaker was also a big fan of Reg's wife Pearl's performances at the Fox and Hare pub, where she took to the small stage each month during normal times, playing guitar and singing rock tunes.

The detective answered on the third ring. "AJ Bailey, to what do I owe this pleasure?" he asked tentatively.

"I'm really sorry, Roy, but this is a business call," she apologised. "I have a situation I'm afraid."

AJ went on to explain everything to Whittaker as Reg oversaw the binding of Pascal's hands and feet with the zip ties Drew brought him. Pascal was stirring and finally waking up when AJ walked back to the group, his eyes rolling around as he fought to regain consciousness.

"Right then, get him in the van, we need to get to your dock in West Bay, Reg," AJ said.

"Why don't we leave from here?" Reg asked.

"I'll explain on the way, we gotta be quick about it," she replied. "Is anyone over there that can bring in one of our boats from their mooring?"

Reg scratched his head. "Pearl might be, call her and see."

Pascal groaned and muttered something from the pier where he lay curled up, his hands and feet securely bound.

AJ leaned down. "What's that, arsehole?" she asked.

"That's how you surprise someone," he repeated.

Reg grabbed the man under the arms and hauled him to his feet, where Pascal tottered and wriggled about.

"Hold still you bugger," Reg cursed at him. "We're gonna carry you to the van."

Pascal's eyes darted about and he continued to tug his arms from Reg's grasp.

AJ swung with all her might and clocked Pascal with a right hook to the opposite cheek to the shiner Reg had just given him. Pascal stopped squirming and Reg caught him as his legs buckled beneath him.

"Surprise, wanker," AJ told him as Reg and Thomas dragged him towards the van, leaving Drew bemused in their wake.

24

GRAND CAYMAN – SATURDAY

Pascal was sprawled across the bench seat behind AJ who was driving, and Reg in the passenger seat. Thomas sat in the third row, keeping an eye on their felon. AJ wheeled the fifteen-passenger van as fast as she dared, leaving the marina and taking West Bay Road north towards Reg's dock, which they both used, on the other side of the narrow strip of land dividing Seven Mile Beach from the North Sound. She had given Whittaker the quick version of the day's events and persuaded him reluctantly to go along with her plan. She was sure he would be setting up plans B and C while they all rushed to rendezvous at the dock.

"You're going to regret this," Pascal snarled from the back seat.

"Let me guess, it would be better for us if we let you go and forgot all about today?" Reg replied. "How about you be quiet or I'll find something to gag you with."

"Fine, ignore me, but I'm telling you, this will end badly," Pascal persisted.

"Bloody right it will," Reg retorted. "Attempted murder is taken seriously around here, mate, you're gonna get real familiar with the same four walls pretty soon."

Pascal laughed sarcastically. "You idiots have no idea."

Reg looked at AJ, who returned a glance and shrugged her shoulders before swinging the van into the tiny car park at the dock. She braked hard to a stop and looked at her watch. 5:35pm. The sun was getting low, throwing warm hues across the horizon as the sky above them turned a deeper blue.

"What's he on about?" Reg asked.

"I dunno, Reg. Whittaker was sending Bobbies around to the girl's house, and we're heading for the fishing boat. As long as we get there before six they shouldn't suspect anything."

She turned and looked down at Pascal. Both sides of his face were swelling, making him look even pudgier. "This tosser likes his mind games, he's just trying to bugger us up."

Pascal smirked. "Sure, go with that. Just remember, I warned you."

AJ felt a lump in her throat as she second guessed herself. Any normal person would have left this solely in the hands of the police, she thought, but that's not what she had chosen to do. Now, Jackson's life depended on her decision, and the plan that she had talked Whittaker into allowing. If this went wrong, it would be on her. No one would ever know what would have taken place had she left it to someone else. They would only know the result of what they were about to do. She was relieved to see a car turn in and park next to them, wrenching her from the demons of self-doubt and the tendrils that wrapped around her confidence and mired her in hesitation. She opened her door and stepped out to meet Whittaker.

Reg kept staring at Pascal. "Alright, let's hear it. What exactly are you proposing?" Reg said. "We'll pretend I'm interested for a minute."

Thomas looked at Reg in surprise, and Pascal peered up at him, grinning. "Let's go back to the other marina, take me out to my boat, and trade me for her boyfriend. Straight-up swap, both parties leave in their boats and go on with their lives."

Reg looked thoughtful for a moment before replying, "Tell you what, I hear what you're saying, but let's do this instead. We hand you over to the Ol' Bill here, and you rot in jail. And, for good measure, let me tell you, if anything goes sideways out there, you're first overboard, all trussed up like you are. So I hope you can hold your breath for a really long time."

Pascal cursed a stream of obscenities at Reg, who ignored him and stepped out of the van, followed by Thomas, who was the one grinning now.

AJ was shaking hands with Detective Whittaker, a tall, slim, light-brown-skinned Caymanian with close-cropped salt and pepper hair and glasses. He was uncharacteristically wearing jeans and a golf shirt.

"Hey Roy, I'm sorry to muck up your Saturday evening," she said in greeting.

"Comes with the job I'm afraid, so don't worry yourself over it," he replied with a brief smile. "Where's this fella then?"

"Evening, Roy," Reg said, extending a hand. "He's in the van. Got him tied up."

"Hello Reg," the policeman replied, shaking Reg's bear-like paw. "Let's get him out and we'll leave him with one of the constables that should be here any moment."

Whittaker's words had barely fallen when two Royal Cayman Islands Police Service cars pulled in and parked, filling the remaining spaces in the small car park. Reg and Thomas manhandled Pascal from the side door of the van and held him up for Whittaker to see. Two constables joined the detective from one of the cars and two other officers in bulletproof vests, helmets, and carrying assault rifles exited the other.

"I have no idea what's going on here," Pascal started. "But I was witness to this woman attempting a hit and run this afternoon and they've held me hostage all day."

"I see," Whittaker said with a serious expression. "And how is it you're here on our lovely island at the moment, sir? Can you show me your passport with the entrance visa and proof of required quarantine?"

Pascal's expression dropped. "Of course, yes... I don't have them with me right now, you understand."

"Perhaps you can tell me your name, sir? That way I can verify your status with a quick call to immigration," Whittaker continued politely.

Pascal stood in silence as behind them one of Reg's 36-foot Newton custom dive boats pulled up to the small pier jutting out from the ironshore coastline into the clear blue water.

"Pascal is all he went by, I don't know his real name," AJ said, turning to see Reg's wife, Pearl, carefully docking the boat and Thomas running down the dock to help her tie in. "But we need to go."

Whittaker turned to the constables. "Gentlemen, please take this fellow into custody and put him in a holding cell. Illegally entering the island for now and I'll sort the rest out later this evening."

The two policemen walked over to where Reg was still holding Pascal by the arm.

"Hold up," Reg said. "Let's take him with us, Roy. Never know, he might be useful. Not like he's going anywhere."

Whittaker thought for a moment before nodding and waving to the two armed officers. "Alright, we'll take him. If you two wouldn't mind getting him aboard, we need to push off," he said, and looked at the two constables who had stepped back. "Thank you anyway gentlemen, we shouldn't require any more of your time, the Marine Unit will be our back-up."

The group moved swiftly down the pier and boarded the boat. Pearl, a curvy, blonde woman in her fifties, with a concerned look on her pretty face, kissed Reg as he came aboard, then stepped over to the dock. A dog, oblivious to the gravity of the situation, enthusiastically greeted Reg, who scratched his ears then pointed towards the dock.

"Coop, go with your mum, go on now."

Coop, still only six months old, paused to run around AJ's legs and wag his tail furiously before obeying Reg and jumping to the pier.

"Thanks love," Reg said with a quick smile to his wife. "I'll call as soon as we're heading back."

Pearl gave them a wave and tossed the line to Thomas as AJ reversed the boat from the dock.

"Thanks, Pearl," AJ called down, and swung the twin diesel-engined vessel around to face the open ocean.

She pushed the throttles forward, and the props thrashed at the water until they found traction and drove the boat across the shallows, heading north towards the corner of the island.

The officers sat on the benches lining the covered deck below the fly-bridge, Pascal uncomfortably sandwiched between them. Reg, Thomas, and Roy joined AJ up top and huddled in close to hear themselves talk as she opened up the motors to full throttle once they were over deeper water.

"So what's the plan gonna be here, Boss?" Thomas shouted over the wind and engine noise.

"Okay, so the worry is they spot a suspicious boat approaching, and run for it, right?" AJ began. "If they do that, as we've learnt before, it's really hard to stop a boat, short of blowing them out of the water, which I don't think we're geared up to do, or would want to do."

"That's true, I can't authorise that level of aggression based on a single eyewitness account," Whittaker confirmed.

"Understandable," AJ said. "So best thing we can do is disable the fishing boat so it can't leave, and to do that we have to get in close."

"Sure, but what makes you think they won't bolt if any boat comes close?" Reg asked, his deep growl easy to hear even over the ruckus.

"Yeah, so we won't pull right up to them," AJ continued, "We'll come through the cut and you and me, Reg, will slide in and dive over to the fishing boat. It's getting dark so they won't see us even in the clear, shallow water. We just won't be able to use a light. They're on Valley of the Rays, which is only a few hundred yards from the cut. We'll foul their prop with some line while Thomas takes his client, Roy here," she said, nodding towards the detective, "over to the second buoy and makes a fuss of tying up."

"Then what are we doing?" Thomas asked, looking at his watch. "Gonna be awful close to six o'clock when you say they're supposed to be getting a call, right?"

"The timing is tight and I don't know how we can signal you once we've got the prop wrapped up," AJ said thoughtfully. "But when we do, you zoom over to the fishing boat and take them by surprise."

"Got to be on time, not a signal, ain't it?" Reg added. "And what about the blokes downstairs with the guns?"

"They hide in the cabin until we surprise them, right Boss?" Thomas said, looking at AJ.

"Exactly," she replied, and they all looked at Whittaker, who hadn't said a word.

He grinned. "I'd say you lot have had too much practice at this sort of thing lately."

AJ rolled her eyes. "You're telling me."

Whittaker lost the grin. "Okay, I think fundamentally that all sounds reasonable, and I agree with Reg, we'll need to set a time on which to move in rather than a signal. My two main concerns are both in regard to safety, of course. The first being with the prop. If they get spooked and take off while you're working down there, well, I don't want to see you turned into chum."

"No problem there," Reg interrupted. "Before they can turn the prop, they have to start the engine, and we'll hear it right away."

"Okay, perfect," Whittaker said. "Just don't push your luck if you hear the engine fire up, we'll deal with it if they try to leave. The second concern is according to AJ they are armed, with at least a handgun, which means we can't rule out more firepower. I need Thomas to be especially careful when we do approach. If I'm not mistaken, this boat is made of fibreglass, which won't give you much protection."

"Don't worry about me, Mr. Whittaker, I'll be ducking and weaving like a boxer up here," Thomas assured the detective.

"Well, make sure you do, young Bodden."

The sun dropped out of sight over the island as they cleared the land to their right and paralleled the shallow reef that separated the North Sound from the open ocean. Ahead, several dive boats still lingered at buoys, either entering for night dives or finishing up their afternoon adventures. The cut loomed before them, with two channel markers blinking brightly either side of the opening in the reef. Whittaker, Reg and AJ scurried down the ladder, leaving Thomas to bring the Newton into the North Sound. As Reg flung scuba gear up from the cabin, the detective explained the plan to the two officers. The boat slowed as Thomas lined up outside the cut and they all looked up when a reggae cover of Three Doors Down's 'Here Without You' came over the boat's speakers.

"Bloody hell, Thomas," Reg shouted up.

"Authentic, man," Thomas yelled down. "No self-respecting Caymanian boat captain wouldn't play the tourists some reggae."

AJ laughed and Reg shook his head as they mounted the BCDs on dive tanks.

"The lad's right," Whittaker agreed with a smile.

25

GRAND CAYMAN – JUNE 1997

Simon and Renee took their time walking along the pavement behind the harbour, with peeks of the calm ocean between the shops and restaurants lining the waterfront. Just past a tiny beach, where local fishermen sold their catch beneath the shade of an old tarpaulin, they stopped for a drink in Hammerheads, a casual bar and restaurant. Renee ordered a glass of wine and Simon tried a Caybrew, the local beer, and they chatted as they sipped their drinks overlooking the water with the sun sinking in the sky.

"Do you want to order food here?" she asked.

Simon looked around the place. There was a mixture of locals and tourists, mainly a younger crowd with lively pop music playing. He imagined the bar was going to liven up even more as the night wore on, and he made a note to recommend the place to Russell. 'MMMBop' by Hanson started on the sound system, which helped Simon decide.

"Let's go somewhere else," he said. "Name a nice restaurant you've never been to and always wanted to try."

"That's a big list. I eat at home or at the small, local cafes." She laughed. "It may surprise you to know my salary at the activities desk doesn't fund fancy dinners."

He smiled. "I guessed as much, so here's a chance to try one of them. My treat."

"Well," she said thoughtfully, "The Wharf is supposed to be amazing, and it has a perfect view of the sunset. It's about half a mile north, if we hurry we could make it in time."

Simon was glad he had optimistically planned ahead and worn a collared shirt with his cotton shorts. As he had frantically readied himself at the hotel, he had vacillated between staying tee-shirt casual, or preparing for the possibility of the afternoon extending into the evening. As he hurriedly paid the bill and swigged the last of his beer, he considered pinching himself to make sure he wasn't lying in the lounger by the pool, dreaming the whole afternoon. He started down the pavement at a keen clip and Renee, with her long slender legs, had no problem keeping up. Without thinking, he extended his hand and clasped hers as they strode along. She took his hand, and he missed a few breaths. A horn honked from behind them and she stopped.

"Hold up, here's our ride," she said, and he stopped and looked.

Renee waved to a small passenger van that pulled over and the side door slid back. Two other locals in the van moved to the rear seat to make room, and they both hopped inside.

"Just to da Wharf please," she said to the driver, who nodded in return.

"Is this the local bus service?" Simon whispered.

Renee nodded. "Bus, shuttle, whatever you want to call it. They run up and down West Bay Road all day. There's no schedule, you just wave them down. If you look like you need a ride they honk."

Simon chuckled. He couldn't imagine the double-decker buses in England cruising high streets, honking the horn at every old lady walking along. In two minutes they were outside the restaurant, and Renee slipped the driver a few coins before Simon could ask about paying. A nautical logo with a life ring surrounded by the words 'The Wharf' guarded a covered walkway leading through palm trees to the restaurant entrance. Simon asked for an ocean view and after much hunting through the reservations list, the maître d' deemed them worthy of his last waterfront table. Their timing was perfect. The sun had turned the horizon a glow of deep orange and yellow, and by the time their drink order arrived, the burning orb was setting, and the sky began to dim. Once nature's colourful art show concluded, they studied the menu, and both chose local fish dishes, giving the waiter their order when he came back by. Renee asked what Simon's friends were up to this evening and he realised he hadn't thought about them. He had told them he was out for the afternoon, but they were undoubtedly wondering where he had got to. Russell would shrug his shoulders, and Paul would fret about it all evening, he thought with a grin.

"I'm sure they've found themselves some trouble to get into," he replied.

He found Renee incredibly easy to talk to. Perhaps the vastly different worlds they came from gave them plenty to ask about, he considered, but it didn't seem to matter what subject they discussed, they fell into an intelligent and interesting conversation each time. He was never fond of talking about himself, and he had always believed his work to be excruciatingly boring, but Renee seemed to find it fascinating. Something still nagged at the back of his mind, and as much as he tried to shake it, there was a bridge that needed to be crossed, and in a quiet moment he found the words were leaving his lips before he could stop them.

"I have to ask you," he started awkwardly. "I realise we're probably a few years apart in age, but how old are you?"

There, he thought, you bumbled it about as badly as anyone could, but the question has been asked. Her expression changed and he couldn't tell if she was embarrassed, disappointed or something altogether different. He was sure he had just ruined what had been a brilliant day.

"What's your guess?" she asked coyly, sipping her wine.

He looked at her soft, girlish face, that would likely lean out in time like the rest of her perfect figure, and her sparkling eyes so full of youthful exuberance. In contrast, her demeanour was mature, and she conversed and carried herself with the elegance and grace of a woman. A lady. She seemed perfectly at home in the fancy restaurant, as though it were a regular occurrence, which he knew wasn't the case.

"I'm terrible at this," he began. "So I'm sure I'm way off, but I'd put you three or four years older than me."

Her jaw dropped, and she laughed loudly as she threw her napkin across the table at him. "You are terrible at this."

"Okay, okay," he said, handing her the napkin back, "I'd guess early twenties."

He then held his breath, waiting for her answer, believing he had optimistically aimed high.

"How about that," she said, holding her glass up. "You're actually good at this after all."

Simon felt a weight leave his shoulders. He had no idea what number would have been unacceptable, but somehow anything in the teens would have felt creepy, he guessed.

"How old are you?" she asked without hesitating.

"I just turned 33, not long before this trip," he replied.

She raised her glass again. "Happy recent birthday."

He clinked his glass to hers. "Thank you."

She smiled. "You can relax now we have all that out of the way."

He shook his head, grinned and felt like the younger of the two at the table. "That obvious, huh?"

"Something was on your mind," she said warmly, then leaned over the table and spoke quietly. "And just so there's no other weirdness. I'm choosy about my dates, I don't date boys, and I certainly don't sleep around. So, if you're banking on getting lucky, you better be planning on coming back to the Cayman Islands."

Renee sat back and looked boldly at Simon, the flickering candle in the centre of the table dancing mischievously in her eyes. For a moment she had him speechless again. He finally pulled his thoughts together.

"I'm thoroughly enjoying your company," he replied confidently. "I'll take as much of it as you're willing to give, and it'll take an act of God to stop me coming back to your island."

They clinked glasses again. The rest of the evening was spent in relaxed conversation, with a lot of laughter, and Simon wondering when he could possibly take a break from the new contract they would be starting the day the three returned to England. This trip was turning into a string of firsts in more ways than he could ever have imagined. He had left Oxford with a feeling of guilt, and his mind firmly focused on the work they would face on their return. A couple of days later, and he couldn't stand the idea of leaving, and work was the furthest thing from his mind.

After dinner, they watched in amazement as floodlights lit the ocean below the sea wall where they sat, and the restaurant staff fed the tarpon. These large, silvery fish, some over four feet long, splashed and jostled as they squabbled over the free evening meal. The water seemed to churn over with glittery scales and they both decided they wouldn't want to fall in amongst the melee. Simon paid the bill, and they walked slowly out to the front of the restaurant.

"Where do you live?" he asked. "I assume it's close by."

"Not far from here," she said. "Just the other side of the harbour. Opposite direction to you, I'm afraid."

"I feel bad, not escorting you to your door, as a gentleman should do," he replied.

"That's okay," she said, stepping a little closer to him. "I'm going to get the bus."

Simon placed his hands softly on her hips and pulled her closer still. She looked into his eyes as he leaned in and kissed her gently. He felt her arms around his neck and she pressed her lips more firmly to his. The honk of a car horn surprised them both, and she pulled away.

"That's your ride," she said, laughing, and waved to the van driver who pulled into the car park.

He reluctantly released her and walked towards the van. "Tomorrow?" he asked.

"Tomorrow is my other day off," she replied.

"I know. What are we doing on your other day off?" he persisted.

"I was going to sleep in, do laundry, clean house," she teased.

He opened the van door, but didn't get in. "I have it on good authority that all that responsible, boring stuff has been postponed. Possibly even cancelled, due to far more interesting things to do."

She laughed. "Well, in that case, I'll pick you up outside the hotel at 10."

Elated, he stepped into the van. "You have a car?" he called out as the van began moving with the door still open.

She shrugged her shoulders, "I have transport," she shouted back with a grin.

Simon closed the door as the van pulled back onto the road. He turned and looked in the back row of seats where two older, dark-skinned ladies stared back at him.

"Sorry for holding us up there," he apologised.

"Dat's a pretty girl," one lady said.

"She be Thompson's girl, you know," her friend said, as they both continued to stare at Simon.

"I thought it be her. Pretty girl and all."

"Thompson don't take kindly to no man messing wit his baby girl, mister," the friend added.

"I assure you, my intentions are honourable, ladies," Simon stuttered, unprepared for the conversation.

The women looked at each other, then back at Simon, before bursting out laughing.

"Be dah first man ever if you are, mister," the friend cackled, still laughing.

"That be dah truth right der, sister."

Simon smiled and was glad they couldn't see him blushing in the dark van as he turned around to face the front.

26

GRAND CAYMAN – SATURDAY

AJ looked up at the dark blue sky to the north with brighter stars already showing as silvery pinpricks in the blanket of night slowly draping itself across the island. With a nod to Reg, and a quick thumbs up to the fly-bridge, the two waited for Thomas to knock the boat into neutral before sliding off the swim step into the darkening water of the North Sound. With no air in their BCDs, they dropped straight below the surface and began descending to the sandy floor of the sound, just 20 feet below. AJ heard the engine note pick back up and knew Thomas had continued on. Shortly, he would be attempting to sell the charade to the two Jamaicans on the fishing boat. She fought back the nerves once again, as the weight of her own decision tried to anchor her in place. She felt a nudge on her arm and could just make out Reg's dark figure beside her, his arm extended with his compass in hand. He pointed with his other hand in the direction he held the compass, and nodded to her. AJ unclipped her own compass to double check Reg's heading, reading the dial by its luminescent arrow and figures. She turned the bezel until the dual marks lined up on north, then held the compass straight ahead with the lubber line facing 300 degrees, the heading they had established on the boat. It lined up with Reg's heading and they wasted no time kicking swiftly in that direction, staying a few feet off the sandy bottom. Her nerves were soon forgotten as the task at hand consumed her thoughts.

The drone of the Newton's diesel faded, leaving their steady inhalations and exhausting of bubbles through their regulators an eerie soundtrack to their dimly lit movie. The water was crystal clear, but with little light their path was a sightless journey into a murky blackness. They both glanced up occasionally, the twilight playing on the rippling surface above, telling them they hadn't reached the fishing boat. They kept their arms out ahead, streamlined guides to maintain their direction and kicked in long sweeping strokes with their legs, letting their fins propel them hastily along. They were working hard and covering ground at a rapid pace. AJ felt another bump, but this time from her left side, and a large shadow swept across the front of them both. She checked up and took a gulp of air as the movement startled her. She sensed Reg looking around as another shadow blocked the token light from above, before gliding down in front of them. Stingrays, she quickly realised. The stingrays were so used to divers and humans in the water around Stingray City and Valley of the Rays, they flocked to see if a free evening meal was being served. The two divers checked their heading and kicked on, ignoring the large grey creatures grazing by them.

AJ was breathing heavily when a deeper darkness fell upon them and remained. She looked up and grabbed Reg's arm. They were finally under the hull of a large boat. They ascended slowly and kicked back to the stern where they could barely make out the single prop in the gloom. AJ unclipped a roll of 1/2 inch braided nylon mooring line from her BCD and began wrapping it tightly around the exposed prop shaft. She then strapped it around the prop itself, weaving it snugly around the curved blades to render them ineffective. Reg helped her hold the line tight while she tied it to itself, leaving a bundled mass, almost completely hiding the stainless steel beneath. AJ looked around and felt around the stern of the old boat. Behind the prop was the tall rudder, pivoting from the underside of the hull above and supported by a metal arm below. Taking the excess line from the knot on the prop, she looped it twice around the metal arm then pulled it above the rudder where she felt for the pivot shaft. She was about to wrap the line around it, when the old diesel motor cranked over and spluttered into life. Reg tapped her shoulder, signalling her to pull away. AJ looked at her handiwork. The prop would still spin but wouldn't create much drive all swaddled in rope, but if she could secure the end of the line, it might stop it turning at all – unless the power of the engine ripped the line free. She hurriedly looped the line around the rudder pivot and began tying it off as securely as possible. She heard a clunk as Reg's big hands yanked her backwards, clear of the prop, as the torque of the diesel tried to turn the prop shaft. The stern of the boat shuddered, the motor coughed and strained, and the engine note began to rise. But the prop didn't turn. The clutch was slipping as her lashing held, and the boat sat idle in the water.

The familiar sound from the twin Caterpillar diesels of the Newton grew louder through the water, and AJ was wondering where they should surface, when she sensed more than heard a splash close by. Reg must have been aware of it too as he looked around. Sound travels through water at a different speed than in air, confusing the human brain which uses the split-second difference in arrival time to each ear to determine the direction the noise came from. They had no idea where the splash originated, and now the engine note was rapidly rising and falling as the confused men on the boat tried to get their drive to engage, drowning out everything else. AJ had a bad feeling she knew what was being thrown into the sea, and kicked back down to the sandy bottom beneath the fishing boat. Looking up, she could make out the silhouette of the hull and began swimming around the perimeter of the shape above, starting down the port side of the 50-foot vessel. She kicked with all her might, sweeping broad strokes with arms to pull herself through the water, but also reaching for what might lie ahead in the darkness. If she was right, there was very little time.

Or, if Pascal's threats were correct, time was of no significance at all. It was unlikely they would have heard a gunshot from above the surface. Her heart raced as she willed herself to swim faster. A shadow swept in from her left side and bumped her firmly before pulling ahead, the single stingray barely visible, leading her into the black water to her right. She stole a glance up, and realised she was cutting across from port towards starboard, passing under the centre of the vessel. She began veering back to continue her perimeter sweep, but the stingray quickly circled and bumped her again, pushing her to her right. Several years before, AJ had followed a couple of sharks and found a WWII submarine, lost to the world for over 70 years. She had no idea why she had been compelled to follow them on that day, but she felt the same compulsion to follow the stingray now. Allowing the ray to direct her, it took two more strong kicks before she met a swirl of stingrays just above the sandy bottom below the starboard midship of the fishing boat. Lying below them in the sand, she felt the body of a human being.

AJ couldn't breathe; she was too late. Pascal hadn't been lying. They had shot Jackson at the first sign of trouble and thrown him overboard. She cried into her regulator and slipped her hands beneath his limp figure, raising him from the sea floor as the stingrays widened their circle and opened a path to the surface. Jackson rolled in her arms and something jolted her to a halt. His hand reached out and touched her face.

"Bloody hell!" she blurted into her mouthpiece, and yanking the spare regulator from its tether, she purged it and shoved it into Jackson's face, dropping him back to the sand. The sweetest sound she had ever heard was the long inhalation he took from the reg. She tried hugging him, but their reg lines tangled, so she made do with holding his head and trying to lift him once again. The same tug resisted her, and she swept an arm beneath him and slapped the line tied around his ankles, which extended down to the sand, where an anchor held him. AJ took her dive knife and cut the line with a strong sawing motion, then found the bindings around his ankles and severed them. They must have run out of time to bind his hands, she assumed, as they now wrapped around her and held her as close as the scuba gear would allow. The stingrays parted and a large dark figure appeared. Reg helped AJ haul Jackson up and the three carefully ascended to the surface, unsure what they would find.

AJ could see a brighter light above them as they broke the surface and when her mask cleared, she saw Reg's Newton alongside the fishing boat on the opposite side. A policeman in full tactical gear swung his automatic weapon in their direction and AJ heard Whittaker's voice call out.

"Hold up, hold up, that's our divers."

Detective Whittaker looked over the side and smiled. "I see you found the one that got away. Thank God you did. They tossed him over as we pulled up. Thomas was about to go in after him."

Thomas's beaming face appeared next to the detective. "Hi Boss."

"Thomas, drop the ladder on our boat so we can climb up," Reg said and started around the bow of the fishing boat towards the Newton.

Jackson handed AJ back her spare regulator as the two bobbed in the warm water. "Thanks for that," he said and grinned.

"I thought you were gone," AJ said, her voice breaking. "You were just lying there."

He reached over and brushed her cheek. "I tried to swim up but the anchor was too heavy and the rope around my ankles was too tight. By the time I hit the sand, I knew I couldn't break myself free."

AJ groaned, imagining that desperate feeling of realising there was no hope.

"I didn't want to leave in a cloud of panic and fear, so I committed myself to a peaceful death. I figured if I relaxed, I had a minute or two of air in my lungs, so I would spend that time the best way I could," he said softly and smiled. "I lay down and I thought of you."

She leaned over and kissed him, holding his head to hers with a firm but tender hand, never wanting to let go. They began to sink in the water and she finally released him, tears streaming down her face. He wiped the tears away with a finger as she inflated her BCD to keep them buoyant.

"Don't cry. It was beautiful. I couldn't see without a mask in the dark, but I could feel the stingrays brushing against me as they circled. And then these strong arms scooped me up when I was almost out of air, and I thought I was being carried to the afterlife. It was a like this crazy, wonderful dream. I was stoked, but sad, and then I reached out and felt your face." He laughed. "Then a regulator about knocked my teeth out."

AJ splashed him. "That was me, saving you."

"And I'm glad you did," he replied, and kissed her again.

By the time they had climbed the ladder and AJ had dumped her scuba gear in the rack, the Marine Police Unit boat had pulled alongside and tied to the starboard side of the fishing boat. Reg threw both AJ and Jackson a towel and they dried off as they looked over at the two Jamaican crew in handcuffs, being transferred to the police boat.

"Sold them good, we did." Thomas boasted. "The music, that made it real for sure."

Reg shook his head. "Bloody racket, but suppose it was a good idea," he said and couldn't hide a smirk under his thick beard.

"Wait," Jackson called out to Whittaker. "Where's the other guy?"

The detective looked over and pointed to Pascal, who they already had aboard the police boat. Pascal scowled back at them.

"No, not him, the other guy," Jackson repeated urgently.

Whittaker looked at the officer next to him on the deck of the fishing boat.

"We've been through the boat, there's no one else, sir," the man assured him.

"There was someone else?" Whittaker asked Jackson.

"Oh yeah," Jackson confirmed. "He's a scary-looking dude. Tall, muscular guy with a shaved head. He stayed below most of the time, but he was definitely aboard."

AJ looked across the sound, where she could see the lights from several of the boats they had spotted on their way in that were finally heading for the marina.

They all heard laughter from the police boat, and turned that way. One of the officers pulled Pascal towards the cabin, but he dug his heels in and stopped laughing enough to talk.

"I warned you, but you wouldn't listen," he said, grinning. "Now you've got trouble."

"Who is he?" Whittaker asked. "Who is the other man?"

The officer let Pascal be so he could answer.

Pascal made a spooky sound. "He's a ghost. See how he disappeared? You'll never see him again." He lifted his shackled hands and waggled a finger at AJ. "You should have listened. You, that girl, this island, you'll all wish you'd listened to me. Now you'll deal with the Ghost."

27

GRAND CAYMAN – SATURDAY

Whittaker looked around at the black waters surrounding the three boats tied together in the North Sound. They were a bobbing island of light amongst an ocean of darkness. In the distance, speckles of light marked the homes at Rum Point to the east, Governors Creek to the south-west, and Grand Harbour far to the south. He had three prisoners, the fishing boat to secure, and now a potentially dangerous man on the loose. His men had thoroughly searched the fishing boat again and found no one hidden away.

Whittaker looked across the fishing boat to AJ standing on the Newton, tied to the opposite side. "Your fellow, Pascal, has clammed up now. Won't say anything about why they're here or who this other man is. We had a policeman at the Shaws' house, but I've radioed for a couple more armed guards to replace him."

"Poor girl has to be scared out of her wits," AJ called back to him. "Who is she, anyway?"

Whittaker held up his hands. "We've got no idea why she would be a target, just a normal family as best we can tell. I spoke with the girl's mother, Renee Shaw, before you called me, and she was dumbfounded. Told me her daughter is just a regular kid, finishing university. Outstanding student, never been in any trouble."

"What's the girl's name?" AJ asked, purely out of curiosity.

"Tenley," Whittaker replied. "Tenley Shaw."

He turned and talked to the Police Marine Unit captain for a moment. AJ looked at Reg.

"Suppose we better muddle off back to the dock. Have you called Pearl? She'll be worried sick."

Reg nodded. "I texted her. But she'll still be fussing until she sees us all."

"The girl," Whittaker called over again. "She's Renee's daughter, but Shaw isn't her father. I doubt it matters, but the mother said Sam Shaw adopted her after they were married."

AJ shrugged her shoulders. "Alright if we shove off?"

Whittaker scratched his head and paused a moment. "Reg, think you can pilot that fishing boat?" he called over.

Reg looked at the big old wooden boat. "Don't see why not," he replied.

Whittaker nodded thoughtfully. "Okay then, would you mind taking it in to the Yacht Club marina, and I'll have some men meet you there to secure it?"

Without waiting for Reg's answer, he turned back to the police marine boat captain. "We'll take a quick sweep of the water here, then head in. We need to check the boats returning to the island from this side, it's likely he's slipped aboard or forced his way aboard one of them. Is there another marine unit on this side of the island?"

The captain shook his head, "No sir, they're in George Town."

"Well, that makes it more difficult. In that case, I suppose it needs to be us," Whittaker said more urgently.

Reg had stepped over to the fishing boat and checked the helm inside the enclosed wheelhouse. He stepped back to the deck.

"Key's in it. As long as they didn't kill the clutch, we should be fine once we clear the prop."

AJ was already putting her gear on. "Guess I'll go undo that mess, seeing as I made the mess."

Reg looked over at Thomas. "Mind taking the Newton back to West Bay, Thomas?"

Thomas waved. "No problem, Big Boss."

The group became a blur of activity as boats were untied, engines started, and the marine unit boat swung its big floodlights across the gently ebbing water.

Whittaker was on the VHF radio in one hand and his cellphone in the other. He lowered both and yelled above the noise.

"AJ's fella!"

Jackson looked up from the Newton where he was helping AJ get in the water. "Yes, sir."

"Can you go with Thomas?" Whittaker called out. "I'll have a sketch artist meet you at Reg's dock. Give her the best description you can recall."

Jackson gave him a thumbs up.

AJ turned and gave Jackson a quick kiss. "I'll see you as soon as we get this tub to the marina. The van keys are on the console up top," she said, nodding towards the fly-bridge of the Newton. "Pick us up, would you?"

She grinned, and stepped off the back of the dive boat with a splash.

Within two minutes, the three boats were separated. Thomas and Jackson headed towards the cut, Whittaker and the police were making a wide sweep in search of the missing man, and Reg was left alone on the fishing boat, while AJ cleared the rope. He busied himself checking out the helm and snooping around the wheelhouse.

AJ cursed herself for tying hurried knots, not intended to be undone. The strain from the engine had pulled everything so tight she finally gave up and cut the line away. She was fumbling in the dark, as holding the torch wasn't really an option while she was cutting. Every once in a while she would turn her beam on and check her progress, then let it hang from its tether on her BCD while she hacked away some more. Below her the stingrays still circled curiously, which made her smile. After five minutes of cutting, tugging and unwrapping, she finally had all the line free and made sure she kept hold of the pieces so they didn't end up on the sea floor. The fishing boat didn't have a swim step, or a ladder – at least one that was readily available from her perspective in the water – so she threw the pieces of rope over the transom and hung on the stern.

"Reg!" she yelled. "Need a bit of a hand back here!"

She heard footsteps across the deck until a large shadow appeared over her, silhouetted by the deck light off the back of the wheelhouse. It occurred to her there was still a man at large that they probably didn't want to meddle with, and it was an assumption he had hitchhiked towards the island.

"Stop buggering about down there and get in the boat," Reg's gruff voice teased her, much to her relief.

"See a ladder anywhere?" AJ asked.

"Nah," he replied. "Slip your gear off in the water so I can lift it in, then I'll haul you up."

She did as Reg suggested and with some heaving and swearing, everything and everyone wound up on the deck of the fishing boat. AJ shoved her dive gear against the gunwale, and Reg went back to the wheelhouse to start the motor. The old diesel cranked over slowly but fired after a few seconds and spluttered to life. Reg put the boat in gear and held his breath. AJ stayed at the stern and looked over the transom at the water beginning to churn behind the boat, turning to give him an okay sign. She made her way to the bow and untied them from the mooring buoy, curling the line up in a neat circle on the forward deck. She looked up as she made her way around the narrow walkway alongside the wheelhouse, and spotted the Police Marine Unit boat heading towards the shore. It was already up on plane, the powerful outboards driving the boat forward at over 50 knots. They may get there in time to intercept a few of the dive and fishing boats heading in, she thought.

Reg swung the old wooden boat towards Governors Creek and

brought the throttle up gently. AJ joined him and started playing with the GPS unit in the console, seeing if she could set their destination.

"Not a bad old boat, this," Reg said, looking around at the varnished teak panels in the wheelhouse, dimly lit by the light of the gauges.

"Have you been down in the cabins?" AJ asked, looking at the narrow stairs leading into the blackness below deck.

Reg shook his head. "Nah. Poked around up here a bit, but figured I didn't ought to plaster my fingerprints all over the place."

"Jackson said they kept him on deck all day," she continued, making idle conversation. "Played backgammon with the two Jamaican blokes. He said they didn't seem to know what it was all about, they were just hired to bring the other two over here and back to Jamaica."

Reg grinned. "I'd say this boat belongs to the two Jamaicans. I can tell you, it's been a while since it was used for fishing," he replied, sniffing the warm, muggy air and detecting another odour mixed in. "Moving weed around more like."

"Or consuming at least." AJ laughed.

She fell quiet for a few minutes, lost in thought after the crazy day it had been and they plodded along to the drone of the old diesel motor. Pretty soon she spotted the channel markers up ahead, leading to the mangrove-lined passage into Governors Creek. AJ could see the Police Marine Unit boat was to their north, at the entrance to Salt Creek, checking a returning pleasure cruiser.

When she finally spoke again, her voice was quiet and subdued.

"I didn't know if I'd ever see him again, Reg. All day I had to keep convincing myself he would be okay."

Reg put a beefy hand on her shoulder and listened patiently.

"Then, when they threw him in, he wasn't moving at all. I was sure I was too late," she said and leaned against the big man. "I came up with the stupid plan, and I thought I'd killed him."

He slipped his arm around her and squeezed her to him. His embrace was firm, but gentle, and made her feel safe and distanced from the trauma they had endured. It always surprised her how the bear of a man could be so tender.

"Idiot told me he was all 'zenned out'. Had himself ready to go." She wiped a tear from her cheek. "I would have been thrashing about like a loony, but not Jackson, he said he wanted a peaceful death."

She felt his barrel chest shudder as he tried to stifle a laugh. "Bloody hippie," he said.

"Yeah," she said, pulling away and thumping Reg on the arm, "bloody hippie."

He let out his laugh. "He's a keeper though, that one. Told you before, if you screw it up, Pearl and me is still havin' him over for tea."

He reached over and ruffled her hair, teasing her the way he would a child, but his voice turned serious. "It was thanks to you he's alright. You did get to him in time. Your plan was solid."

"It was, thanks to the stingray," she replied, her voice brightening. "I know we're all one with the animals and nature and all that Jackson, karmic stuff, but I tell you, Reg, the stingray took me straight to him. If she hadn't, I might have been too late."

"Then I suppose his karma theory holds water, don't it?" he said. "Still means you made the right call. Besides, if me or Whittaker had thought it was balmy, we wouldn't have gone along with it."

"I guess," she mumbled before looking over at him. "Do you believe in karma then?"

Reg laughed. "I'm an old Navy tar, we're not supposed to believe in anything namby-pamby like that. We believe in swabbing decks and shooting big guns."

AJ gave him a firm nudge, which didn't move him at all. "Yeah, yeah, big tough bloke, but seriously, Reg, do you?"

He looked at her with a grin. "I'd say you're proof there's something to it," he said, then turned back to the front window as they approached the channel markers. "But if you tell a living soul I said that, I'll have your guts for garters."

AJ laughed. "Fair enough."

She scanned the darkness ahead, but didn't see any boats. The lights from a few luxury homes lining the channel cast a glow across the water's edge, otherwise there was no sign of life.

"I wonder where Whittaker wants us to pull up with this thing?" she asked.

"You're not going to the marina," came a deep, accented voice behind them. "Turn to port, stay in the sound."

28

GRAND CAYMAN – JUNE 1997

Ten o'clock seemed to be a lot further from breakfast than normal. Simon had been awake at 5am, which was his usual time at home, so he went for a run when he couldn't go back to sleep. He couldn't believe how much sweat could be expelled from a human being in the muggy pre-dawn heat, but managed to log his usual five miles, although slower than his regular pace. He didn't mind. The scenery was exciting and different, a far cry from the often drizzly, damp streets of Oxford. Running was his time alone to think and organise himself for the day. His best ideas and clearest logic often came to him during his morning run. This morning, his mind was completely occupied with thoughts of Renee. She had knocked his world from its axis, and he doubted he was being either logical or clear thinking. It had taken forty-five minutes in the air-conditioned room before sweat ceased to leak from his pores and he was able to shower. He had gone downstairs for breakfast and found the restaurant a lonely place at 7:15am. Eating alone took a frustratingly short amount of time, so he'd topped off his coffee, and sat outside where the sun was high enough in the east to light the ocean and cast long shadows from the palm trees across the beach. What an amazing part of the world, he thought, as he sipped his coffee and imagined the bustling reef below the acres of calm blue water stretching away before him.

At 9:50am, he was standing out front of the hotel, strategically away from the foyer entrance so he wasn't bothered by the ever-helpful staff, and Renee wouldn't be seen when she arrived. He strained to look inside each car that pulled around, and by 10am he was beaded with sweat again, standing in the sun with little shade. He stepped out the way of a scooter coming by, but the scooter stopped, and he realised it was Renee grinning at him from under a silver, open-faced helmet. The scooter was a Red Honda Elite of eighties vintage, with several scuffed panels held in place with duct tape. Its seat was just big enough for two, and behind it was a small wire rack where her rucksack was held with a bungee cord. Renee was wearing black cut-offs, a lacy white shirt and flip-flops. Simon laughed.

"I'm pretty sure this is how fifty percent of personal injury insurance claims in the Italian Riviera start."

Renee scowled at him. "I've never been to the Italian Riviera, but in the Cayman Islands this is how many of us get around, and we do just fine." She held out a helmet. "I'm eating that picnic in my bag on a nice quiet beach," she said, throwing a thumb towards her rucksack. "You can join me or not. Up to you."

She was trying hard not to grin, but when he took the helmet and put it on, she couldn't stop herself from laughing.

"You couldn't let me wear the silver one?" he asked, buckling the strap.

"This is my helmet, which fits me. Your big, manly head wouldn't squeeze into it," she said, still laughing. "Besides, you look good in fuchsia."

He shook his head. "You can call it fuchsia, but to the rest of the world it's pink. The rainbow stripe is a nice touch too. Whose helmet is this, anyway?"

"It's my mother's." She grinned.

"Your dad didn't have one?" he asked, throwing up his hands. "Something more masculine perhaps?"

"He won't ride a scooter, says they're dangerous," she said matter-of-factly, trying to keep a straight face again. "Are you getting on, or what?"

"I presume there's no chance I could drive?" he asked.

"Ride," she said. "You ride motorcycles and horses, you drive cars and buses. And no."

He swung his leg over and once he was seated behind her, he decided he might like being back there after all. She pulled away, wobbling slightly with the extra weight, but to his relief, appeared under control. He fumbled behind him for the luggage rack and found the frame to hang on to as she paused at the car park exit. Once she had swung out onto West Bay Road and accelerated up to speed, she called out over the wind noise.

"You can hold on to me if you need to."

He leaned into her and let go of the luggage rack, putting his hands on her slender waist.

"Don't know that I need to, but I'd certainly like to," he replied.

They rode north, with the wind rushing over them, carrying the salty smell of the ocean. Simon glimpsed the water between low-rise hotels and condos, which gave way to a strip of mangroves after Public Beach, until they approached West Bay. He could faintly hear Renee humming a tune to herself as she whizzed along the road and hoped it was a sign that she was as happy as he felt. By West Bay dock the road narrowed and became Town Hall Road, and from there he had no idea where they went. Renee zigged and zagged down roughly paved roads, lined with small, block-built homes with colourful roofs. She slowed and waited at a junction while a lady pushed her pram across the intersection. When she reached their side of the road Simon could see the woman was pregnant.

"Hi there, Mrs. Bodden," Renee said with a wave, and peered into the pram.

Oh, hello Renee, how you bin?" the lady asked. "How's your Mami and Papi? I have some curtains of hers I been sewin' up. Tell her they ready anytime she wants to come by."

"I tell her tonight," Renee replied. "What's her name?" she asked, tickling the baby's tummy.

"That's Regina Sydney, right there, and she's a good one. This other one ain't been in there long, and he already given me trouble," she said, rubbing the paunch in her stomach.

"It's a boy?" Renee asked.

"Doc don't know yet, but I already named him Thomas 'cos I know he gotta be a boy. No girl don't wriggle and kick around this much," she said with a smile and looked at Simon on the back of the scooter.

"Oh, this is my friend, Simon," Renee said, seeing the woman's curious look. "I'm giving him a tour."

"Hello, Mrs. Bodden," Simon said politely, and she looked up at the helmet, then back down at the Englishman.

"Hello there," she said, forcing a smile. "Well I best be getting home with dis one. Tell your Mami now."

"I will, Mrs. Bodden. Good seeing you," Renee replied, and the lady waved a hand in the air as she waddled away, pushing the pram.

"I don't think she approves," Simon said quietly.

Renee put her hand on his leg. "Don't worry about her, she's a lovely lady. Folks are just protective around here. It's a small island."

She motored away, and after a few more twists and turns she took a right on Conch Point Road and slowed as she approached a restaurant on the right, signed Ristorante Pappagallo. Simon looked over her shoulder and saw the pavement ended ahead.

"Hang on, it'll get a little rough," Renee said, and bounced onto the rutted trail that continued between the mangroves.

The surface was greyed white limestone, with patches of scrub clinging to sandy soil by the edges and thick shrubs, small trees and mangroves on both sides. Occasionally, a sandy path led away to the left and after a few minutes, Renee turned on a trail barely wide enough for a car, and carefully manoeuvred the scooter along the raised middle between the tracks made by vehicle tyres. Fifty yards ahead the trail ended, and Simon could see clear blue sky. Renee stopped short of a raised berm and they got off the scooter. Simon could see calm turquoise ocean. They took off their helmets, Renee unstrapped her rucksack, and they walked over the berm to a narrow stretch of sand meeting the Caribbean Sea. The only sound was the breeze rustling in the trees and the water lapping softly against the shoreline. From where they stood, they couldn't see another human being, or any sign of mankind. Not a building, boat or trace of activity. To Simon, it felt like they were the only two people in their own island paradise.

Renee unpacked her rucksack, spreading a blanket on the sand and handing Simon a bottle of water. They sat, and she put a container of fruit between them. Simon ate a few pieces of the fresh mango and inspected a small, yellowish green fruit that looked like a tiny apple.

"What is this?" he asked, smelling the odd-looking fruit.

"That's a ju plum," she replied, and bit one in half herself.

Simon tried one and smiled as he chewed. "It's sweet."

Renee nodded. "Only ripe to eat twice a year," she said, grinning. "You timed it right."

Simon laid back on the blanket and savoured the lingering taste of the ju plum. The overhead sun was hot, and even with sunglasses on he was squinting. He closed his eyes and soaked up the sounds and smells around him. Beside him he felt Renee move about and he peeked one eye open. She had taken off her shirt, revealing a black bikini top, and laid down on her side looking at him.

"What?" he asked, smiling.

"Just checking you out. Thinking," she replied, quietly.

"What's on your mind?" he asked, rolling to his side, facing her.

She took a moment before replying. "I'm wondering, what's important to you?"

He laughed. "Wow. That's a rather deep thought for a day at the beach."

"Well," she said slowly. "You're not here very long, so if I want to get to know you, there are things I need to ask."

"I'm taking that as good news that you'd like to get to know me," he replied lightly.

"You should," she said, grinning for a second before her expression turned serious.

He thought for a moment, wondering what exactly she was looking for. What was important to him? Good question, he thought, what is important to me. She stayed silent, just looking at him patiently as he mulled the idea around in his mind.

"Success," he finally said. "But not success as in money and accolades. I mean successfully completing things I commit to. I don't like things left incomplete, and I don't like to fail. So, I think carefully before taking on a project or a commitment, and I'm quite determined once I do. I hate loose ends."

She nodded. "What else?"

He considered the question again, and realised he had never asked himself this. It dawned on him that although he naturally applied lessons learnt from his personal life into his business world, it could and should work both ways. His business should reflect and support his personal ethics and not fall purely into the hands of competitive corporate strategy.

"Truth," he said firmly. "My mother taught me the importance of truth and honesty, even at the cost of things we hold dear. When I was young, I told a fib about not having homework because I wanted to go outside and play football, not sit in the house and do schoolwork. She knew I had homework to do. She asked me, 'Are you sure you don't have homework you need to do first?'"

He smiled, recollecting the memory. "She was giving me a second chance. I lied again. But it bothered me the whole time I was out playing with my friends, and when I came home, she sat me down again. I wasn't scared of the punishment, although she wasn't opposed to giving me a whack on the backside, but the guilt of disappointing her was far worse. She asked me how my game was, and my first thought was that maybe I'd got away with it.

That made me feel even more guilty. I couldn't stand it and I confessed."

Simon rolled over onto his back and Renee leaned in closer. "What did she do?" she asked softly.

"She pulled her chair in close and told me I was about to hear the most important lesson she could ever teach me," he said, recalling her words perfectly. "'Truth is a responsibility to others, but more importantly to yourself. Without truth you can never take responsibility, and without responsibility for your words and actions, you will never have self-respect.'"

Renee rested her head on Simon's shoulder, and he put his arm around her. She didn't say a word.

They spent the afternoon at their secluded spot on the beach, cooling off in the balmy water, walking along the sand collecting shells and lying on the blanket dozing in each other's arms. When the sun began to lower in the sky to the west, they packed everything up and Renee let Simon ride them back through West Bay. She directed him to a small restaurant called Silver Sands Cafe where she introduced him to jerk chicken and conch stew.

It was dark when they pulled into the car park at the Westin, and Renee parked the scooter in a dimly lit corner. They took off their helmets and Simon pulled her close to kiss her good night. The day had been another flood of new experiences, leaving him overwhelmed by Renee's presence in his every thought and emotion. He kissed her deeply and felt her arms holding him tightly to her. She pulled slightly away and nestled her face into his neck, whispering softly.

"I can't go through the foyer with you, go ahead without me. I'll be up to your room in a few minutes."

29

GRAND CAYMAN – SATURDAY

Startled, Reg and AJ both whipped around to face the man. He stood near the top of the stairs, and even in the dimly lit wheelhouse they could tell he was a large, broad-shouldered man with a shaved head. His most outstanding feature, AJ quickly noticed, was the handgun which he pointed at them. AJ couldn't abide guns. Especially ones aimed at her.

"Steer hard to port," the man repeated. "Then remove your mobile phones from your pockets and throw them on the floor behind you," he instructed calmly.

They both complied and Reg swung the boat to the left, just before the channel markers, and headed south along the coastline.

"You are a bloody ghost," Reg said, keeping his gaze out the front window. "Never heard you coming. You been down below this whole time?"

AJ heard the man gather up their mobile phones and open the wheelhouse door to the deck. Bugger, she thought to herself, there goes another mobile. The shop on the island had threatened to stop allowing her to take out the replacement insurance on their phones. She seemed to lose one every six months or so. The door closed, and the man made no effort to respond to Reg.

"Where are we going?" AJ asked as they continued to motor along with more homes and the Grand Caymanian Hotel on their right.

"Where I tell you," the man answered.

"The police are expecting this boat to arrive at the marina in a few minutes," Reg said. "They'll be on the lookout. Not exactly a stealthy vessel to sneak around in."

AJ guessed Reg was trying to engage the man in some kind of conversation just to figure out his intentions, but she hoped pointing out the error of his plans wouldn't make the two of them superfluous. She noticed a glow from behind her, brightening the side wall of the wheelhouse, and presumed it came from a mobile phone in the man's hand. Once more, he had ignored Reg, and the rumble of the motor was the only sound in the confined, humid space. AJ had been running on adrenaline most of the day and had finally relaxed on the run across North Sound. Now, thrown back into the middle of a drama they were yet to understand, her tired body was back on high alert. The fact that the man hadn't directed them out of the North Sound towards international waters could only mean one thing. Pascal was right, his cohort was planning to finish what they had come for. They passed by mangrove and scrub land broken only by a channel leading to docks where many of the Stingray City boats left from, and the Ritz-Carlton development surrounded their own golf course. Far ahead, the lights of Owen Roberts International Airport glowed in the sky and AJ knew the next channel they would come to was the one leading into Snug Harbour.

"What has this girl, Tenley, possibly done that would warrant you and your mate trying to kill her?" AJ asked.

"Be quiet," the man replied in an even tone. "Stop the boat and take it out of gear."

Reg pulled the throttle back to idle and disengaged the gear. The boat slowed and coasted slowly forward, clearing the end of the mangroves on their right to reveal the lights of the homes on Snug Harbour. AJ heard the man move behind them.

"Down below," he ordered, and the two turned around.

He pointed to the stairwell with the gun and AJ started down the steep steps into the blackness.

"Light switch on your left," the man called down and AJ fumbled around on the wall until her hand brushed a switch and a low voltage light bathed the stairwell in a yellow glow. At the bottom of the steps, facing the stern, was a door marked 'engine room' and to her right it opened up into the galley with a small dining area. Under the stairs on the starboard side, a hallway ran towards the bow, and she could see several cabin doors on the left side of the hall. Reg followed her down, and they both stood clear of the steps in the galley. The man came down and waved the gun towards the hallway. She could see him clearly now, and Jackson's description had been accurate. He had a deep tan, a chiselled jaw and the athletic physique of a prize-fighter. She noticed a scar on his temple and his eyes were calm but intense. He waved the gun again, and she walked down the hallway as directed, hearing Reg's feet clomping behind her.

"Last cabin, go inside," the man said, and AJ opened the heavy wooden door on the left where the hallway ended.

Inside, she found the light switch and turned it on. The cabin was small, with a single bunk bed against the opposite wall, which was the port side hull, and a wardrobe and small table to her left. To the right was an opening in the wall with the removed panel laid on the bottom bunk. The vertical wood planks lining the room made it easy to disguise the seams of the hidden panel, which explained why the police didn't find the man during their search. Reg stepped into the tiny cabin and the man stood in the doorway. He reached inside the cabin and turned out the light.

"Unscrew the bulb," he said, looking at Reg.

Reg looked up, and from the thin light coming from the hall, he could see the bare bulb above his head. He reached up and unscrewed the hot bulb, tossing it to the man who deftly caught it and threw it to the floor where it smashed to pieces.

"Be quiet and I won't shoot you," he explained, as though he were ordering a coffee. "Make a noise, or try to break out, and I will come back down and shoot you both."

He closed the door, and AJ heard a key turn in the lock. A hint of light seeped under the door, otherwise the room was pitch black. They both waited, barely breathing, listening for the man's footsteps to ascend the stairs. They never heard a single creak or footfall, but the boat clunked into gear and the engine note rose so they knew he must have made it to the wheelhouse.

"Bloody hell, he is a ghost. The bloke doesn't make a sound," AJ whispered.

"Must weigh over 14 stone too," Reg added as he gently tried the door handle. The door didn't budge.

AJ's eyes were beginning to become accustomed to the dark cabin, and she could make out Reg's form and the outlines of the furniture.

"What can we do?" she asked, feeling the boat gently rocking as it moved through the water.

"Not sure," Reg answered in a hushed tone. "I might be able to bust this door down, but I can't do it without him hearing, that's for sure. Not much point getting out, just to be shot."

"You know he's going after Tenley again, right?" she said, feeling around the edge of the door for the hinges.

"Yeah, guessed that when we came up on Snug Harbour. Hopefully Whittaker has her well guarded by now," Reg replied. "Or moved her."

AJ found no hinges. She realised the door opened into the hallway so the hinges were on the outer side.

"Can't imagine how he's going to sneak up to her house in a 50-foot fishing boat without being spotted," AJ said. "Hardly stealthy, as you said. That canal isn't very wide either, he'd have to find a spot without boats tethered both sides if he wants to turn around to leave."

"Maybe he's planning on leaving it at the end. He could tie up by Turtle Cove condos and go on foot from there," Reg whispered. "We'll wait until he ties up, then I'll try to knock this door down."

"How the hell we gonna know he's left the boat?" AJ replied, wondering how the man of his size could make so little noise.

Reg stayed quiet for a moment and AJ knew he was thinking it through. "Don't suppose we will. Are we willing to take the risk?"

It was AJ's turn to ponder for a minute, but she ran through her thoughts aloud. "It's possible, if we stay quiet and don't make a fuss, he'll tie up, go about his business and the police will be by and find us. But, if he abandons this boat, how would he leave the island? There are no flights, and he'd have to go through immigration and they'd see he was here illegally. Not to mention they're looking for him. He could steal another boat, I suppose."

"All good points," Reg grunted.

She continued. "Makes me think he'll be back for this boat, which means we need to get off it as soon as we can."

"Without getting shot," Reg added.

"Without getting shot," AJ agreed. "But the reason he's back here is to kill that poor girl, so we can't sit here and do nothing, right? We're the only ones who know what he's really up to, and where he is. We might be the only ones who can stop him."

"True," Reg replied. "But not sure how we stop an armed professional killer when we're locked in here. Not sure how we stop one if we were out there either, mind you. Maybe he'll get bored using up all his bullets shooting at us and give up?"

"That would be a crappy way to save someone," AJ agreed again.

"Yeah," Reg mused. "But you're right, we can't sit here and wait forever. I say we give him two minutes after he stops, just enough time to get tied up, then we bash down the door."

"When you say we, I hope you don't mean using the eight-and-a-half stone girl to knock the door down?" AJ chuckled.

"I was planning on using your noggin as a battering ram," Reg replied. "It's the hardest thing I know of in this world."

She punched him playfully, although, in the dark cabin, she wasn't altogether sure which part of him she had punched. They both listened for a bit, but all they could hear was the steady droning of the diesel, plodding along.

"We've been going a while now, don't you think?" AJ said. "Surely, he must have gone past Snug Harbour."

"I was thinking the same thing," Reg replied slowly. "Unless he turned into the canal."

AJ listened intently again, for what, she had no idea, but maybe, she figured, there would be some indication of their whereabouts. In the movies, she thought, they always hear a train or a foghorn or something completely distinctive. All she could hear was a fifty-year-old diesel chugging away; she couldn't even hear the water against the hull, idling as slowly as they were.

"I still can't imagine how he would sneak this boat by anyone. If Whittaker posted more guards at the house, they'll see it coming the moment it turns into the canal."

Just as her words came out, the diesel engine note climbed, and the big wooden boat noticeably picked up speed, causing them both to take a step back to catch their balance.

"What on earth?" AJ mumbled. "Reckon he's being chased?"

"Bollocks," Reg shouted, and moved back to the bunk beds. "Get out the way, AJ, I'm taking a run at the door."

She stepped aside. "What are you doing, Reg? He'll hear you!"

"He's not sneaking anywhere," Reg shouted back. "He's using the bloody boat as a distraction. Hang on to something!"

Reg lowered his shoulder and started towards the door just as the boat shuddered to a stop in a violent crash. The force threw them flailing to the back of the cabin where they hit the table and wall, before tumbling to the floor.

30

GRAND CAYMAN – SATURDAY

The ear-piercing sounds of splintering wood and crunching fibreglass died away, leaving the strained throbs of the diesel engine, hunting up and down in its attempt to continue driving the vessel forward. AJ used the table for support and picked herself up from the floor.

"Reg? You alright?" she groaned.

"Feels like everything is about as old and broken as it was before we were in a shipwreck," he mumbled from the floor to her right.

The boat creaked and crunched some more and AJ felt it list to port, staggering to keep her balance as the floor tilted beneath her. The poor diesel laboured and with a shudder through the whole vessel, the motor ground to a stop and the faint light from under the door flickered, before extinguishing completely. She stood still for a moment in the inky blackness, keeping the cabin's orientation clear in her mind. She heard Reg shuffling and moaning next to her.

"Are you off the floor?" she asked.

"Yeah, I'm standing between the wardrobe and the table. Where are you?" he replied, and she felt his hand touch her right arm. "There you are."

"Think you can take another run at that door?" she asked.

"Don't know," he said. "Bit harder now we're listed over. Gotta run uphill. Would have been handy if it had settled the other way."

"When we get out, I'll give it a shove and tilt it the other way for you if you like," she replied. "But for now we'd better hurry up and get that door open."

"Alright, alright, these old bones don't move about like they used to," he complained, and she felt him move in front of her towards the bunks.

"Don't mean to nag you, old man, but it's just that my feet are getting wet," she said and tapped her foot on the floor, making a splashing sound.

"Yeah, well, that's because we're sitting on the bottom of the canal," Reg replied, and she could hear his feet sloshing through water as well.

"Good job this canal's not very deep," she said optimistically.

He scoffed. "Probably 6 or 7 feet, which puts it over my breathing parts, don't know about you."

She laughed. She was barely 5' 4", and Reg towered over her. "Have you got that door open yet?"

"Would help if I could see where it is," he mumbled. "Reckon I'll charge uphill and hit something up there and hope it's the door."

"Hang on," AJ said, and shuffled up to the starboard side, feeling her way along the small cabin wall until she felt the door. "Can you hear where my voice is coming from?"

"Sort of," Reg said, over the growing sound of rushing water.

"Aim for the knock," she said. "I'm off to the side now, and I'll reach over and knock on the door, okay?"

She began methodically knocking loudly on the wooden door.

"Right," he said. "Here I come. You might want to move your hand now."

She knocked twice more until she heard Reg start his charge with a splash of water and thumping feet on the floor. The splashing and a louder thump startled AJ, who was bracing for the impact, which didn't come.

"What happened?" she called out.

"It's bloody slippery over here," he spluttered. "I fell arse over tea kettle before I made it halfway."

"Blimey Reg, you need me to knock it down for you? I'm only letting you do it so you can feel all manly and Navy like," she teased and began knocking again.

"Don't tempt me, you cheeky wench, or I *will* use your noggin as a ram," he said, and she heard him getting to his feet, "Let's try this again."

AJ heard him step more carefully forward before picking up speed in the three steps it took to cross the cabin. She pulled her hand back as the big man crashed into the door with a dull thud that reverberated throughout the room. The door didn't budge.

"You all right?" she asked.

"Yeah," he replied, and she heard him trudge back down the sloping floor, meeting the rising water after a single pace. "Tap again."

She resumed her knocking and heard him charge again. This time the dull thud was accompanied by a cracking of wood and they both felt around the door in the darkness to see what damage he had inflicted. AJ felt a sharp edge at the top of the right side of the door.

"Here," she said excitedly, "It's breaking apart up top."

She felt his big paw find her hand, and she moved so he could check it out.

"Good, that's the lock side," he said. "It's held by three hinges on the left, but just in the middle by the lock on the right. I'll try to clobber it again upper right, so knock up there, okay?"

"Got it," she replied, and knocked higher on the right side of the door.

"Bollocks," Reg muttered. "Water's too deep, I can only get two steps now."

"It's over my ankles up here," AJ added. "You'll get it, Reg, couple more good hits."

She heard him take a step, and she pulled her hand clear before he bashed against the door again.

"Owww," he bellowed.

"You alright?" she asked again.

"Got a bit of door, and a lot of door frame," he groaned. "Knock again, come on, we're running out of time."

AJ knocked loudly, a little farther from the frame this time, and she waited till the last second to pull her hand away. Reg hit with a resounding smack that made AJ fall backwards into the water that was now almost up to her knees.

"Did you get it?" she asked from the floor.

She heard him fumble around with his hands, checking the damage. "Yeah, getting there," he said, and she heard a loud thump.

"What are you doing?" she asked, getting back to her feet, hearing another thump.

"Stay back," he answered, breathing heavily. "I think I can punch a hole."

Wood creaked and began to splinter under each blow, and AJ could only imagine the carnage it was causing to Reg's fists. Finally, she heard something break away.

"Bugger," Reg yelped, and she heard him sucking wind.

"Can I do something?" she asked as the water lapped around her thighs.

"Here," he said. "Pull this splinter out would you, I'm shaking too bad to get it."

"Splinter?" she said, thinking now is not the time to mess about with a splinter.

She found his outstretched hand in the dark and felt around. It was wet and sticky and he growled when her finger knocked a large, jagged piece of wood jutting from the top of his hand.

"Oooohhh," she squealed, feeling her stomach clench and her

knees go weak. "You know I'm squeamish, Reg. This ain't a splinter, it's half the bloody boat sticking out of your hand."

"I know, I know, just yank it out so I can get on, will you? I don't need the gory description."

"Alright," she said, shakily taking hold of the shard. Then she paused. "Hey, be rather funny if they found us both passed out in here, eh? They'd be scratching their heads, and I bet they'd never figure out we both fainted 'cos we're too squeamish."

"What the bloody hell are you yammering…" Reg started but never finished as AJ pulled the sliver of wood from Reg's hand. He groaned loudly and clutched his hand to his chest.

"Sorry, Reg. My mum's trick she used when she'd pull a plaster off when I was a kid," she whispered, but all she heard back was his body ramming against the door again.

He bashed and kicked and used the hole he'd made in the top as a handhold to gain leverage now running across the cabin was impossible with the water reaching their waists. AJ heard the wood giving, cracking and splintering.

"Here, here, can you fit through there?" Reg said and grabbed AJ's shoulder.

"Where?" she asked.

"Down low, I've kicked a hole through it," he urgently explained. "If you can get outside, you can kick downhill at the lock, with your back against the hull out there."

AJ felt around under the water and found the ragged hole Reg had made. It seemed tight, but she thought it might be big enough to wriggle through.

"Move over a bit, Reg," she said and took a few deep breaths before filling her lungs and ducking under the warm, salty water with her eyes closed.

She felt around the hole, poked her head through until both shoulders hit the door. She curled her shoulders in as tight as she could and pushed with her feet on the slippery, flooded floor. She felt the wood scraping her arms as she squeezed through the narrow gap.

She cringed at the thought of the cuts and scrapes that were forming down the beautiful artwork of her tattooed arms, then berated herself as she recalled the wound Reg had in his hand. The scrapes will heal, she reminded herself, and pushed harder with her feet. Her arms sprung through the hole and she lurched forward until her hips met the same resistance. The effort made her lungs strain, and she realised, with a moment of panic, she was only halfway through the hole. Backing out would be harder than continuing forward, but she cursed her shapely female hips that ground to a halt in the rough wood. She couldn't gather her hips in narrower as she had her shoulders, so she pushed on the back of the door with her hands and ground her way forward, wincing at the jagged wood cutting into her skin. Finally, her hips and thighs made it through the hole and she pulled her feet to the hallway and stood to take a gasp of air.

"I'm through," she shouted at the door.

"Good girl," Reg said. "Now go up and get help."

"You wily old bugger," she cursed. "I'm not leaving you in there! Now stand back while I kick this door down."

"Don't be silly, AJ, get up top and get some help," Reg shouted from the cabin.

AJ looked down the hallway, where a faint light glistened off the sea water that was now up to her waist on the higher starboard side. Several pots, pans and pieces of debris floated on the water by the galley. She wondered if it might be better to get help from the shore, and maybe some tools. She could hear a distant sound of sirens and remembered the man was out there somewhere. She turned back to the door and was about to tell Reg she would be back in two minutes when something burst inside the cabin and the sound of rushing water echoed loudly around below decks. The water AJ stood in surged and slopped around, rising dramatically.

"What just happened," she yelled.

"I think the hull just caved in up by the bow," Reg called back, and she heard him thumping his fist against the wood. "Get out AJ, I'll be right behind you."

AJ pushed her back against the hull behind her, and felt with her left foot until it rested just outside the door frame. She levered herself with her foot until she was jammed between the two surfaces, then raised her other leg from the water. She kicked at the wooden cabin door with all her might. It felt disappointingly solid, and the water continued to move up the wall, covering her back-side. Pretty soon she'd be immersed and would have no power kicking through the water. She thumped and beat on the door with her heel, moving the blows around, searching for a weak spot. She felt the water surge over her lap and shuffled her left leg and back-side farther up the walls until her head bumped the ceiling of the hallway. There was only three feet of airspace left, and it was diminishing rapidly. She struck out with her right foot, which hit nothing, flying through the hole Reg had made towards the top of the door. She pulled it back, ignoring the cuts and wounds from the broken planks, and kicked with all her might, aiming just below the hole. The wood gave but didn't break away and she rammed forward again, skimming through the top of the rising water as it took another foot of precious air away. This time the wood buckled beneath her heel, and she tipped her head to the side, shuffling higher on the wall to clear the water.

"You have to get out, AJ," Reg shouted from inside the cabin. "Ain't no good girl, I'll figure something out. Go up and get some help."

But AJ knew there was no figuring anything out, and no time to get help. The cabin and the hallway would be completely flooded before she reached the shore. She kicked with every ounce of strength she had, then pulled back and kicked again. The guilt she had hidden from under the relief of saving Jackson washed back over her like the sea water that reached her chest. They had been at Valley of the Rays because of her. If they hadn't been there on her hare-brained scheme, they wouldn't be here now; where Reg was about to drown on the other side of the stubborn wooden door she couldn't break down. AJ felt tears welling in her eyes, and she gritted her teeth and screamed loudly, fighting them back. She wasn't one to cry, and it made her mad when she succumbed. The adrenaline surged and her anger burst into violent jabs and blows with her bare foot that bled and throbbed in pain. The water slapped against her chin and she screamed again in rage, thrashing madly with her battered foot. Wood splintered, planks moved, and she kept pounding away with her aching leg. When resistance gave, she moved over and bashed again.

"Stop!" Reg yelled from inside the cabin. "Stop kicking!"

AJ took the pressure off her left foot and fell into the water. She clawed her way back to the surface and her head hit the ceiling with the top of her shoulders barely above the surface. She felt something bowl into her below the water, and Reg's head popped up next to her.

"Well, move then!" he spluttered, and she threw her arms around his big soggy, grey-haired head.

"Ha! You're out!" she yelled and let him go.

"I'm half out, and if you get a bloody move on, I'll get the rest of me out," he coughed and spluttered.

AJ pulled and kicked her way down the hallway, hearing Reg splashing along behind her. She shoved and batted kitchenware and floating rubbish from her path to reach the base of the stairs where the water was less than a foot from the ceiling. Using the stair rail, she pulled herself up and out of the water towards the wheelhouse, and once her feet cleared the water she turned back and looked down at Reg trudging up the stairs behind her, water raining from his shaggy beard, but a beautiful grin on his face.

They opened the wheelhouse door to the listing deck of the fishing boat and met a chaotic scene. Red and blue lights flashed in the sky behind the house on the shore, the fishing boat was speared into a sailboat whose deck was underwater with the mast reaching at an odd angle towards the heavens, and a policeman was pointing an automatic rifle at them. Again.

"Arms up, hold it right there," the policeman ordered.

"Where is he?" AJ shouted back, raising her tired arms.

"Hold it right there," the man repeated. "Where's who?"

"The assassin man!" AJ called out, looking beyond the policeman at the house. "He had us locked in a cabin."

The policeman frowned, clearly confused. "Back-up is on its way. You two are staying right there until we can sort this mess out. You're the only ones I've seen coming out of that boat."

"You better check on the girl, mate," Reg shouted. "We're telling you, the man you need to worry about is after the girl."

31

GRAND CAYMAN – JUNE 1997

The last few days of the holiday flew by agonisingly quickly as Simon tried to cling to every moment he had with Renee. While she worked during the day, the three friends took a few excursions, dived with Keith and Casey one more time, and lazed by the pool. Russell worked far too hard at finding his own island romance, finally declaring success when he hooked up with a girl from Solihull, on holiday with two of her workmates. Paul insisted it didn't count as he could have driven an hour up the M40 back home and chatted her up in a pub. In the evenings, Renee would meet Simon outside the hotel and took him to a different restaurant each time, usually a local food shack, as she introduced him to an array of local dishes and Caribbean flavours. Russell and Paul joined them one evening, which was far less romantic, but they laughed endlessly, thoroughly entertained by their contradictory retelling of the day's adventures. Each night, Simon would return to his room and Renee would join him shortly after, using the stairwell and avoiding the staff. They would share a bottle of wine, take a bath in the large oval tub, or shower together, washing away the salty sweat of the humid days. She would then spend the night in his arms. He had never before felt such a sense of loss and longing as he did watching her leave his room each morning, when she quietly slipped away to go to work.

Saturday loomed like a black cloud slowly approaching from the horizon. As much as Simon tried to enjoy each moment, he couldn't help seeing the cloud inch closer, and feel the impending change that would come. Once he set foot on that aeroplane, what would happen next? The question weighed on him constantly and wouldn't leave his mind. Millions of people had holiday flings every year. But how many people did he know that spent the rest of their lives with that person, or even continue a relationship? He knew of none. He had known this girl just a matter of days, in the most idyllic set of circumstances anyone could invent. Logically, he knew the chances of them sharing the same passion, fascination and attraction for each other away from the island, were remote. And yet, he felt more for this woman than anyone he had ever dated. There was something uniquely different about his feelings he struggled to identify. In the early hours of Saturday morning, as he lay awake with her sleeping by his side, he finally realised what it was. He had never needed a woman before. He had desired, lusted, felt challenged, and a host of other emotions that drive someone to pursue the attention of another, but he had never felt an overwhelming need to be with anyone. He had always been comfortable in walking away, or letting them walk away from him.

He tried to picture her in his flat in Oxford, her smiling face greeting him when he came through the door. The door he often didn't step through until late in the evening, and left again early the next morning. What life could he offer this beautiful young woman? How could it possibly compare to the paradise she had grown up knowing? Would she be willing to trade spending her mornings in clear blue waters, swimming and playing with majestic stingrays, for working in a dreary office in an English town? Would she be willing, or more importantly, would she be happy? She was at least ten years younger than he was, surely she would desire nightclubs, bars, dancing and socialising, all the things most young adults call normal. He had done all of that. He had very little interest in returning to that scene. His idea of a night out was a good meal and a fine wine. But she hadn't pushed him to go to any of those places on the island, and they had passed by noisy bars and even a nightclub. In fact, she had never even mentioned it. She seemed happy to take him to quiet cafes and be back in the room with just the two of them.

In uncharacteristic flights of fantasy, Simon imagined himself moving to the island and running his business from there. Could he live on a relatively remote island? Holidaying somewhere was a bad way of judging if you could live there; the waiters, pools and excursions disappeared from your day when it was back to the reality of working and making a living, but it was certainly a brighter prospect than imagining Renee wintering in England. The Internet was the issue that brought any chance of him running his business from the island to a screeching halt. One day, he was sure, the Internet would be fast enough, and cheap enough, to work from anywhere in the world, but that was years away from being a reality. Besides, he thought, every programmer is dreading the problems that the year 2000 will bring to the computing world.

Step by step, he made a decision, lying there in bed, feeling her warm, soft brown skin against him. There was too much he didn't know and very little he did, so all they could do was move forward based on what they had built in their few days together. He was sure he didn't want to say goodbye, and sensed she didn't want to either, although neither had spoken of it. He would find a way to come back to the island as soon as he could, even if it was for a brief visit. If he leaned on Russell and Paul, and trusted them with more responsibility, he may be able to slip away for a week in a few months' time. Once the new project was under way and they had the scope of the tasks mapped out, he would take a short trip. He would offer the same to the other two, and they could each have a week's sanity break every few months. They all deserved it, and after the multi-year slog they had just completed, they needed to find some balance. He would talk about hiring one more person with his partners, someone who could take some of the workload from each of them.

Renee stirred next to him and Simon glanced at the bedside clock. It was 6:10am. They both needed to be up.

"If I go back to sleep, will you be here when I wake up?" she mumbled, and rolled over against him, putting her hand on his chest.

"I'd like nothing more than to stay," he said and kissed the top of her head, her wild mop of hair tickling his face.

"Then stay," she whispered.

"I think I've come up with a plan that will allow me to come back sooner than I thought I could," he said tenderly, "if that's what you want."

"I want you to stay," she replied. "But I'll take 'come back sooner' if that's the only option."

She was talking quietly, and it was hard for him to read the inflection in her voice. He desperately wanted her to desire that he stayed, but hoped she could understand that it simply wasn't possible without letting a lot of people down, including his two best friends.

"Believe me, Renee, if I could stay, I would," he said, stroking her back. "You've no idea what this time with you has meant to me."

She squeezed him tightly, then lifted herself up and kissed him softly. He felt a tear fall from her cheek to his, before she rolled out of bed, and walked quickly to the bathroom, closing the door. His emotions felt raw and open, something he had never experienced before. If she begged him to stay, he wasn't sure he could bring himself to board the plane. It would mean rolling a grenade through their company's plans and commitments, and he knew in time that would tear him apart, but leaving Renee was destroying him in other ways. He hauled himself out of bed, slipped on a pair of boxer shorts, and reluctantly began packing his suitcase. He heard the shower turn on and he longed to join her, but he knew it would only make it harder to leave. By the time she came out of the bathroom, he was packed, and she was dressed in her shorts and polo shirt, ready for work. She stuffed last night's clothes into her rucksack and looked around the room for anything she was forgetting. He had another twenty minutes before he needed to be out front and meet Russell and Paul to take the shuttle to the airport, just enough time for him to shower. He walked over and went to put his arms around her, but she reached up and put her hands firmly on his chest, stopping him. He saw tears in her eyes again.

"There's something I have to tell you, and I'm scared to say it," she said, her voice broken and shaky.

He tried to wipe the tears from her cheeks, but she turned her head away. "You have to listen to me."

Simon stepped back, a lump started rising in his throat. What on earth could she possibly be about to say that would be so bad, or so difficult? She didn't want to see him again was all he could fathom, and his heart desperately sank.

She looked up, her eyes moist, and her lips quivering. "I lied about something," she said. "I don't know why I did." She stopped and sniffled, wiping her face with the back of her hand, "Well I do know why I did, but after I did, I realised it was stupid, but by then it was too late."

Simon was dumbfounded. He couldn't find anything to say because he didn't really know what she was talking about. He wanted to tell her it was okay, and take her in his arms to let her know everything was fine, but he dare not. He was terrified it wasn't fine.

"I didn't lie exactly," she continued, barely managing to say the words. "But I let you believe something that wasn't true. I'm not twenty-something." She couldn't look him in the eyes anymore, and her head dropped. "I'm eighteen."

Simon felt paralysed. Their relationship had pivoted from attraction, flirting and possibility, to the most important relationship of his life so far, based on a lie.

"I start college in the autumn. This is my summer job," she muttered between sniffles.

He searched for words, but they weren't there. His mind was a frenzy of thoughts and emotions, yet none of them made sense. He had no idea at what point 'like' became 'love', but he was further along the line than he'd ever been before, and it had all happened in a handful of days; which had now been torn apart in a handful of seconds. He wanted nothing more than to hold her and say it didn't matter. But it did matter. The age itself mattered, but just as devastating was the lie. All the arguments and points he had thrown around his mind as to why this couldn't work came flooding back, and landed in the two feet that separated them in his hotel room.

"The truth is too important," he thought, and realised he had said the words out loud.

Renee turned and ran to the door, sobbing. Simon stood still in a stupor, and watched her leave.

32

GRAND CAYMAN – SATURDAY

The policeman stood on the dock looking back and forth between the two people who had just emerged from the crashed boat and the house behind him, where Sam and Renee Shaw stood watching from behind the large sliding glass door of their living room.

"Come over to the dock, but keep your hands where I can see them," he ordered.

AJ could see the young, dark-skinned man was probably in his mid-twenties and had likely never faced a situation like the one he now had to deal with. The majority of crime on the island was domestic disputes, occasional altercations between locals, and every once in a while a drug bust. She was sure he had never fired his weapon outside of the practice range, and she hoped his first time wouldn't be while it was pointed in their direction. At least, she thought as she leapt the four feet from the gunwale to the concrete dock, it's one of the good guys holding the gun this time. Still, she really didn't care for it being aimed her way. Reg lumbered over to the dock and they both stood there, looking at the policeman.

"Who's inside with them?" Reg asked, nodding towards the house.

"Don't you worry about them," the policeman snapped. "My partner's watching them."

The sirens AJ had heard from inside the boat still sounded a mile away and she scanned the garden of the house, wondering where the man could be. The area was a large patio with an in-ground swimming pool in the centre, and a set of outdoor furniture and several sun loungers between the pool and the house.

"Radio Whittaker," she blurted. "Radio Detective Whittaker and tell him you have AJ and Reg, he'll explain what's going on."

The policeman looked back at the house again, nervously shifting his feet.

"Radio him, damn it, man," Reg barked in his deep voice and the policeman swung back to face them. He finally reached up and keyed the microphone clipped to his bulletproof vest.

"Detective Whittaker, this is Sergeant Rhodes, over."

AJ looked at Reg's hand that was bleeding profusely, dark red blood trickling down his raised arm. She glanced back at the patio window and noticed the Shaws must have stepped back from the glass, as she couldn't see them anymore. She noticed the policeman touched his earpiece and hoped it was Whittaker.

"Yes sir, big fella and a young lady, both Caucasians. Both came out of the fishing boat after it crashed here, sir. Over."

It was driving AJ crazy waiting for the conversation to play out and not hearing what Whittaker was saying on the other end. Where was he, she wondered? Was he still on the marine police boat in the sound? Surely he was on his way. The sirens continued to get closer, but across the flat island the sound carried, and she knew they could still be minutes away, and the Ghost already had a head start. Every minute counted. The policeman's gun slowly lowered, and he turned and faced the house as he listened through his earpiece.

"Yes, sir. Over," he called into the microphone and swung back to AJ and Reg.

"I'm sorry, I had no way of knowing who you were. Please stay

212 | NICHOLAS HARVEY

here and I'll check on my partner. Whittaker is a few minutes away."

Rhodes keyed his mic again. "Hingston, do you copy? Everything okay in there? Over."

There was silence.

He keyed the mic one more time. "Hingston, do you copy?" he said more urgently and the three of them held their breath.

After what felt like ages, he touched his ear and looked back at AJ and Reg. "He's okay, says everything's fine inside."

AJ breathed again and relaxed for two seconds. And then they all heard the gunshot.

Rhodes ran towards the house, trying to stay clear of the windows. Reg bolted behind him at an impressive pace for a big man. He picked up a chair from the patio set as he passed by, without missing a step, and flung it at the sliding glass door with all his might. Both men careened into the wall next to the sliding door as the chair bounced off the hurricane-proof glass and clattered across the paving stones of the patio.

"Go around the side," Reg hissed at Rhodes and pointed to the left side of the house. "I'll cover the back."

AJ stood watching it all unfold, paralysed to the spot, unsure what to do that would be remotely helpful. Reg looked back at her, and waved for her to take cover somewhere. She managed to move her feet, staying out by the dock; she ran to the right-hand side of the garden, noticing the marine police boat entering the canal several hundred yards away as she reached the low wall and hedge lining the side of the property. She could hear a commotion inside the house and Rhodes talking urgently into his radio. He was on the opposite side of the house and she couldn't understand exactly what he was saying, but was sure part of it was 'man down'. Sirens wailed loudly as the police back-up were finally close by and the red and blue lights still flashed in the sky from Rhodes and Hingston's police car in front of the house. Reg was trying to slide the patio door open, and she heard a crashing sound she presumed was Rhodes breaking into the house. She looked over at Reg, who had opened the sliding patio door and now ran across the back of the house instead of going inside. A door flung open from the right side of the house and Tenley stumbled out, regained her footing, then took off sprinting straight towards AJ. A few beats behind her, the Ghost flew out of the same door and ran to the corner of the house, where he raised his gun and aimed just as AJ leapt at Tenley and bowled her over.

They landed with a scraping thud on the paving stones, and AJ rolled once before dropping into the swimming pool with a loud splash. Spluttering and choking, she kicked off the bottom and surfaced to see Tenley back on her feet and running towards the canal. AJ began to climb out and saw the Ghost pick himself up off the patio near the house, look around the ground for a second, then sprint after Tenley. Reg lay in a heap against the wall and was trying to clamber back to his feet. She guessed he had bowled the man over and knocked the gun from his hand, as she never heard a shot go off. As AJ stood up, she saw Tenley reach the canal and realise she was trapped. The girl swung around to dive in when the Ghost crashed into her at full sprint, carrying them both into the dark water.

AJ stared at the churned-up surface where they had entered, and knew Tenley didn't stand a chance against the muscular man. She ran towards the fishing boat as Reg arrived at the edge of the canal.

"Where did they go?" he yelled.

AJ leapt to the deck of the fishing boat awash with water and scooped up her dive gear, floating against the gunwale. She swung the BCD across her back, quickly buckled the strap, released her mask from its clip, and stepped over the transom into the canal. She bobbed back to the surface and slipped her mask over her face.

"They're down there somewhere!" she yelled at Reg. "Stay up on the dock," she added, before shoving her regulator in her mouth and dropping below the surface.

She hadn't bothered with her fins, and her bare feet quickly hit the silty bottom of the canal. She released her torch from her BCD and turned it on. The light beam didn't penetrate far into the stirred-up water, with particulate scattering from where she had landed on the bottom. Small fish flitted in and out of the illumination, with every movement making AJ jump. She flashed her torch around but couldn't see anyone. The drone of the police marine boat's engine resonated through the water and she hoped Reg pulled them up short before they ran her over, her head just a few feet below the surface. Leaning forward at a steep angle, she was able to walk herself along the bottom, and headed away from the fishing boat, in the direction Tenley and the man had plunged into the canal. Beneath her toes she could feel small rocks and debris amongst the sand, and eel grass brushed against her ankles as she pushed her way forward. A bold movement to her right startled her, and she whipped her torch beam in an arc, just seeing the grey disk shape of a ray scooting away. She kept moving forward, slowly plodding against the resistance of the water. It felt like the dream where she tried to run, but the world was treacle and everything was restrained in agonising slow motion. She knew Tenley wouldn't have long with the breath undoubtedly knocked out of her when she was bowled into the water. AJ swept the torch in an arc before her and spotted a large dark shape just six feet away. She pushed harder with her feet and lowered her shoulders to reach the two figures.

Tenley was pinned to the sandy bottom, with the Ghost kneeling on top of her, with his hand shoving her head back. Tenley's eyes were wide open in terror. The Ghost had his eyes closed and appeared to be in a trance. Of course, AJ realised, if he held a lungful of air they would float to the surface; he would have to expel almost all the air from his lungs to stay submerged. Like a competitive freediver, he had reduced his heart rate and his body's demand for oxygen, all while taking the life of another human being. AJ knew she had to attack. It went against all her beliefs, and every instinct in her brain; except one. The same way she couldn't sit back and watch Pascal take an innocent life, the adrenaline pumped and determination took over, driving her forward. She pulled her three-inch titanium dive knife from its sheath and lunged towards the assassin. His eyes shot open when the beam from the torch in her left hand lit his face, just as her right arm swung through the water. His reaction was slowed by his meditative state, but his left arm raised to deflect the blow, and his right arm left Tenley's head and shot towards AJ. She felt the knife hit something just before his powerful arm knocked her hand away and he wrenched the reg from her mouth with his other hand. Her momentum carried her into the man's torso and the two of them tumbled over with Tenley still trapped under the man's legs as the world lit up around them with bright flood lights penetrating the water from above. AJ felt like she was in a violent washing machine, being tumbled around with limbs flying, blood mixing with the billowing sand and the grey and white whoosh of a startled stingray flashing by.

AJ tried to strike the blade at the man, determined to hit any part of him she could, but he was now fully conscious and was easily pushing her arm away. She noticed he was grabbing for the regulator with his free hand and figured he must be out of air. What little he had kept in his lungs to stay on the bottom was used up when she had surprised him, and now he desperately needed air. She allowed his left arm to push her knife hand farther away, which sent them both rolling to her left with the regulator flailing in the water behind her, out of his reach. Without a mask, he was effectively blind, and not finding the reg, he turned his attention back to the knife. They spun around in the water and his right arm lunged for her left hand where his other arm was holding her at bay. In a desperate effort, AJ pulled back with her right arm, spinning them both further around, and jammed her left hand towards the man's throat. His muscular grip twisted her forearm, and she unwillingly released the knife and gritted her teeth against the pain as it felt like he would break her arm. Without him being able to deflect her blow, she drove her hand into his throat, using her feet in the sand as leverage, pushing him down to the bottom where the sea floor appeared to explode in a cloud of sand and debris, sending a grey mass shooting away with its long tail whipping. Disarmed, and up against a far stronger opponent, AJ could only hope she had knocked the man clear of Tenley, so at least the girl could escape. She knew the Ghost would easily out-wrestle her now, but if she could kick clear, maybe she too could make the surface where help was waiting. She wanted to recover her reg as her own lungs burned, but she dare not let go of his throat. And then she realised he was no longer fighting her.

His throat convulsed under her grip, and his hands released her arm. I'm killing him, she thought in a panic. She had attacked with all her might, but had never considered the possibility of killing the assassin. She had never imagined killing anyone. All she wanted to do was save Tenley and try to stay alive herself. Could she actively throttle another human until they were dead? The idea repulsed her, and she reflexively let go of his neck. But he continued to convulse with a stream of blood wafting from the back of his neck, and it dawned on her what had happened. She had inadvertently shoved him down against the stingray as it had swooped by. The gentle creatures rarely ever used their stingers, but a sure way was to step on them. The Ghost had stepped on one with the back of his neck; with AJ's help. She wondered if the stingray was okay. The man's mouth was opening and closing in a strange gulping motion, like a beached goldfish. His eyes stared blankly into the murky water and his arms hung limply by his side. AJ sensed movement to her left, and saw Tenley was still under the man's legs, weakly pulling and shoving to get clear. AJ swept her arm behind her, recovered her regulator, she purged it, and took two gulps, before thrusting it into Tenley's mouth and purging it again. Tenley's first reaction was to defend herself, but her weakened, oxygen-starved muscles could put up little resistance, and she quickly realised she was breathing again. AJ felt the girl's arms wrap around her neck and cling tightly. She slid Tenley clear of the man's legs and pulled them both to their knees. To her side, AJ could still see the Ghost, floating lightly above the sand. His mouth was no longer moving. A stingray glided over his still body and AJ reached out a hand. The ray brushed gently over her and she stroked along its belly.

They broke the surface to a mass of chaos, shouting and furious activity. AJ ignored it all and softly removed the regulator from Tenley's mouth, the girl still clinging to her with quivering arms.

"Hello Tenley, I'm AJ," she said quietly.

"Where is he?" Tenley asked, her voice weak and trembling.

AJ nodded at the water behind her. "He's staying down there, you're safe now."

The girl rested her head on AJ's shoulder. "Thank you. I thought I was dead."

"Not for the first time today, I'm sure," AJ whispered. "I apologise for my van trying to run you and your lovely dog over. I wasn't driving."

"The detective told me it was you that saved me then too." The girl leaned back and looked at AJ. "You must be some kind of guardian angel."

AJ laughed. "No. I just have a habit of being in the wrong place sometimes. Well, a lot of the times, it seems."

"Bring her to the side, AJ," Reg's voice boomed over all the other ruckus.

AJ swam them the ten feet over to the dock wall and began taking in the scene. Reg's big paw reached down and, with the help of Rhodes, pulled Tenley from the water and sat her on the dock where her mother and father rushed over. Another policeman in scuba gear was sitting on the dock slipping his fins on with Whittaker standing next to him, peering over at AJ.

"What did you do with him?" Whittaker asked.

"I left him down there," she replied.

Whittaker looked at her confused. "You overpowered that guy? I heard he was a big fella."

AJ looked offended, "The Ghost? Yeah, he's pretty big."

"Land," Whittaker said. "His real name is Tony Land."

AJ grinned. "Well, Tony landed on a stingray, and it didn't agree with him," she said as she kicked along the sea wall to a metal ladder leading into the water. "He does have a nick on his shoulder which is my handiwork though," she added, and flexed her bicep for Whittaker.

33

OXFORD, ENGLAND – MONDAY

The Levers' home was a renovated farmhouse on the outskirts of Oxford, and despite Simon's desire to be upstairs in their large master bedroom, the hospital bed was far too heavy and unmanageable to manoeuvre up the narrow stairs. He had settled for the lounge where they had removed a pair of armchairs to make room, and Tamsin could sleep on the sofa if she wanted to stay downstairs with him. The morning had been chaotic and tiring. The ambulance ride was only a few miles from John Radcliffe Hospital to their home, but getting to and from the ambulance had been an ordeal in his weakened state. Lots of people picking up, sliding and manhandling him had left Simon exhausted and sore. His pride had gone by the wayside weeks ago. There was no room for ego, he had realised a while back, when your body fails you and your basic needs fall to others.

Once he was settled in the lounge, tucked in the rental hospital bed, the caregivers and ambulance drivers finally left and he drifted off to sleep for a couple of hours. When he awoke, he was alone in the room. Martin was at school. His son had wanted to stay home and help with the move, but they had been worried how traumatic it might be, and the boy had enough memories of his broken father. Simon hoped the visual of the healthy man cheering Martin on from the sideline of the football pitch would be strong enough to override the picture of the final weeks. He listened for movement in the house, but didn't hear anyone, and wondered where Tamsin was. He looked around the room that had been the centre of their life since shortly after their marriage. This was the only home Martin had ever known. He looked down at the hospital bed, a stark, modern metal contrast to the softwoods and earth tones of the furniture and decor that emanated warmth and familiar comfort. He wondered about the bed's resume. How many terminal occupants had preceded him? He made a mental note to ask Tamsin if she could dig up a nice blanket to drape over the white sheets, something that matched the room and dulled the clinical contrast.

He heard the back door open and close. He wanted to call out and have his wife with him while he was awake, but he was too weak to speak much above a whisper. He was also aware that she already felt an obligation to be by his side, and she needed some time to herself. He knew this battle, as people liked to call it, was a relentless emotional drain, and must constantly feel like hands around her throat. He heard her feet slowly ascending the creaky old stairs. One thing about a house originally built in the 1700s, everything let you know its age. There was no creeping about on the time-trodden, uneven floors. The kitchen, dining area, and bedroom above, were built nearly 300 years ago. Somewhere in the late 1800s the rest of the house was added on, and throughout the 1900s and 2000s the farmhouse had been modernised with electricity, updated plumbing, rewired and so on.

With another series of creaks and complaints, the steps announced Tamsin's arrival back downstairs, and she stood in the doorway to the lounge.

"Hello, dear," he greeted her, and smiled.

Tamsin looked pale, her eyes were red and her make-up had run from tears. She held a piece of paper in her hand.

"What's wrong, my love?" he asked.

It was a question they had all been avoiding for a while, the reason being obvious; but this seemed different to him. For months, Tamsin had tried to hide her grief and show strength in his presence. She wouldn't enter the room if she was in the middle of a breakdown. She walked slowly over and he barely recognised the expression on her face. He had never seen her this way. She looked beaten down, he thought, scared even. She sat in the chair by the bed and handed him the piece of paper.

"You need to read this," was all she said.

Simon took the paper and looked at the document. It was a printout of an email. He began to read.

Dear Simon,

I'm sorry for contacting you after so many years, I'm sure you don't want to hear from me with the way things ended. I had resigned myself to that fact, but something I hadn't expected happened. Today, your four-year-old daughter, Tenley, asked about her father. She is finally old enough that other kids at kindergarten are talking about their families and she has realised hers is different.

I realise this must be quite a shock, and if I don't hear back, then I know you would prefer to remain anonymous, and I will find a way to handle the situation with our daughter. I want to be clear, I'm not looking for help, I don't want money and I do not expect anything for the two of us. But your daughter wants to know her father, and it would be unfair and wrong of me to deny her that opportunity.

I came so close to contacting you after you left, especially when I found out I was pregnant, but I could never formulate the words. I would always remember the look on your face when I last saw you, and that seemed to say everything, but now I feel I should at least try.

Your daughter is a beautiful, healthy young lady, full of joy with a strong will. She is smart beyond her years. I have known her question would come one day, but I certainly didn't expect it this soon. I hope the last five years have been kind to you, you've found happiness, and the balance you were seeking in your life.

I hope to hear from you, but I will try to understand if I do not.

Renee Thompson

Simon didn't know what to do or say. He looked at the date of the email. November, 2002. He looked over at his wife.

"I'm so sorry, Simon," she said quietly. "You had just divorced, and we were starting to have drinks together, and this showed up in your spam folder. I wasn't sure what to do, so I printed a copy, then deleted the email. When we became serious, I considered showing you, but I didn't know how to explain why I hadn't before."

Tamsin reached a hand over and took his, but he pulled away.

"This girl is now in her twenties," he said. "Renee thinks I turned my back on my own daughter. For eighteen years she's believed I wanted no part of this girl's life."

"I'm so sorry, Simon," Tamsin muttered, with tears streaming down her face. "I wish I could change all this, but I've screwed up so badly."

For years, Simon had fought with his decision to leave Grand Cayman behind him, and the first woman he had ever loved. He had tried to replace those feelings with other women, and had married 18 months later, knowing it wasn't the same. Four years later, growing distant, she found solace in another man's arms, and he faced another set of lies. But Tamsin had been different. In Tamsin he had felt the spark and intensity of his first love, and although it happened soon after his divorce, he knew it wasn't rushed, or for the wrong reasons. Yet now, everything he believed and had held true was collapsing. He asked himself over and over, why would she tell me this now? Let me die in blissful ignorance. Why turn their marriage, their wonderful life together for all these years, into another relationship built on a lie? He had to find Renee and explain. The idea barrelled into him and filled him with a purpose; a reason to hang on. He had Martin to think of, and now he had to find Renee and their daughter. He had to meet her before this awful disease took him. He heard the sound of a car on the gravel driveway outside and Tamsin moaned.

"Are you expecting someone? I'm really not up for visitors with this dropped on me," he said, holding up the letter.

Tamsin nervously shuffled in the chair, still sobbing. "I'm so sorry, Simon. You always said Martin comes first. We had to do everything we could for him," she babbled, and he struggled to follow her.

"What's that got to do with hiding this from me?" he replied.

"Because that's not all I've screwed up," she shouted as a loud knock came on the front door.

"Who could that be?" he asked, confused and frustrated. Tamsin had a fiery side, but he'd never seen her like this.

"I thought you'd want Martin to have it all," Tamsin blurted, her tears replaced with anger. "He was getting everything, he would have the company."

"What on earth are you saying?" Simon asked, and another knock came from the door, louder this time.

"I couldn't let some island hussy take half of everything we've built for our son, Simon," Tamsin spat angrily. "She didn't deserve you, and she wasn't going to take anything away from Martin. I wouldn't let some holiday fling with a young tramp from years ago compromise our son's future."

Simon was bewildered. He couldn't comprehend what she was saying, but the person at the door knocked again.

"Mrs. Lever, can you open the door please, this is the police."

34

GRAND CAYMAN – MONDAY

AJ stirred and slowly woke to the feel of Jackson next to her, and the faint clucking of a chicken from the kitchen. The odd sound from her ancient coffee maker was a comforting reminder that the mayhem of Saturday, and the exhausting police interviews and statements from Sunday, were behind them. With the island slowly and carefully opening its borders to visitors, business was still sporadic, but she did have a customer planned for later that morning. She rolled out of bed and plodded the handful of paces across her tiny cottage to the kitchen, enjoying the luxury of sleeping in until 8am. She fixed a coffee to go in her stainless-steel travel mug before hunting around in the dark room for shorts and a shirt to wear. She tried not to wake Jackson, but by the time she came out of the bathroom after washing her face and brushing her teeth, he was pouring himself a coffee too.

"Hey," she said quietly and stood on her tiptoes to kiss him.

"Morning," he replied and gently pushed her purple-streaked blonde hair from her face.

She kissed him again. "I slept much better last night."

"Good," he said, looking into her eyes. "You seem more peaceful this morning."

"I am. I think I have it sorted in my mind and I feel as good about it all as I probably ever will," she said thoughtfully. "He was responsible for putting us all in that situation, I was responsible for defending our lives. I can live with that."

"You can only claim an assist anyway, the stingray gets the credit for the score," Jackson said with a grin.

She punched him playfully on the arm. "I won't be long."

"Can I help Thomas get ready?" he asked.

"If you'd like," she replied, scooping up her rucksack and van keys. "I'll meet you both at the dock at 10."

He nodded and smiled as she stepped out of the front door into the muggy morning air. She walked across the garden of the large holiday home in which the little guest cottage was situated. She glanced over her shoulder at the calm ocean beyond the palm trees lining the property, before going through the gate to Boggy Sand Road where her van was parked. Playing a role in taking the life of another human was not something she could ever feel good about, but 'comfortable' with the outcome was a compromise she could live with. AJ fired up the van and sat for a few moments, sipping her coffee. Yesterday, she had been agitated and ill at ease all day, but this morning she felt more like herself, which she credited to Jackson and his calming manner and intuitive support. She realised she was smiling as she put the van in gear and drove slowly up Boggy Sand Road. It felt good to smile.

Once on West Bay Road heading south towards George Town along the back of Seven Mile Beach, she was about to play some music from her mobile when the device rang loudly through the van's speakers. The caller ID showed Roy Whittaker. She hit accept, and hoped it wasn't leading to another trip to the police station for more statements.

"Good morning AJ, I hope I'm not calling too early?" the detective asked, his voice sounding tired but in good spirits.

"No, I'm out and about, just driving into town," she replied over the van's hands-free system. "How's your officer doing? The one who was hit."

"He's fine, thank you for asking. He has a mighty bruise on his chest, but his vest saved him," Whittaker replied. "In all honesty, I'm guessing Land intended to temporarily disable Hingston instead of killing him. I'm certain at that close range he could have taken a kill shot."

"I suppose," AJ said. "By everyone's accounts he could have shot the parents too, but stayed focused on Tenley."

"It does appear that way. Anyway, my officers had some real-world training that we can't simulate. Hingston and Rhodes will be better prepared if they ever face something like that again," Whittaker added. "Hopefully they won't."

The line fell silent for a moment before Whittaker continued. "Well, I just wanted to update you on some progress in the case. We've been fortunate to wrap things up quickly," he said. "The UK police arrested a woman just a short time ago, based on the confession we got from the man who called himself Pascal."

"Really? He told you who paid him?" AJ said, surprised.

"He was very helpful, as it turned out," Whittaker explained. "His real name is Roy Ellis, and together with his partner Tony Land, they formed a team that ranked pretty highly on Interpol's most wanted list. Apparently he had a preference on where he should be extradited to. It seems the pair were wanted in many countries, but some more keenly than others. We agreed to send him to the UK to face manslaughter charges there, in return for information on who hired them. They were paid from an account in Spain, which was easily traced to the owners in the UK."

"It was a woman, you say? Why on earth was she after Tenley?" AJ asked.

"It's a sad story, really," Whittaker continued. "Tenley's biological father was a fellow who visited the island back in the late nineties and had a relationship with Renee Thompson, now Renee Shaw of course. Sadly, the man's now dying of cancer. His wife knew about Tenley, and as best as we can gather so far, he didn't. They have a son, who stood to inherit everything, and she was worried the Shaws would show up after the fellow passed away to claim part of his company and their estate. So it appears she tried to remove the problem. The UK police tell me she had connections to a crime family, but had distanced herself for many years. Looks like she used those connections one more time."

"Bloody hell, that's awful," AJ said, as she stayed on West Bay Road instead of getting on the bypass. One benefit of the pandemic had been a huge reduction in tourist traffic. "Poor girl must be devastated. She just found out who her father is, and then discovers the bloke's wife is the one that wanted her dead."

"Exactly, and now he's dying of cancer. I'm told he was just moved home under hospice care," the Detective added.

AJ thought for a moment. "Well, I guess I'll see how she's holding up. I'm taking her diving later this morning."

"That's good. I hope she doesn't cancel after all the news she's received in the past twenty-four hours. The girl needs a break from the drama," Whittaker replied. "We should be able to leave her be the rest of the day, so enjoy your morning with her. She seems like a lovely young lady. Are you heading there now?"

"No, I have an errand to run across town, just something that's been bothering me that I need to clear up," AJ said.

"Okay, well, I'll try to leave you both alone." Whittaker paused a moment and AJ waited, unsure if he was going to say something more. "I'm sorry you got mixed up in this mess, I'm sure there's some baggage you'll carry because of it. But there are a few people, me included, who are glad you were. You saved that girl's life, AJ," Whittaker said. "Have a good day now."

He hung up before she could even thank him for his kind words. It left her with a lump in her throat, but a good feeling to help wrestle with the mixed emotions the events had created.

AJ passed through downtown George Town by the harbour and continued on South Church Street until she found the left turn she was looking for. Turning up the street, she quickly found the small house on the left and parked the van out front. Walking to the door, she scooped up the newspaper lying in the front garden where the delivery driver had thrown it from the road. The *Cayman Compass*'s front page was the big news about 'assassins caught on the island'. AJ rang the doorbell and waited a few moments until the door was opened by the lady at 45 Melmac.

"Hello Kate," AJ greeted her.

"Oh, hello there," the lady replied. "You're the young lady who came by looking for the Thompsons, aren't you? Did you have any luck?"

"I am," AJ said. "And yes, I did as a matter of fact, but if you have a minute or two, I owe you an explanation."

"Oh," Kate said, stepping back to allow AJ to come inside, "Come on in and I'll make us some tea. How does that sound?"

AJ stepped into the woman's perfectly kept home. "That sounds absolutely perfect, Kate."

35

OXFORD, ENGLAND – THURSDAY

Simon's strength had understandably taken a downward turn after Tamsin was arrested. Martin had stayed home from school and a nurse was on hand full time. Simon had done his best to explain the situation to his son, but there was no way to sugar-coat what lay ahead. The boy was about to lose both his parents. Russell and Paul had come by every day when they left the office, but although he looked forward to the company, Simon found the visits becoming more of a strain. The three days since Monday had ebbed by so slowly, and now he lay propped up in the bed trying to conserve all his strength for his next visitors. When the knock finally came on the front door, he felt a surge of nervousness, mixed with embarrassment for his appearance and the circumstances. Martin rushed down the stairs and beat the nurse to the front door. Simon could hear voices as Martin introduced himself. His son stepped into the room, closely followed by a beautiful, slim, dark-skinned woman in her early forties, who he instantly recognised with a flood of memories. Behind her, was a lighter-skinned girl, the spitting image of her mother, who could easily have been the person filling those memories.

Renee walked slowly over and nervously smiled. "Hello, Simon."

In the back of his mind he knew the drugs and emotional trauma he was going through were amplifying his feelings, but he felt more certain than ever before in his life that his true soulmate stood before him. Any guilt associated with wishing his life had been different, was overwhelmed by the fact that it hadn't been. He wouldn't trade Martin for anything, but he was leaving this world knowing his true love had slipped through his stubborn fingers.

"Hello, Renee. I cannot begin to express how much I appreciate you being here, and I cannot apologise enough for what I've put you and your family through."

Renee appeared to be lost for words and ushered her daughter forward instead. "Simon, this is Tenley."

Tenley smiled, and the resemblance blew Simon's mind. After more than twenty years, his mental picture of her mother had faded and become tainted with other images and memories, but seeing them both brought visions of 1997 back crisply in focus.

"I'm very late introducing myself to you, and I wish these circumstances were different in so many ways, but I am truly blessed we are able to finally meet."

Tenley nodded, and looked at her mother. "What should I call you?" she asked.

Simon laughed, which was little more than a wheeze. "I expect your mother has had an assortment of names for me over the years, but how about we stick with Simon?"

They both laughed and a layer of tension left the room.

"Here, please have a seat," Martin said, and pulled a second chair close by.

Simon noticed the way his son was looking at the two women. His expression was filled with curiosity, without a trace of disapproval or jealousy. With everything poured on the young lad in the last few days, he was filled with pride at Martin's fortitude and understanding. Renee and Tenley sat, and Martin pulled up a third chair around the other side of the bed for himself.

"So, Tenley," Simon said, leaning towards her. "Tell me what you've been up to for the past 22 years."

They all talked, laughed and shed a tear or two over the next hour until Simon could stay in the moment no longer. The nurse fussed around several times but he repeatedly shooed her away with a smile and an assurance he was fine. But finally, he had no shooing left, and she suggested the visitors take a break and maybe have some lunch while Simon slept and regained his strength. As they rose to leave, Simon raised a hand and mumbled for them to wait.

"Please, I have two requests I must ask of you," he said, weakly.

All three leaned over the bed to hear him clearly, and he continued.

"The first is, please give my heartfelt thanks to your husband for raising my daughter in such a wonderful way. I know he is your father Tenley, and he's truly earned the right to be. He has done what I failed to do and I am eternally grateful."

He swallowed a few times and cleared his head for a moment, "The second," he said, looking at Martin, and then Tenley. "My lad here has some challenging times ahead, and it would mean the world to me if I knew he had his sister to lean on and talk to from time to time."

Tenley placed her hand on Simon's. "How about we start by taking him to lunch?"

Simon nodded and smiled as he slipped into the most peaceful sleep he had experienced all week.

Renee and Tenley stayed as planned for two more days, visiting twice a day and spending all the time Simon's energy would allow. That time lessened a little each day and on their way to the airport they received a phone call from Russell to tell them Simon was gone. They turned the car around, changed their travel arrangements, and stayed through the funeral early the following week. Tenley met her biological father and attended his service all within five days. Hastily arranged after Tamsin's arrest, Russell and his wife, a delightful Finnish woman he'd met on a trip to Scandinavia, took Martin in alongside their own two children, and promised to guide him through university. Tenley and Martin email frequently, and have a standing Internet call once a week. They have planned a trip for Martin to Grand Cayman over the holidays, during which Tenley promised to introduce him to her new passion of scuba diving.

ACKNOWLEDGMENTS

Sincere thanks…

…as always to my amazing wife, dive buddy and partner in crime, Cheryl.

…to my family for all their love and support.

…to my great friend James Guthrie. May your eyes stay far ahead, and your knees drag smoothly on the pavement.

…to my Royal Latin School friends who find many of their names scattered throughout characters in this novel. A fine bunch of misfits you are.

…to my old mate Russell Eacott. The character Russell in this novel is not based on you. I almost typed that whole sentence without laughing.

…to the Viñas family for their support, and a special nod to Tenley, the little AJ.

…to my rock-star editor Andrew Chapman. I couldn't do this without you. He can be found at PrepareToPublish.

…to Drew McArthur for another great cover.

…to Keith and Casey Keller for their help, friendship over many years, and endless hours of fun aboard their boats.

…to Roy Powell for his friendship and advice over many years.

…to the real Tony Land who's not a vicious hitman, but a great bloke and an accomplished photographer.

…to my advanced reader copy (ARC) group, whose input and feedback is invaluable. It is a pleasure working with all of you.

Above all, I thank you, the readers: none of this happens without the choice you make to spend your precious time with AJ and her stories. I am truly in your debt.

LET'S STAY IN TOUCH!

To buy merchandise, find more info or join my Newsletter, visit my
website at
www.HarveyBooks.com

If you enjoyed this novel I'd be incredibly grateful if you'd consider
leaving a review on Amazon.com
Find eBook deals and follow me on BookBub.com

Visit Amazon.com for more books in the
AJ Bailey Adventure Series,
Nora Sommer Caribbean Suspense Series,
and collaborative works;
The Greene Wolfe Thriller Series
Tropical Authors Adventure Series

ABOUT THE AUTHOR

A *USA Today* Bestselling author, Nicholas Harvey's life has been anything but ordinary. Race car driver, adventurer, divemaster, and since 2020, a full-time novelist. Raised in England, Nick has dual US and British citizenship and now lives wherever he and his amazing wife, Cheryl, park their motorhome, or an aeroplane takes them. Warm oceans and tall mountains are their favourite places.

For more information, visit his website at HarveyBooks.com.

Printed in Great Britain
by Amazon